823.8
S

Stoker, Bram, 1847-1912
The Bram Stoker bedside companion; 10 stories by the author of Dracula, edited and with an introd. by Charles Osborne. New York, Taplinger Pub. Co., 1973.
224 p. 21cm.

I. Osborne, Charles, ed. II. Title.

rn

THE BRAM STOKER BEDSIDE COMPANION

THE BRAM STOKER BEDSIDE COMPANION

10 stories by the author of *Dracula*

Edited
and with an
Introduction by

Charles Osborne

TAPLINGER PUBLISHING COMPANY
NEW YORK
1973

First published in the United States in 1973 by
TAPLINGER PUBLISHING CO., INC.
New York, New York

Printed in Great Britain

Library of Congress Catalog Card Number: 72-7717

ISBN 0-8008-0963-7

CONTENTS

INTRODUCTION

Bram Stoker and his Work

Dracula, published in 1897, was Bram Stoker's most successful novel. It ran to several editions during his lifetime, and was translated into a number of languages. After his death, it became a play, and the subject of scores of films. The Transylvanian vampire, it seems, is here to stay. But the name of Bram Stoker is hardly known at all, while most of his other works are equally neglected today. It is to acquaint the reader with some of the best of Stoker's other stories that this selection has been made; and the purpose of this introduction is to provide a brief sketch of the life and career of the Irish author who began life as the son of a government clerk, was incurably stage struck yet at the same time extremely level-headed, and who died of exhaustion at the age of sixty-four after a long and arduous career.

His father was Abraham Stoker, a clerk in the Civil Service, employed at Dublin Castle. Abraham junior, whose first name soon became shortened to Bram, was born in Dublin on 24 November 1847, nine years before George Bernard Shaw, seven years before Oscar Wilde, those two other Dubliners of his time who, like Bram, were to become involved in the theatre in England. As a child he was sickly, as an adolescent shy and bookish. But by the time he went to University—Trinity College, Dublin—he had developed a large, healthy physique and an interest in theatre. From childhood, he had tried to write poetry, stories and articles, and had hoped for some kind of career perhaps in literary journalism. His father, however, preferred to see the boy safely tucked away in the Civil Service, and so, after graduating in 1870, Bram followed his father into Dublin Castle. By this time, he had encountered the two men who were greatly to influence his life: Henry Irving on the stage, and Walt Whitman on the printed page.

He first saw Irving as a member of Miss Louisa Herbert's company who came from London to play a season at the Theatre Royal, Dublin. The twenty-nine-year-old actor played Captain Absolute in Sheridan's *The Rivals,* and his performance quite bowled over the young Irishman, who wrote: 'What I saw, to my amazement and delight, was a patrician figure as real as the person of one's dreams, and endowed with the same poetic grace. A young soldier, handsome, distinguished, self-dependent, compact of grace and slumbrous energy.' His discovery of Whitman came only a few months later when he borrowed from a fellow-student a copy of the recently published English edition of *Leaves of Grass,* and found himself overwhelmed by the richness of the poet's imagery, the daring of his form and subject-matter, and the life-enhancing exhilaration of his message. The young Stoker began to busy himself in the service of these two artists, the creative poet, the interpretative actor. He wrote articles about Whitman, and even letters to Whitman. When Irving returned to Dublin with a comedy called *Two Roses,* he went to see it three times in two weeks, and, indignant that no review of the performance had appeared in the Dublin press, talked the editor of the *Dublin Mail* into taking him on as drama critic, to rectify the situation. As the post was an unpaid one, its only perquisite being the free theatre tickets, Bram continued to work as a clerk at Dublin Castle. To supplement his meagre income, he persevered with the stories he had been writing for years. One of them, a romantic adventure story called 'The Chain of Destiny', was accepted for publication as a four-part serial by a weekly magazine, *Shamrock.* With such ingredients as a curse and a fiendish phantom, it pointed clearly to the direction Bram Stoker was to take as a writer of fiction. Towards the macabre, towards horror, towards, in the fullness of time, *Dracula.*

Meanwhile, the threads linking him with Whitman and Irving were taken up again. After delivering a talk on Whitman one evening to a Dublin debating society, Bram wrote a long letter to the American poet. This time, the poet replied: 'My dear young man, your letters have been most welcome to me—welcome to me as a person and then as author—I don't know which most. You did right to write to me so unconventionally, so fresh, so manly. . . . My physique is entirely shattered—doubtless permanently—from paralysis and other ailments. But I am up and dressed, and get out every day a little, live here quite lonesome but hearty, and in good spirits.' Whitman's letter coincided with the return to Dublin of Henry Irving, now a star, as Hamlet. Stoker wrote of him in the *Mail* that 'in his fits of passion there is a realism that no one but a genius can ever effect'. As a result, the actor asked to meet the critic, and they quickly became friends. The following year, 1877, Stoker, now thirty years old, went to London on holiday, and spent much of his time at the Lyceum Theatre, watching Irving's rehearsals and performances, and talking to the actor in his dressing room. A year later, again on holiday in London, he saw Irving in *Vanderdecken*, a play based on the legend of the Flying Dutchman. It was only some months afterwards that Irving, having decided to take over the lease of the Lyceum Theatre himself, sent a telegram to Stoker: 'Will you give up the Civil Service and join me, to take charge of my business as acting-manager?' The answer, of course, was yes. Hastily, yet methodically, Bram Stoker resigned from his job, married the girl he had become engaged to, finished writing a book on the Civil Service, and arrived, a few weeks later, in England.

Stoker worked with Irving until the actor's death twenty-seven years later. He proved to be an admirable manager, controlling the company's expenditure, negotiating its tours, advising Irving on plays, and acting generally as amiable and dependable father-figure to the other actors and actresses. It was a style of life he revelled in, and the relaxation and freedom from care that it brought him were to lead to his being able to turn again to his other love, the written word, and to begin writing again. He enjoyed, too, the meetings with famous men of the theatre and of literature. He got to know Tennyson, and the great poet's sons became frequent visitors at the house Bram and his wife Florence had acquired in

Cheyne Walk, Chelsea. Whistler and Oscar Wilde were among their other regular guests. Bram's Civil Service book, *The Duties of Clerks of Petty Sessions in Ireland,* had been published, and now he was at work on what he regarded as his first 'real' book, a collection of his stories. These were published in 1881, as *Under the Sunset.* Ostensibly a book of stories for children, this was a collection of fantasies, some of them strangely poetic, others grim and frightening. The reviews were encouraging: 'A collection of delicate and forcible allegories'; 'The style is characterized throughout by remarkable purity and grace'. 'The Invisible Giant' comes from this volume.

Life in London was not without its dangers. On a Thames steamer one autumn evening, Bram saw an elderly man jump from the deck into the river. He immediately dived in, and managed to bring the man back on board, but was unable to revive him. When the steamer docked, Bram had the body taken into his house in Cheyne Walk, to the consternation of his wife, Florence. There the man was found to be dead. The incident made newspaper headlines the following day, and Bram Stoker was awarded the bronze medal of the Royal Humane Society. To the excitement of unexpected adventure was added the adventure of travel. Bram found himself visiting the continent with Irving in connection with the actor's forthcoming production of *Faust.* He also took Irving and the full company of forty actors to the United States. In Philadelphia he was thrilled to be able at last to meet Walt Whitman, and on a second visit to the States the following year he and Whitman met again, this time in the poet's home in Camden, New Jersey. Whitman was in straitened circumstances, and Bram attempted to persuade the poet to allow *Leaves of Grass* to be published in an expurgated edition for wider sale. Whitman refused.

Another of Bram's literary friendships was with Hall Caine. The two writers, and Henry Irving, were known to sit up late at night telling one another tales of the occult. Bram continued to write whenever he found the opportunity. A novel, *The Snake's Pass,* was published in 1891, to great critical acclaim. From this adventure story set in the west of Ireland, the chapter called 'The Gombeen Man' has been selected for this volume. A gombeen man is a voracious money lender, and the one in *The Snake's Pass* is eventually punished by forces of nature for his greed and viciousness. It was shortly after publication of this novel that Bram met Doctor Arminius Vambery, Professor of Oriental Languages at the University of Budapest. Vambery was a strange and fascinating man with an intense interest in the supernatural. He had a great deal to tell Bram about the weird superstitions of eastern Europe, for he had travelled widely in places where old beliefs lingered on, for instance in Transylvania.

In the summer of 1893, Bram spent two weeks in August exploring the east coast of Scotland. He discovered a remote little fishing village, Cruden Bay on the Aberdeenshire coast, and fell in love with his first sight of it. There he stayed, and there he began to write a long story, 'The Watter's Mou' ', setting it in that locality and even utilising actual places and people. The title, 'the water's mouth' in Scottish dialect, refers to the Water of Cruden which ran down to the sea between the castle and the village. Included in this present volume, it is a tale of smuggling which ends in tragedy. Also included here are two other stories written in the mid 1890s, but conceived some years earlier. One, 'The Burial of the Rats', is a macabre tale for which Bram had made notes in Paris in 1874, while the other, 'The Squaw', is the result of his visit to Nuremburg with Irving. Grim and masochistic, it tells of the revenge of a cat, and involves a torture device which Bram had examined in Nuremburg, a contraption known as 'the Iron Virgin'.

In 1897, Bram Stoker's masterpiece, *Dracula*, was published. Bram had involved himself in an immense amount of research into Transylvanian vampire legends, and had also enlisted the aid of his curiously named friend Doctor Vambery in Budapest. The book that resulted, written in the form of letters and diaries, was an immediate and overwhelming success. 'In seeking a parallel to this weird, powerful and horrible story', wrote the *Daily Mail* critic, 'our minds revert to such tales as *The Mysteries of Udolpho, Frankenstein, Wuthering Heights, The Fall of the House of Usher* and *Marjery of Quelher*. But *Dracula* is even more appalling in its gloomy fascination than any one of these.' In the seventy-six years since it was first published, *Dracula* has never been out of print, and has been translated into several languages. It also, of course, though not until after Bram Stoker's death, became even more famous in stage and film adaptations. Reprinted here is 'Dracula's Guest', a chapter which was removed from the book before publication, and has never been reinstated. It is a self-contained episode recounting a horrifying incident which occurred to the narrator, Jonathan Harker, during his journey across Germany and Hungary to Transylvania.

Another two of the stories in this volume date from the months immediately following *Dracula.* They are 'Crooken Sands' which, like 'The Watter's Mou' ', was set in Cruden Bay, and 'The Secret of the Growing Gold'. Both are ghost stories of an unusual power and vividness. At Cruden Bay, Bram Stoker worked on a romantic novel, *Miss Betty,* set in Cheyne Walk, Chelsea, in the eighteenth century. His sentimental style, however, was less effective and individual than his way with the macabre and the supernatural. Neither *Miss Betty* nor his later romances were to achieve the success of *Dracula. The Jewel of Seven Stars,* however, another venture into the occult, involving this time the mysteries of ancient Egypt, drew praise from Sir Arthur Conan Doyle.

On 13 October, 1905, Bram and Henry Irving were in Bradford, where that evening Irving performed Tennyson's *Becket.* Returning to the Midland Hotel after the performance, Irving collapsed in the front hall. Bram was summoned, but by the time he arrived his old friend was dead. Bram sought refuge in work. The company had to be kept together, and there was also his own writing to turn to. He wrote another romantic novel, *The Man,* and then devoted his time to working on *Personal Reminiscences of Henry Irving* which was published in two volumes. Next, he wrote *Snowbound,* a series of stories linked together to form a kind of novel. A touring theatrical company, snowbound overnight in a train somewhere between Aberdeen and Perth, passes the time by telling stories. The one included here, 'A Star Trap', is the contribution of the Master Machinist. Many of the stories were based on Bram Stoker's own experiences on tour with the Irving company.

In 1908, Bram published another romantic novel, *Lady Athlyne,* and also wrote, for the *Nineteenth Century,* an article advocating censorship of fiction. 'A number of books have been published in England,' he claimed, 'that would be a disgrace to any country even less civilised than our own. They are meant by both authors and publishers to bring to the winning of commercial success the forces of evil inherent in man. The evil is a grave and dangerous one, and may, if it does not already, deeply affect the principles and lives of the young people of this country.' Relinquishing his interest in the theatre, he now spent most of his time writing. Two more novels in the style of *Dracula,* though less spine-chilling and therefore less successful, were to appear. *The Lady of the Shroud* is a vampire story, set in the Balkans, but cheats somewhat in having as its heroine a princess who merely poses as a vampire for political reasons. *The Lair of the White Worm* was, after *Dracula,* Bram Stoker's most successful novel. Set in modern Staffordshire, which is supposed to have formed part of the ancient kingdom of Mercia, it tells of a woman, Lady Arabella, who is really the White Worm, many thousands of years old.

The Lair of the White Worm was to be Bram Stoker's last novel. While working on it, he was also finishing *Famous Impostors,* a collection of essays on frauds throughout the ages, including the Tichborne claimant, the legend of the Wandering Jew, Cagliostro, Mesmer, and the story of 'The Bisley Boy' which, he seemed to suggest, was not a fraud. The legend that Henry VIII's daughter Elizabeth had died as a child at Bisley, and that her governess, frightened to tell the King, substituted a boy who grew up to be Queen of England, was one that appealed to Bram Stoker's temperament. His researches failed to disclose any fraud, and he concluded 'That this story impugns the identity—and more than the identity—of Queen Elizabeth, and hints at an explanation of circumstances in her life which have long puzzled historians, will entitle it to the most serious consideration.'

He planned more books, and in April 1912 was sorting out

some earlier published stories (including 'The Judge's House', to be found in this volume) when he suddenly died. He was sixty-four years old, and the cause of death on his death certificate was given simply as 'exhaustion'. The very last article of his to appear in print before his death was, appropriately, a piece on Irving in the *Nineteenth Century.* He lives on, however, not as the biographer, friend and associate of that great actor, but as the creator of ***Count Dracula.***

C.O.

THE SECRET OF THE GROWING GOLD

When Margaret Delandre went to live at Brent's Rock the whole neighbourhood awoke to the pleasure of an entirely new scandal. Scandals in connection with either the Delandre family or the Brents of Brent's Rock, were not few; and if the secret history of the county had been written in full both names would have been found well represented. It is true that the status of each was so different that they might have belonged to different continents—or to different worlds for the matter of that—for hitherto their orbits had never crossed. The Brents were accorded by the whole section of the country a unique social dominance, and had ever held themselves as high above the yeoman class to which Margaret Delandre belonged, as a blue-blooded Spanish hidalgo out-tops his peasant tenantry.

The Delandres had an ancient record and were proud of it in their way as the Brents were of theirs. But the family had never risen above yeomanry and although they had been once well-to-do in the good old times of foreign wars and protection, their fortunes had withered under the scorching of the free trade sun and the 'piping times of peace'. They had, as the elder members used to assert, 'stuck to the land', with the result that they had taken root in it, body and soul. In fact, they, having chosen the life of vegetables, had flourished as vegetation does—blossomed and thrived in the good season and suffered in the bad. Their holding, Dander's Croft, seemed to have been worked out, and to be typical of the family which had inhabited it. The latter had declined generation after generation, sending out now and again some abortive shoot of unsatisfied energy in the shape of a soldier or sailor, who had worked his way to the minor grades of the services and had there stopped, cut short either from unheeding gallantry in action or from that destroying cause to men without breeding or youthful care—the recognition of a position above them which they feel unfitted to fill. So, little by little, the family dropped lower and lower, the men brooding and dissatisfied, and drinking themselves into the grave, the women drudging at home, or marrying beneath them—or worse. In process of time all disappeared, leaving only two in the Croft, Wykham Delandre and his sister Margaret. The man and woman seemed to have inherited in masculine and feminine form respectively the evil tendency of their race, sharing in common the principles, though manifesting them in different ways, of sullen passion, voluptuousness and recklessness.

The history of the Brents had been something similar, but showing the causes of decadence in their aristocratic and not their plebeian forms. They, too, had sent their shoots to the wars; but their positions had been different and they had often attained honour—for without flaw they were gallant, and brave deeds were done by them before the selfish dissipation which marked them had sapped their vigour.

The present head of the family—if family it could now be called when one remained of the direct line—was Geoffrey Brent. He was almost a type of worn out race, manifesting in some ways its most brilliant qualities, and in others its utter degradation. He might be fairly compared with some of those antique Italian nobles whom the painters have preserved to us with their courage, their unscrupulousness, their refinement of lust and cruelty—the voluptuary actual with the fiend potential. He was certainly handsome, with that dark, aquiline, commanding beauty which women so generally recognise as dominant. With men he was distant and cold; but such a bearing never deters womankind. The inscrutable laws of sex have so arranged that even a timid woman is not afraid of a fierce and haughty man. And so it was that there was hardly a woman of any kind or degree, who lived within view of Brent's Rock, who did not cherish some form of secret admiration for the handsome wastrel. The category was a wide one, for Brent's Rock rose up steeply from the midst of a level region and for a circuit of a hundred miles it lay on the horizon, with its high old towers and steep roofs cutting the level edge of wood and hamlet, and far-scattered mansions.

So long as Geoffrey Brent confined his dissipations to London and Paris and Vienna—anywhere out of sight and sound of his home—opinion was silent. It is easy to listen to far off echoes unmoved, and we can treat them with disbelief, or scorn, or disdain, or whatever attitude of coldness may suit our purpose. But when the scandal came close home it was another matter; and the feelings of independence and integrity which is in people of every community which is not utterly spoiled, asserted itself and demanded that condemnation should be expressed. Still there was a certain reticence in all, and no more notice was taken of the existing facts than was absolutely necessary. Margaret Delandre bore herself so fearlessly and so openly—she accepted her position as the justified companion of Geoffrey Brent so naturally that people came to believe that she was secretly married to him, and therefore thought it wiser to hold their tongues lest time should justify her and also make her an active enemy.

The one person who, by his interference, could have settled all doubts was debarred by circumstances from interfering in the matter. Wykham Delandre had quarrelled with his sister—or perhaps it was that she had quarrelled with him—and they were on terms not merely of armed neutrality but of bitter hatred. The quarrel had been antecedent to Margaret going to Brent's Rock. She and Wykham had almost come to blows. There had certainly been threats on one side and on the other; and in the end Wykham, overcome with passion, had ordered his sister to leave his house. She had risen straightway, and, without waiting to pack up even her own personal belongings, had walked out of the house. On the threshold she had paused for a moment to hurl a bitter threat at Wykham that he would rue in shame and despair to the last hour of his life his act of that day. Some weeks had since passed; and it was understood in the neighbourhood that Margaret had gone to London, when she suddenly appeared driving out with Geoffrey Brent, and the entire neighbourhood knew before nightfall that she had taken up her abode at the Rock. It was no subject of surprise that Brent had come back unexpectedly, for such was his usual custom. Even his own servants never knew when to expect him, for there was a private door, of which he alone had the key, by which he sometimes entered without anyone in the house being aware of his coming. This was his usual method of appearing after a long absence.

Wykham Delandre was furious at the news. He vowed vengeance—and to keep his mind level with his passion drank deeper than ever. He tried several times to see his sister, but she contemptuously refused to meet him. He tried to have an interview with Brent and was refused by him also. Then he tried to stop him in the road, but without avail, for Geoffrey was not a man to be stopped against his will. Several actual encounters took place between the two men, and many more were threatened and avoided. At last Wykham Delandre settled down to a morose, vengeful acceptance of the situation.

Neither Margaret nor Geoffrey was of a pacific temperament, and it was not long before there began to be quarrels between them. One thing would lead to another, and wine flowed freely at Brent's Rock. Now and again the quarrels would assume a bitter aspect, and threats would be exchanged in uncompromising language that fairly awed the listening servants. But such quarrels generally ended where domestic altercations do, in reconciliation, and in a mutual respect for the fighting qualities proportionate to their manifestation. Fighting for its own sake is found by a certain class of persons, all the world over, to be a matter of absorbing interest, and there is no reason to believe that domestic conditions minimise its potency. Geoffrey and Margaret made occasional absences from Brent's Rock, and on each of these occasions Wykham Delandre also absented himself; but as he generally heard of the absence too late to be of any service, he returned home each time in a more bitter and discontented frame of mind than before.

At last there came a time when the absence from Brent's Rock became longer than before. Only a few days earlier there had been a quarrel, exceeding in bitterness anything which had gone before; but this, too, had been made up, and a trip on the Continent had been mentioned before the servants. After a few days Wykham Delandre also went away, and it was some weeks before he returned. It was noticed that he was full of some new importance—satisfaction, exaltation—they hardly knew how to call it. He went straightaway to Brent's Rock, and demanded to see Geoffrey Brent, and on being told that he had not yet returned, said, with a grim decision which the servants noted:

'I shall come again. My news is solid—it can wait!' and turned away. Week after week went by, and month after month; and then there came a rumour, certified later on, that an accident had occurred in the Zermatt valley. Whilst crossing a dangerous pass the carriage containing an English lady and the driver had fallen over a precipice, the gentleman of the party, Mr. Geoffrey Brent, having been fortunately saved as he had been walking up the hill to ease the horses. He gave information, and search was made. The broken rail, the excoriated roadway, the marks where the horses had struggled on the decline before finally pitching over into the torrent—all told the sad tale. It was a wet season, and there had been much snow in the winter, so that the river was swollen beyond its usual volume, and the eddies of the stream were packed with ice. All search was made, and finally the wreck of the carriage and the body of one horse were found in an eddy of the river. Later on the body of the driver was found on the sandy, torrent-swept waste near Täsch; but the body of the lady, like that of the other horse, had quite disappeared, and was—what was left of it by that time—whirling amongst the eddies of the Rhone on its way down to the Lake of Geneva.

Wykham Delandre made all the enquiries possible, but could not find any trace of the missing woman. He found, however, in the books of the various hotels the name of 'Mr. and Mrs. Geoffrey Brent'. And he had a stone erected at Zermatt to his sister's memory, under her married name, and a tablet put up in the church at Bretten, the parish in which both Brent's Rock and Dander's Croft were situated.

There was a lapse of nearly a year, after the excitement of the matter had worn away, and the whole neighbourhood had gone on its accustomed way. Brent was still absent, and Delandre more drunken, more morose, and more revengeful than before.

Then there was a new excitement. Brent's Rock was being made ready for a new mistress. It was officially announced by Geoffrey himself in a letter to the Vicar, that he had been married some months before to an Italian lady, and that they were then on their way home. Then a small army of workmen invaded the house; and hammer and plane sounded, and a general air of size and paint pervaded the atmosphere. One wing of the old house, the south, was entirely re-done; and then the great body of the workmen departed, leaving only materials for the doing of the old hall when Geoffrey Brent should have returned, for he had directed that the decoration was only to be done under his own eyes. He had brought with him accurate drawings of a hall in the house of his bride's father, for he wished to reproduce for her the place to which she had been accustomed. As the moulding had all to be re-done, some scaffolding poles and boards were brought in and laid on one side of the great hall, and also a great wooden tank or box for mixing the lime, which was laid in bags beside it.

When the new mistress of Brent's Rock arrived the bells of the church rang out, and there was a general jubilation. She was a beautiful creature, full of the poetry and fire and passion of the South; and the few English words which she had learned were spoken in such a sweet and pretty broken way that she won the hearts of the people almost as much by the music of her voice as by the melting beauty of her dark eyes.

Geoffrey Brent seemed more happy than he had ever before appeared; but there was a dark, anxious look on his face that was new to those who knew him of old, and he started at times as though at some noise that was unheard by others.

And so months passed and the whisper grew that at last Brent's Rock was to have an heir. Geoffrey was very tender to his wife, and the new bond between them seemed to soften him. He took more interest in his tenants and their needs than he had ever done; and works of charity on his part as well as on his sweet young wife's were not lacking. He seemed to have set all his hopes on the child that was coming, and as he looked deeper into the future the dark shadow that had come over his face seemed to die gradually away.

All the time Wykham Delandre nursed his revenge. Deep in his heart had grown up a purpose of vengeance which only waited an opportunity to crystallise and take a definite shape. His vague idea was somehow centred in the wife of Brent, for he knew that he could strike him best through those he loved, and the coming time seemed to hold in its womb the opportunity for which he longed. One night he sat alone in the living-room of his house. It had once been a handsome room in its way, but time and neglect had done their work and it was now little better than a ruin, without dignity or picturesqueness of any kind. He had been drinking heavily for some time and was more than half stupefied. He thought he heard a noise as of someone at the door and looked up. Then he called half savagely to come in; but there was no response. With a muttered blasphemy he renewed his potations. Presently he forgot all around him, sank into a daze, but suddenly awoke to see standing before him someone or something like a battered, ghostly edition of his sister. For a few moments there came upon him a sort of fear. The woman before him, with distorted features and burning eyes seemed hardly human, and the only thing that seemed a reality of his sister, as she had been, was her wealth of golden hair, and this was now streaked with grey. She eyed her brother with a long, cold stare; and he, too, as he looked and began to realise the actuality of her presence, found the hatred of her which he had had, once again surging up in his heart. All the brooding passion of the past year seemed to find a voice at once as he asked her:

'Why are you here? You're dead and buried.'

'I am here, Wykham Delandre, for no love of you, but because I hate another even more than I do you!' A great passion blazed in her eyes.

'Him?' he asked, in so fierce a whisper that even the woman was for an instant startled till she regained her calm.

'Yes, him!' she answered. 'But make no mistake, my revenge is my own; and I merely use you to help me to it.' Wykham asked suddenly;

'Did he marry you?'

The woman's distorted face broadened out in a ghastly attempt at a smile. It was a hideous mockery, for the broken features and seamed scars took strange shapes and strange colours, and queer lines of white showed out as the straining muscles pressed on the old cicatrices.

'So you would like to know! It would please your pride to feel that your sister was truly married! Well, you shall not know. That was my revenge on you, and I do not mean to change it by a hair's breadth. I have come here tonight simply to let you know that I am alive, so that if any violence be done me where I am going there may be a witness.'

'Where are you going?' demanded her brother.

'That is my affair! and I have not the least intention of letting you know!' Wykham stood up, but the drink was on him and he reeled and fell. As he lay on the floor he announced his intention of following his sister; and with an outburst of splenetic humour told her that he would follow her through the darkness by the light of her hair, and of her beauty. At this she turned on him, and said that there were others beside him that would rue her hair and her beauty too. 'As he will,' she hissed; 'for the hair remains though the beauty be gone. When he withdrew the lynch-pin and sent us over the precipice into the torrent, he had little thought of my beauty. Perhaps his beauty would be scarred like mine were he whirled, as I was, among the rocks of the Visp, and frozen on the ice pack in the drift of the river. But let him beware! His time is coming!' and with a fierce gesture she flung open the door and passed out into the night.

Later on that night, Mrs. Brent, who was but half-asleep, became suddenly awake and spoke to her husband:

'Geoffrey, was not that the click of a lock somewhere below our window?'

But Geoffrey—though she thought that he, too, had started at the noise—seemed sound asleep, and breathed heavily. Again Mrs. Brent dozed; but this time awoke to the fact that her husband had arisen and was partially dressed. He was deadly pale, and when the light of the lamp which he had in his hand fell on his face, she was frightened at the look in his eyes.

'What is it, Geoffrey? What dost thou?' she asked.

'Hush! little one,' he answered, in a strange, hoarse voice. 'Go to sleep. I am restless, and wish to finish some work I left undone.'

'Bring it here, my husband,' she said; 'I am lonely and I fear when thou art away.'

For reply he merely kissed her and went out, closing the door behind him. She lay awake for awhile, and then nature asserted itself, and she slept.

Suddenly she started broad awake with the memory in her ears of a smothered cry from somewhere not far off. She jumped up and ran to the door and listened, but there was no sound. She grew alarmed for her husband, and called out: 'Geoffrey! Geoffrey!'

After a few moments the door of the great hall opened, and Geoffrey appeared at it, but without his lamp.

'Hush!' he said, in a sort of whisper, and his voice was harsh and stern. 'Hush! Get to bed! I am working, and must not be disturbed. Go to sleep, and do not wake the house!'

With a chill in her heart—for the harshness of her husband's voice was new to her—she crept back to bed and lay there trembling, too frightened to cry, and listened to every sound. There was a long pause of silence, and then the sound of some iron implement striking muffled blows! Then there came a clang of a heavy stone falling, followed by a muffled curse. Then a dragging sound, and then more noise of stone on stone. She lay all the while in an agony of fear, and her heart beat dreadfully. She heard a curious sort of scraping sound; and then there was silence. Presently the door opened gently, and Geoffrey appeared. His wife pretended to be asleep; but through her eyelashes she saw him wash from his hands something white that looked like lime.

In the morning he made no allusion to the previous night, and she was afraid to ask any question.

From that day there seemed some shadow over Geoffrey Brent. He neither ate nor slept as he had been accustomed, and his former habit of turning suddenly as though someone were speaking from behind him revived. The old hall seemed to have some kind of fascination for him. He used to go there many times in the day, but grew impatient if anyone, even his wife, entered it. When the builder's foreman came to inquire about continuing his work Geoffrey was out driving; the man went into the hall, and when Geoffrey returned the servant told him of his arrival and where he was. With a frightful oath he pushed the servant aside and hurried up to the old hall. The workman met him almost at the door; and as Geoffrey burst into the room he ran against him. The man apologised:

'Beg pardon, sir, but I was just going out to make some enquiries. I directed twelve sacks of lime to be sent here, but I see there are only ten.'

'Damn the ten sacks and the twelve too!' was the ungracious and incomprehensible rejoinder.

The workman looked surprised, and tried to turn the conversation.

'I see, sir, there is a little matter which our people must have done; but the governor will of course see it set right at his own cost.'

'What do you mean?'

'That 'ere 'arth-stone, sir: Some idiot must have put a scaffold pole on it and cracked it right down the middle, and it's thick enough you'd think to stand hanythink.' Geoffrey was silent for quite a minute, and then said in a constrained voice and with much gentler manner:

'Tell your people that I am not going on with the work in the hall at present. I want to leave it as it is for a while longer.'

'All right sir. I'll send up a few of our chaps to take away these poles and lime bags and tidy the place up a bit.'

'No! No!' said Geoffrey, 'leave them where they are. I shall send and tell you when you are to get on with the work.' So the foreman went away, and his comment to his master was:

'I'd send in the bill, sir, for the work already done. 'Pears to me that money's a little shaky in that quarter.'

Once or twice Delandre tried to stop Brent on the road, and, at last, finding that he could not attain his object rode after the carriage, calling out:

'What has become of my sister, your wife?' Geoffrey lashed his horses into a gallop, and the other, seeing from his white face and from his wife's collapse almost into a faint that his object was attained, rode away with a scowl and a laugh.

That night when Geoffrey went into the hall he passed over to the great fireplace, and all at once started back with a smothered cry. Then with an effort he pulled himself together and went away, returning with a light. He bent down over the broken hearth-stone to see if the moonlight falling through the storied window had in any way deceived him. Then with a groan of anguish he sank to his knees.

There, sure enough, through the crack in the broken stone were protruding a multitude of threads of golden hair just tinged with grey!

He was disturbed by a noise at the door, and looking round, saw his wife standing in the doorway. In the desperation of the moment he took action to prevent discovery, and lighting a match at the lamp, stooped down and burned away the hair that rose through the broken stone. Then rising nonchalantly as he could, he pretended surprise at seeing his wife beside him.

For the next week he lived in an agony; for, whether by accident or design, he could not find himself alone in the hall for any length of time. At each visit the hair had grown afresh through the crack, and he had to watch it carefully lest his terrible secret should be discovered. He tried to find a receptacle for the body of the murdered woman outside the house, but someone always interrupted him; and once, when he was coming out of the private doorway, he was met by his wife, who began to question him about it, and manifested surprise that she should not have before noticed the key which he now reluctantly showed her. Geoffrey dearly and passionately loved his wife, so that any possibility of her discovering his dread secrets, or even of doubting him, filled him with anguish; and after a couple of days had passed, he could not help coming to the conclusion that, at least, she suspected something.

That very evening she came into the hall after her drive and found him there sitting moodily by the deserted fireplace. She spoke to him directly.

'Geoffrey, I have been spoken to by that fellow Delandre, and he says horrible things. He tells to me that a week ago his sister returned to this house, the wreck and ruin of her former self, with only her golden hair as of old, and announced some fell intention. He asked me where she is—and oh, Geoffrey, she is dead, she is dead! So how can she have returned? Oh! I am in dread, and I know not where to turn!'

For answer, Geoffrey burst into a torrent of blasphemy which made her shudder. He cursed Delandre and his sister and all their kind, and in especial he hurled curse after curse on her golden hair.

'Oh, hush! hush!' she said, and was then silent, for she feared her husband when she saw the evil effect of his humour. Geoffrey in the torrent of his anger stood up and moved away from the hearth; but suddenly stopped as he saw a new look of terror in his wife's eyes. He followed their glance, and then he too, shuddered—for there on the broken hearth-stone lay a golden streak as the point of the hair rose through the crack.

'Look, look!' she shrieked. 'Is it some ghost of the dead! Come away—come away!' and seizing her husband by the wrist with the frenzy of madness, she pulled him from the room.

That night she was in a raging fever. The doctor of the district attended her at once, and special aid was telegraphed for to London. Geoffrey was in despair, and in his anguish at the danger to his young wife almost forgot his own crime and its consequences. In the evening the doctor had to leave to attend to others; but he left Geoffrey in charge of his wife. His last words were:

'Remember, you must humour her till I come in the morning, or till some other doctor has her case in hand. What you have to dread is another attack of emotion. See that she is kept warm. Nothing more can be done.'

Late in the evening, when the rest of the household had retired, Geoffrey's wife got up from her bed and called to her husband.

'Come!' she said. 'Come to the old hall! I know where the gold comes from! I want to see it grow!'

Geoffrey would fain have stopped her, but he feared for her life or reason on the one hand, and lest in a paroxysm she should shriek out her terrible suspicion, and seeing that it was useless to try to prevent her, wrapped a warm rug around her and went with her to the old hall. When they entered, she turned and shut the door and locked it.

'We want no strangers amongst us three tonight!' she whispered with a wan smile.

'We three! nay we are but two,' said Geoffrey with a shudder; he feared to say more.

'Sit here,' said his wife as she put out the light. 'Sit here by the hearth and watch the gold growing. The silver moonlight is jealous! See, it steals along the floor towards the gold—our gold!' Geoffrey looked with growing horror, and saw that during the hours that had passed the golden hair had protruded further through the broken hearth-stone. He tried to hide it by placing his feet over the broken place; and his wife, drawing her chair beside him, leant over and laid her head on his shoulder.

'Now do not stir, dear,' she said; 'let us sit still and watch. We shall find the secret of the growing gold!' He passed his arm round her and sat silent; and as the moonlight stole along the floor she sank to sleep.

He feared to wake her; and so sat silent and miserable as the hours stole away.

Before his horror-struck eyes the golden hair from the broken stone grew and grew; and as it increased, so his heart got colder and colder, till at last he had not power to stir, and sat with eyes full of terror watching his doom.

* * *

In the morning when the London doctor came, neither Geoffrey nor his wife could be found. Search was made in all the rooms, but without avail. As a last resource the great door of the old hall was broken open, and those who entered saw a grim and sorry sight.

There by the deserted hearth Geoffrey Brent and his young wife sat cold and white and dead. Her face was peaceful, and her eyes were closed in sleep; but his face was a sight that made all who saw shudder, for there was on it a look of unutterable horror. The eyes were open and stared glassily at his feet, which were twined with tresses of golden hair, streaked with grey, which came through the broken hearth-stone.

DRACULA'S GUEST

WHEN WE STARTED for our drive the sun was shining brightly on Munich, and the air was full of the joyousness of early summer. Just as we were about to depart, Herr Delbrück (the maître d'hôtel of the Quatre Saisons, where I was staying) came down, bareheaded, to the carriage and, after wishing me a pleasant drive, said to the coachman, still holding his hand on the handle of the carriage door:

'Remember you are back by nightfall. The sky looks bright but there is a shiver in the north wind that says there may be a sudden storm. But I am sure you will not be late.' Here he smiled, and added, 'for you know what night it is.'

Johann answered with an emphatic, 'Ja, mein Herr,' and, touching his hat, drove off quickly. When we had cleared the town, I said, after signalling to him to stop:

'Tell me, Johann, what is tonight?'

He crossed himself, as he answered laconically: 'Walpurgis Nacht.' Then he took out his watch, a great, old-fashioned German silver thing as big as a turnip, and looked at it, with his eyebrows gathered together and a little impatient shrug of his shoulders. I realised that this was his way of respectfully protesting against the unnecessary delay, and sank back in the carriage, merely motioning him to proceed. He started off rapidly, as if to make up for lost time. Every now and then the horses seemed to throw up their heads and sniffed the air suspiciously. On such occasions I often looked round in alarm. The road was pretty bleak, for we were traversing a sort of high, wind-swept plateau. As we drove, I saw a road that looked but little used, and which seemed to dip through a little, winding valley. It looked so inviting that, even at the risk of offending him, I called Johann to stop—and when he had pulled up, I told him I would like to drive down that road. He made all sorts of excuses, and frequently crossed himself as he spoke. This somewhat piqued my curiosity, so I asked him various questions. He answered fencingly, and repeatedly looked at his watch in protest. Finally I said:

'Well, Johann, I want to go down this road. I shall not ask you to come unless you like; but tell me why you do not like to go, that is all I ask.' For answer he seemed to throw himself off the box, so quickly did he reach the ground. Then he stretched out his hands appealingly to me, and implored me not to go. There was just enough of English mixed with the German for me to understand the drift of his talk. He seemed always just about to tell me something—the very idea of which evidently frightened him; but each time he pulled himself up, saying, as he crossed himself: 'Walpurgis Nacht!'

I tried to argue with him, but it was difficult to argue with a man who did not know one's language. The advantage certainly rested with him, for although he began to speak in English, of a very crude and broken kind, he always got excited and broke into his native tongue—and every time he did so, he looked at his watch. Then the horses became restless and sniffed the air. At this he grew very pale, and, looking around in a frightened way, he suddenly jumped forward, took them by the bridles and led them on some twenty feet. I followed, and asked why he had done this. For answer he crossed himself, pointed to the spot we had left and drew his carriage in the direction of the other road, indicating a cross, and said, first in German, then in English: 'Buried him—him what killed themselves.'

I remembered the old custom of burying suicides at cross-roads: 'Ah! I see, a suicide. How interesting!' But for the life of me I could not make out why the horses were frightened.

Whilst we were talking, we heard a sort of sound between a yelp and a bark. It was far away; but the horses got very restless, and it took Johann all his time to quiet them. He was pale, and said, 'It sounds like a wolf—but yet there are no wolves here now.'

'No?' I said, questioning him; 'isn't it long since the wolves were so near the city?'

'Long, long', he answered, 'in the spring and summer; but with the snow the wolves have been here not so long.'

Whilst he was petting the horses and trying to quiet them, dark clouds drifted rapidly across the sky. The sunshine passed away, and a breath of cold wind seemed to drift past us. It was only a breath, however, and more in the nature of a warning than a fact, for the sun came out brightly again. Johann looked under his lifted hand at the horizon and said:

'The storm of snow he comes before long time.' Then he looked at his watch again, and, straightway holding his reins firmly—for the horses were still pawing the ground restlessly and shaking their heads—he climbed to his box as though the time had come for proceeding on our journey.

I felt a little obstinate and did not at once get into the carriage.

'Tell me,' I said, 'about this place where the road leads,' and I pointed down.

Again he crossed himself and mumbled a prayer, before he answered, 'It is unholy.'

'What is unholy?' I enquired.

'The village.'

'Then there is a village?'

'No, no. No one lives there hundreds of years.' My curiosity was piqued, 'But you said there was a village.'

'There was.'

'Where is it now?'

Whereupon he burst out into a long story in German and English, so mixed up that I could not quite understand exactly what he said, but roughly I gathered that long ago, hundreds of years, men had died there and been buried in their graves; and sounds were heard under the clay, and when the graves were opened, men and women were found rosy with life, and their mouths red with blood. And so, in haste to save their lives (aye, and their souls!—and here he crossed himself) those who were left fled away to other places, where the living lived, and the dead were dead and not—not something. He was evidently afraid to speak the last words. As he proceeded with his narration, he grew more and more excited. It seemed as if his imagination had got hold of him, and he ended in a perfect paroxysm of fear—white-faced, perspiring, trembling and looking round him, as if expecting that some dreadful presence would manifest itself there in the bright sunshine on the open plain. Finally, in an agony of desperation, he cried:

'Walpurgis Nacht!' and pointed to the carriage for me to get in. All my English blood rose at this, and, standing back, I said:

'You are afraid, Johann—you are afraid. Go home; I shall return alone; the walk will do me good.' The carriage door was open. I took from the seat my oak walking-stick—which I always carry on my holiday excursions—and closed the door, pointing back to Munich, and said, 'Go home, Johann—Walpurgis Nacht doesn't concern Englishmen.'

The horses were now more restive than ever, and Johann was trying to hold them in, while excitedly imploring me not to do anything so foolish. I pitied the poor fellow, he was deeply in earnest; but all the same I could not help laughing. His English was quite gone now. In his anxiety he had forgotten that his only means of making me understand was to talk my language, so he jabbered away in his native German. It began to be a little tedious. After giving the direction, 'Home!' I turned to go down the cross-road into the valley.

With a despairing gesture, Johann turned his horses towards Munich. I leaned on my stick and looked after him. He went slowly along the road for a while: then there came over the crest of the hill a man tall and thin. I could see so much in the distance. When he drew near the horses, they began to jump and kick about, then to scream with terror. Johann could not hold them in; they bolted down the road, running away madly. I watched them out of sight, then looked for the stranger, but I found that he, too, was gone.

With a light heart I turned down the side road through the deepening valley to which Johann had objected. There was not the slightest reason, that I could see, for his objection; and I daresay I tramped for a couple of hours without thinking of time or dist-

* *

ance, and certainly without seeing a person or a house. So far as the place was concerned, it was desolation itself. But I did not notice this particularly till, on turning a bend in the road, I came upon a scattered fringe of wood; then I recognised that I had been impressed unconsciously by the desolation of the region through which I had passed.

I sat down to rest myself, and began to look around. It struck me that it was considerably colder than it had been at the commencement of my walk—a sort of sighing sound seemed to be around me, with, now and then, high overhead, a sort of muffled roar. Looking upwards I noticed that great thick clouds were drifting rapidly across the sky from North to South at a great height. There were signs of coming storm in some lofty stratum of the air. I was a little chilly, and, thinking that it was the sitting still after the exercise of walking, I resumed my journey.

The ground I passed over was now much more picturesque. There were no striking objects that the eye might single out; but in all there was a charm of beauty. I took little heed of time and it was only when the deepening twilight forced itself upon me that I began to think of how I should find my way home. The brightness of the day had gone. The air was cold, and the drifting of clouds high overhead was more marked. They were accompanied by a sort of far-away rushing sound, through which seemed to come at intervals that mysterious cry which the driver had said came from a wolf. For a while I hesitated. I had said I would see the deserted village, so on I went, and presently came on a wide stretch of open country, shut in by hills all around. Their sides were covered with trees which spread down to the plain, dotting, in clumps, the gentler slopes and hollows which showed here and there. I followed with my eye the winding of the road, and saw that it curved close to one of the densest of these clumps and was lost behind it.

As I looked there came a cold shiver in the air, and the snow began to fall. I thought of the miles and miles of bleak country I had passed, and then hurried on to seek the shelter of the wood in front. Darker and darker grew the sky, and faster and heavier fell the snow, till the earth before and around me was a glistening white carpet the further edge of which was lost in misty vagueness. The road was here but crude, and when on the level its boundaries were not so marked as when it passed through the cuttings; and in a little while I found that I must have strayed from it, for I missed underfoot the hard surface, and my feet sank deeper in the grass and moss. Then the wind grew stronger and blew with ever increasing force, till I was fain to run before it. The air became icy-cold, and in spite of my exercise I began to suffer. The snow was now falling so thickly and whirling around me in such rapid eddies that I could hardly keep my eyes open. Every now and then the heavens were torn asunder by vivid lightning, and in the flashes I could see ahead of me a great mass of trees, chiefly yew and cypress all heavily coated with snow.

I was soon amongst the shelter of the trees, and there, in comparative silence, I could hear the rush of the wind high overhead. Presently the blackness of the storm had become merged in the darkness of the night. By-and-by the storm seemed to be passing away: it now only came in fierce puffs or blasts. At such moments the weird sound of the wolf appeared to be echoed by many similar sounds around me.

Now and again, through the black mass of drifting cloud, came a straggling ray of moonlight, which lit up the expanse, and showed me that I was at the edge of a dense mass of cypress and yew trees. As the snow had ceased to fall, I walked out from the shelter and began to investigate more closely. It appeared to me that, amongst so many old foundations as I had passed, there might be still standing a house in which, though in ruins, I could find some sort of shelter for a while. As I skirted the edge of the copse, I found that a low wall encircled it, and following this I presently found an opening. Here the cypresses formed an alley leading up to a square mass of some kind of building. Just as I caught sight of this, however, the drifting clouds obscured the moon, and I passed up the path in darkness. The wind must have grown colder, for I felt myself shiver as I walked; but there was hope of shelter, and I groped my way blindly on.

I stopped, for there was a sudden stillness. The storm had

passed; and, perhaps in sympathy with nature's silence, my heart seemed to cease to beat. But this was only momentarily; for suddenly the moonlight broke through the clouds, showing me that I was in a graveyard, and that the square object before me was a great massive tomb of marble, as white as the snow that lay on and all around it. With the moonlight there came a fierce sigh of the storm, which appeared to resume its course with a long, low howl, as of many dogs or wolves. I was awed and shocked, and felt the cold perceptibly grow upon me till it seemed to grip me by the heart. Then while the flood of moonlight still fell on the marble tomb, the storm gave further evidence of renewing, as though it was returning on its track. Impelled by some sort of fascination, I approached the sepulchre to see what it was, and why such a thing stood alone in such a place. I walked around it, and read, over the Doric door, in German:

COUNTESS DOLINGEN OF GRATZ
IN STYRIA
SOUGHT AND FOUND DEATH
1801

On the top of the tomb, seemingly driven through the solid marble—for the structure was composed of a few vast blocks of stone—was a great iron spike or stake. On going to the back I saw, graven in Great Russian letters:

'The dead travel fast.'

There was something so weird and uncanny about the whole thing that it gave me a turn and made me feel quite faint. I began to wish, for the first time, that I had taken Johann's advice. Here a thought struck me, which came under almost mysterious circumstances and with a terrible shock. This was Walpurgis Night!

Walpurgis Night, when, according to the belief of millions of people, the devil was abroad—when the graves were opened and the dead came forth and walked. When all evil things of earth and air and water held revel. This very place the driver had specially shunned. This was the depopulated village of centuries ago. This was where the suicide lay; and this was the place where I was alone—unmanned, shivering with cold in a shroud of snow with a wild storm gathering again upon me! It took all my philosophy, all the religion I had been taught, all my courage, not to collapse in a paroxysm of fright.

And now a perfect tornado burst upon me. The ground shook as though thousands of horses thundered across it; and this time the storm bore on its icy wings, not snow, but great hailstones which drove with such violence that they might have come from the throngs of Balearic slingers—hailstones that beat down leaf and branch and made the shelter of the cypresses of no more avail than though their stems were standing-corn. At the first I had rushed to the nearest tree; but I was soon fain to leave it and seek the only spot that seemed to afford refuge, the deep Doric doorway of the marble tomb. There, crouching against the massive bronze door, I gained a certain amount of protection from the beating of the hailstones, for now they only drove against me as they ricocheted from the ground and the side of the marble.

As I leaned against the door, it moved slightly and opened inwards. The shelter of even a tomb was welcome in that pitiless tempest, and I was about to enter it when there came a flash of forked-lightning that lit up the whole expanse of the heavens. In the instant, as I am a living man, I saw, as my eyes were turned into the darkness of the tomb, a beautiful woman, with rounded cheeks and red lips, seemingly sleeping on a bier. As the thunder broke overhead, I was grasped as by the hand of a giant and hurled out into the storm. The whole thing was so sudden that, before I could realise the shock, moral as well as physical, I found the hailstones beating me down. At the same time I had a strange, dominating feeling that I was not alone. I looked towards the tomb. Just then there came another blinding flash, which seemed to strike the iron stake that surmounted the tomb and to pour through to the earth, blasting and crumbling the marble, as in a burst of flame. The dead woman rose for a moment of agony, while she was lapped in the flame, and her bitter scream of pain was drowned in the thundercrash. The last thing I heard was this mingling of dreadful sound, as again I was seized in the giant-grasp and dragged away, while the hailstones beat on me, and the air around seemed reverberant with the howling of wolves. The last sight that I remembered was a vague, white, moving mass, as if all the graves around me had sent out the phantoms of their sheeted-dead, and that they were closing in on me through the white cloudiness of the driving hail.

Gradually there came a sort of vague beginning of consciousness; then a sense of weariness that was dreadful. For a time I remembered nothing; but slowly my senses returned. My feet seemed positively racked with pain, yet I could not move them. They seemed to be numbed. There was an icy feeling at the back of my neck and all down my spine, and my ears, like my feet, were dead, yet in torment; but there was in my breast a sense of warmth which was, by comparison, delicious. It was as a nightmare —a physical nightmare, if one may use such an expression; for some heavy weight on my chest made it difficult for me to breathe.

This period of semi-lethargy seemed to remain a long time, and as it faded away I must have slept or swooned. Then came a sort of loathing, like the first stage of sea-sickness, and a wild desire to be free from something—I knew not what. A vast stillness enveloped me, as though all the world were asleep or dead—only broken by the low panting as of some animal close to me. I felt a warm rasping at my throat, then came a consciousness of the awful truth, which chilled me to the heart and sent the blood surging up through my brain. Some great animal was lying on me and now licking my throat. I feared to stir, for some instinct of prudence bade me lie still; but the brute seemed to realise that there was now some change in me, for it raised its head. Through my eyelashes I saw above me the two great flaming eyes of a gigantic wolf. Its sharp white teeth gleamed in the gaping red mouth, and I could feel its hot breath fierce and acrid upon me.

For another spell of time I remembered no more. Then I became conscious of a low growl, followed by a yelp, renewed again and again. Then, seemingly very far away, I heard a 'Holloa!

holloa!' as of many voices calling in unison. Cautiously I raised my head and looked in the direction whence the sound came; but the cemetery blocked my view. The wolf still continued to yelp in a strange way, and a red glare began to move round the grove of cypresses, as though following the sound. As the voices drew closer, the wolf yelped faster and louder, I feared to make either sound or motion. Nearer came the red glow, over the white pall which stretched into the darkness around me. Then all at once from beyond the trees there came at a trot a troop of horsemen bearing torches. The wolf rose from my breast and made for the cemetery. I saw one of the horsemen (soldiers by their caps and their military cloaks) raise his carbine and take aim. A companion knocked up his arm, and I heard the ball whizz over my head. He had evidently taken my body for that of the wolf. Another sighted the animal as it slunk away, and a shot followed. Then, at a gallop, the troop rode forward—some towards me, others following the wolf as it disappeared amongst the snow-clad cypresses.

As they drew nearer I tried to move, but was powerless, although I could see and hear all that went on around me. Two or three of the soldiers jumped from their horses and knelt beside me. One of them raised my head, and placed his hand over my heart.

'Good news, comrades!' he cried. 'His heart still beats!'

Then some brandy was poured down my throat; it put vigour into me, and I was able to open my eyes fully and look around. Lights and shadows were moving among the trees, and I heard men call to one another. They drew together, uttering frightening exclamations; and the lights flashed as the others came pouring out of the cemetery pell-mell, like men possessed. When the further ones came close to us, those who were around me asked them eagerly:

'Well, have you found him?'

The reply rang out hurriedly:

'No! no! Come away quick—quick! This is no place to stay, and on this of all nights!'

'What was it?' was the question, asked in all manner of keys.

The answer came variously and all indefinitely as though the men were moved by some common impulse to speak, yet were restrained by some common fear from giving their thoughts.

'It—it—indeed!' gibbered one, whose wits had plainly given out for the moment.

'A wolf—and yet not a wolf!' another put in shudderingly.

'No use trying for him without the sacred bullet,' a third remarked in a more ordinary manner.

'Serve us right for coming out on this night! Truly we have earned our thousand marks!' were the ejaculations of a fourth.

'There was blood on the broken marble,' another said after a pause—'the lightning never brought that there. And for him—is he safe? Look at his throat! See, comrades, the wolf has been lying on him and keeping his blood warm.'

The officer looked at my throat and replied:

'He is all right; the skin is not pierced. What does it all mean? We should never have found him but for the yelping of the wolf.'

'What became of it?' asked the man who was holding up my head, and who seemed the least panic-stricken of the party, for his hands were steady and without tremor. On his sleeve was the chevron of a petty officer.

'It went to its home,' answered the man, whose long face was pallid, and who actually shook with terror as he glanced around fearfully. 'There are graves enough there in which it may lie. Come, comrades—come quickly! Let us leave this cursed spot.'

The officer raised me to a sitting posture, as he uttered a word of command; then several men placed me upon a horse. He sprang to the saddle behind me, took me in his arms, gave the word to advance; and, turning our faces away from the cypresses, we rode away in swift, military order.

As yet my tongue refused its office, and I was perforce silent. I must have fallen asleep; for the next thing I remembered was finding myself standing up, supported by a soldier on each side of me. It was almost broad daylight, and to the north a red streak of sunlight was reflected, like a path of blood, over the waste of snow. The officer was telling the men to say nothing of what they had seen, except that they found an English stranger, guarded by a large dog.

'Dog! that was no dog,' cut in the man who had exhibited such fear. 'I think I know a wolf when I see one.'

The young officer answered calmly: 'I said a dog.'

'Dog!' reiterated the other ironically. It was evident that his courage was rising with the sun; and, pointing to me, he said, 'Look at his throat. Is that the work of a dog, master?'

Instinctively I raised my hand to my throat, and as I touched it I cried out in pain. The men crowded round to look, some stooping down from their saddles; and again there came the calm voice of the young officer.

'A dog, as I said. If aught else were said we should only be laughed at.'

I was then mounted behind a trooper, and we rode on into the suburbs of Munich. Here we came across a stray carriage, into which I was lifted, and it was driven off to the Quatre Saisons—the young officer accompanying me, whilst a trooper followed with his horse, and the others rode off to their barracks.

When we arrived, Herr Delbrück rushed so quickly down the steps to meet me, that it was apparent he had been watching within. Taking me by both hands he solicitously led me in. The officer saluted me and was turning to withdraw, when I recognised his purpose, and insisted that he should come to my rooms. Over a glass of wine I warmly thanked him and his brave comrades for saving me. He replied simply that he was more than glad, and that Herr Delbrück had at the first taken steps to make all the searching party pleased; at which ambiguous utterance the maître d'hôtel smiled, while the officer pleaded duty and withdrew.

'But Herr Delbrück,' I enquired, 'how and why was it that the soldiers searched for me?'

He shrugged his shoulders, as if in depreciation of his own deed, as he replied:

'I was so fortunate as to obtain leave from the commander of the regiment in which I served, to ask for volunteers.

'But how did you know that I was lost?' I asked.

'The driver came hither with the remains of his carriage, which had been upset when the horses ran away.'

'But surely you would not send a search-party of soldiers merely on this account.

'Oh, no!' he answered; 'but even before the coachman arrived, I had this telegram from the Boyar whose guest you are,' and he took from his pocket a telegram which he handed to me, and I read:

Bistritz.

Be careful of my guest—his safety is most precious to me. Should aught happen to him, or if he be missed, spare nothing to find him and ensure his safety. He is English and therefore adventurous. There are often dangers from snow and wolves and night. Lose not a moment if you suspect harm to him. I answer your zeal with my fortune.—*Dracula.*

As I held the telegram in my hand, the room seemed to whirl around me; and, if the attentive maître d'hôtel had not caught me, I think I should have fallen. There was something so strange in all this, something so weird and impossible to imagine, that there grew on me a sense of my being in some way the sport of opposite forces—the mere vague idea of which seemed in a way to paralyse me. I was certainly under some form of mysterious protection. From a distant country had come, in the very nick of time, a message that took me out of the danger of the snow-sleep and the jaws of the wolf.

THE INVISIBLE GIANT

TIME GOES ON in the Country Under the Sunset much as it does here.

Many years passed away; and they wrought much change. And now we find a time when the people that lived in good King Mago's time would hardly have known their beautiful Land if they had seen it again.

It had sadly changed indeed. No longer was there the same love or the same reverence towards the king—no longer was there perfect peace. People had become more selfish and more greedy, and had tried to grasp all they could for themselves. There were some very rich and there were many poor. Most of the beautiful gardens were laid waste. Houses had grown up close round the palace; and in some of these dwelt many persons who could only afford to pay for part of a house.

All the beautiful Country was sadly changed, and changed was the life of the dwellers in it. The people had almost forgotten Prince Zaphir, who was dead many, many years ago; and no more roses were spread on the pathways. Those who lived now in the Country Under the Sunset laughed at the idea of more Giants, and they did not fear them because they did not see them. Some of them said,

'Tush! what can there be to fear? Even if there ever were giants there are none now.'

And so the people sang and danced and feasted as before, and thought only of themselves. The Spirits that guarded the Land were were very, very sad. Their great white shadowy wings drooped as they stood at their posts at the Portals of the Land. They hid their faces, and their eyes were dim with continuous weeping, so that they heeded not if any evil thing went by them. They tried to make the people think of their evil-doing; but they could not leave their posts, and the people heard their moaning in the night season and said,

'Listen to the sighing of the breeze; how sweet it is!'

So is it ever with us also, that when we hear the wind sighing and moaning and sobbing round our houses in the lonely nights, we do not think our Angels may be sorrowing for our misdeeds, but only that there is a storm coming. The Angels wept evermore, and they felt the sorrow of dumbness—for though they could speak, those they spoke to would not hear.

Whilst the people laughed at the idea of Giants, there was one old man who shook his head, and made answer to them, when he heard them, and said:

'Death has many children, and there are Giants in the marshes still. You may not see them, perhaps—but they are there, and the only bulwark of safety is in a land of patient, faithful hearts.'

The name of this good old man was Knoal, and he lived in a house built of great blocks of stone, in the middle of a wild place far from the city.

In the city there were many great old houses, storey upon storey high; and in these houses lived many poor people. The higher you went up the great steep stairs the poorer were the people that lived there, so that in the garrets were some so poor that when the morning came they did not know whether they should have anything to eat the whole long day. This was very, very sad, and gentle children would have wept if they had seen their pain.

In one of these garrets there lived all alone a little maiden called Zaya. She was an orphan, for her father had died many years before, and her poor mother, who had toiled long and wearily for her dear little daughter—her only child—had died also not long since.

Poor little Zaya had wept so bitterly when she saw her dear mother lying dead, and she had been so sad and sorry for a long time, that she quite forgot that she had no means of living. However, the poor people who lived in the house had given her part of their own food, so that she did not starve.

Then after a while she had tried to work for herself and earn her own living. Her mother had taught her to make flowers out of paper; so that she made a lot of flowers, and when she had a full basket she took them into the street and sold them. She made flowers of many kinds, roses and lilies, and violets, and snowdrops, and primroses, and mignonette, and many beautiful sweet flowers that only grow in the Country Under the Sunset. Some of them she could make without any pattern, but others she could not, so when she wanted a pattern she took her basket of paper and scissors, and paste, and brushes, and all the things she used, and went into the garden which a kind lady owned, where there grew many beautiful flowers. There she sat down and worked away, looking at the flowers she wanted.

Sometimes she was very sad, and her tears fell thick and fast as she thought of her dear dead mother. Often she seemed to feel that her mother was looking down at her, and to see her tender smile in the sunshine on the water; then her heart was glad, and she sang so sweetly that the birds came around her and stopped their own singing to listen to her.

She and the birds grew great friends, and sometimes when she had a sung a song they would all cry out together, as they sat round her in a ring, in a few notes that seemed to say quite plainly:

'Sing to us again. Sing to us again.'

So she would sing again. Then she would ask them to sing, and they would sing till there was quite a concert. After a while the birds knew her so well that they would come into her room, and they even built their nests there, and they followed her wherever she went. The people used to say:

'Look at the girl with the birds; she must be half a bird herself, for see how the birds know and love her.' From so many people coming to say things like this, some silly people actually believed that she was partly a bird, and they shook their heads when wise people laughed at them, and said:

'Indeed she must be; listen to her singing; her voice is sweeter even than the birds.'

So a nickname was applied to her, and naughty boys called it after her in the street, and the nickname was 'Big Bird'. But Zaya did not mind the name; and although often naughty boys said it to her, meaning to cause her pain, she did not dislike it, but the contrary, for she so gloried in the love and trust of her little sweet-voiced pets that she wished to be thought like them.

Indeed it would be well for some naughty little boys and girls if they were as good and harmless as the little birds that work all day long for their helpless baby birds, building nests and bringing food, and sitting so patiently hatching their little speckled eggs.

One evening Zaya sat alone in her garret very sad and lonely. It was a lovely summer's evening, and she sat in the window looking out over the city. She could see over the many streets towards the great cathedral whose spire towered aloft into the sky higher by far even than the great tower of the king's palace. There was hardly a breath of wind, and the smoke went up straight from the chimneys, getting further and fainter till it was lost altogether.

Zaya was very sad. For the first time for many days her birds were all away from her at once, and she did not know where they had gone. It seemed to her as if they had deserted her, and she was so lonely, poor little maid, that she wept bitter tears. She was thinking of the story which long ago her dead mother had told her, how Prince Zaphir had slain the Giant, and she wondered what the prince was like, and thought how happy the people must have been when Zaphir and Bluebell were king and queen. Then she wondered if there were any hungry children in those good days, and if, indeed, as the people said, there were no more Giants. So she went on with her work before the open window.

Presently she looked up from her work and gazed across the city. There she saw a terrible thing—something so terrible that she gave a low cry of fear and wonder, and leaned out of the window, shading her eyes with her hands to see more clearly.

In the sky beyond the city she saw a vast shadowy Form with its arms raised. It was shrouded in a great misty robe that covered it, fading away into air so that she could only see the face and the grim, spectral hands.

The Form was so mighty that the city below it seemed like a child's toy. It was still far off the city.

The little maid's heart seemed to stand still with fear as she thought to herself, 'The Giants, then, are not dead. This is another of them.'

Quickly she ran down the high stairs and out into the street. There she saw some people, and cried to them,

'Look! look! the Giant, the Giant!' and pointed towards the Form which she still saw moving onwards to the city.

The people looked up, but they could not see anything, and they laughed and said,

'The child is mad.'

Then poor little Zaya was more than ever frightened, and ran down the street crying out still,

'Look! look! the Giant, the Giant!' But no one heeded her, and all said, 'The child is mad,' and they went on their own ways.

Then the naughty boys came around her and cried out.

'Big Bird has lost her mates. She sees a bigger bird in the sky, and she wants it.' And they made rhymes about her, and sang them as they danced round.

Zaya ran away from them; and she hurried right through the city, and out into the country beyond it, for she still saw the great Form before her in the air.

As she went on, and got nearer and nearer to the Giant, it grew a little darker. She could see only the clouds; but still there was visible the form of a Giant hanging dimly in the air.

A cold mist closed around her as the Giant appeared to come onwards towards her. Then she thought of all the poor people in the city, and she hoped that the Giant would spare them, and she knelt down before him and lifted up her hands appealingly, and cried aloud:

'Oh, great Giant! spare them, spare them!"

But the Giant moved onwards still as though he never heard. She cried aloud all the more,

'Oh, great Giant! spare them, spare them!' And she bowed her head and wept, and the Giant still, though very slowly, moved onward towards the city.

There was an old man not far off standing at the door of a small house built of great stones, but the little maid saw him not. His face wore a look of fear and wonder, and when he saw the child kneel and raise her hands, he drew nigh and listened to her voice. When he heard her say, 'Oh, great Giant!' he murmured to himself,

'It is then even as I feared. There are more Giants, and truly this is another.' He looked upwards, but he saw nothing, and he murmured again,

'I see not, yet this child can see; and yet I feared, for something told me that there was danger. Truly knowledge is blinder than innocence.'

The little maid, still not knowing there was any human being near her, cried out again, with a great cry of anguish:

'Oh, do not, do not, great Giant, do them harm. If someone must suffer, let it be me. Take me. I am willing to die, but spare them. Spare them, great Giant and do with me even as thou wilt.' But the giant heeded not.

And Knoal—for he was the old man—felt his eyes fill with tears, and he said to himself,

'Oh, noble child, how brave she is, she would sacrifice herself!' And coming closer to her, he put his hand upon her head.

Zaya, who was again bowing her head, started and looked round when she felt the touch. However, when she saw that it was Knoal, she was comforted, for she knew how wise and good he was, and felt that if any person could help her, he could. So she clung to him, and hid her face in his breast; and he stroked her hair and comforted her. But still he could see nothing.

The cold mist swept by, and when Zaya looked up, she saw that the Giant had passed by, and was moving onward to the city.

'Come with me, my child,' said the old man; and the two arose, and went into the dwelling built of great stones.

When Zaya entered, she started, for lo! the inside was as a tomb. The old man felt her shudder, for he still held her close to him, and he said:

'Weep not, little one, and fear not. This place reminds me and all who enter it, that to the tomb we must all come at the last. Fear it not, for it has grown to be a cheerful home to me.'

Then the little maid was comforted, and began to examine all around her more closely. She saw all sorts of curious instruments, and many strange and many common herbs and simples hung to dry in bunches on the walls. The old man watched her in silence till her fear was gone, and then he said:

'My child, saw you the features of the Giant as he passed?'

She answered, 'Yes.'

'Can you describe his face and form to me?' he asked again.

Whereupon she began to tell him all that she had seen. How the Giant was so great that all the sky seemed filled. How the great arms were outspread, veiled in his robe, till far away the shroud was lost in air. How the face was as that of a strong man, pitiless, yet without malice; and that the eyes were blind.

The old man shuddered as he heard, for he knew that the Giant was a very terrible one; and his heart wept for the doomed city where so many would perish in the midst of their sin.

They determined to go forth and warn again the doomed people; and making no delay, the old man and the little maid hurried towards the city.

As they left the small house, Zaya saw the Giant before them, moving towards the city. They hurried on; and when they had passed through the cold mist, Zaya looked back, and saw the Giant behind them.

Presently they came to the city.

It was a strange sight to see that old man and that little maid flying to tell people of the terrible Plague that was coming upon them. The old man's long white beard and hair and the child's golden locks were swept behind them in the wind, so quick they came. The faces of both were white as death. Behind them, seen only to the eyes of the pure-hearted little maid when she looked back, came ever onward at slow pace the spectral Giant that hung a dark shadow in the evening air.

But those in the city never saw the Giant; and when the old man and the little maid warned them, still they heeded not, but scoffed and jeered at them, and said,

'Tush! there are no Giants now'; and they went on their way, laughing and jeering.

Then the old man came and stood on a raised place amongst them, on the lowest step of the great fountain with the little maid by his side, and he spake thus:

'Oh, people, dwellers in this Land, be warned in time. This pure-hearted child, round whose sweet innocence even the little birds that fear men and women gather in peace, has this night seen in the sky the form of a Giant that advances ever onward menacingly to our city. Believe, oh, believe; and be warned, whilst ye may. To myself even as to you the sky is a blank; and yet see that I believe. For listen to me: all unknowing that another Giant had invaded our land, I sat pensive in my dwelling; and, without cause or motive, there came into my heart a sudden fear for the safety of our city. I arose and looked north and south and east and west, and on high and below, but never a sign of danger could I see. So I said to myself,

' "Mine eyes are dim with a hundred years of watching and waiting, and so I cannot see." And yet, oh people, dwellers in this land, though that century has dimmed mine outer eyes, still it has quickened mine inner eyes—the eyes of my soul. Again I went forth, and lo! this little maid knelt and implored a Giant, unseen by me, to spare the city; but he heard her not, or, if he heard, answered her not, and she fell prone. So hither we come to warn you. Yonder, says the maid, he passes onward to the city. Oh, be warned! be warned in time.'

Still the people heeded not; but they scoffed and jeered the more, and said,

'Lo, the maid and the old man both are mad;' and they passed onwards to their homes—to dancing and feasting as before.

Then the naughty boys came and mocked them, and said that Zaya had lost her birds, and gone mad; and they made songs, and sang them as they danced round.

Zaya was so sorely grieved for the poor people that she heeded not the cruel boys. Seeing that she did not heed them, some of them got still more rude and wicked; they went a little way off, and threw things at them, and mocked them all the more.

Then, sad of heart, the old man arose, and took the little maid by the hand, and brought her away into the wilderness; and lodged her with him in the house built with great stones. That night Zaya slept with the sweet smell of the drying herbs all around her; and the old man held her hand that she might have no fear.

In the morning Zaya arose betimes, and awoke the old man, who had fallen asleep in his chair.

She went to the doorway and looked out, and then a thrill of gladness came upon her heart; for outside the door, as though waiting to see her, sat all her little birds, and many, many more. When the birds saw the little maid they sang a few loud joyous notes, and flew about foolishly for very joy—some of them fluttering their wings and looking so funny that she could not help laughing a little.

When Knoal and Zaya had eaten their frugal breakfast and given to their little feathered friends, they set out with sorrowful hearts to visit the city, and to try once more to warn the people. The birds flew around them as they went, and to cheer them sang as joyously as they could, although their little hearts were heavy.

As they walked they saw before them the great shadowy Giant; and he had now advanced to the very confines of the city.

Once again they warned the people, and great crowds came around them, but only mocked them more than ever; and naughty boys threw stones and sticks at the little birds and killed some of them. Poor Zaya wept bitterly, and Knoal's heart was very sad. After a time, when they had moved from the fountain, Zaya looked up and started with joyous surprise, for the great shadowy Giant was nowhere to be seen. She cried out in joy, and the people laughed and said,

'Cunning child! she sees that we will not believe her, and she pretends that the Giant has gone.'

They surrounded her, jeering, and some of them said,

'Let us put her under the fountain and duck her, as a lesson to liars who would frighten us.' Then they approached her with menaces. She clung close to Knoal, who had looked terribly grave when she had said she did not see the Giant any longer, and who was now as if in a dream, thinking. But at her touch he seemed to wake up; and he spoke sternly to the people, and rebuked them. But they cried out on him also, and said that as he had aided Zaya in her lie he should be ducked also, and they advanced to lay hands on them both.

The hand of one who was a ringleader was already outstretched, when he gave a low cry, and pressed his hand to his side; and, whilst the others turned to look at him in wonder, he cried out in great pain, and screamed horribly. Even whilst the people looked, his face grew blacker and blacker, and he fell down before them, and writhed a while in pain, and then died.

All the people screamed out in terror, and ran away, crying aloud.

'The Giant! the Giant! he is indeed amongst us!' They feared all the more that they could not see him.

But before they could leave the market-place, in the centre of which was the fountain, many fell dead and their corpses lay.

There in the centre knelt the old man and the little maid, praying; and the birds sat perched around the fountain, mute and still, and there was no sound heard save the cries of the people far off. Then their wailing sounded louder and louder, for the Giant—Plague—was amongst and around them, and there was no escaping, for it was now too late to fly.

Alas! in the Country Under the Sunset there was much weeping that day; and when the night came there was little sleep, for there was fear in some hearts and pain in others. None were still except the dead, who lay stark about the city, so still and lifeless that even the cold light of the moon and the shadows of the drifting clouds moving over them could not make them seem as though they lived.

And for many a long day there was pain and grief and death in the Country Under the Sunset.

Knoal and Zaya did all they could to help the poor people, but it was hard indeed to aid them, for the unseen Giant was amongst them, wandering through the city to and fro, so that none could tell where he would lay his ice-cold hand.

Some people fled away out of the city; but it was little use, for go how they would and fly never so fast they were still within the grasp of the unseen Giant. Ever and anon he turned their warm hearts to ice with his breath and his touch, and they fell dead.

Some, like those within the city, were spared, and of these some perished of hunger, and the rest crept sadly back to the city and lived or died amongst their friends. And it was all, oh! so sad, for there was nothing but grief and fear and weeping from morn till night.

Now, see how Zaya's little bird friends helped her in her need.

They seemed to see the coming of the Giant when no one—not even the little maid herself—could see anything, and they managed to tell her when there was danger just as well as though they could talk.

At first Knoal and she went home every evening to the house built of great stones to sleep, and came again to the city in the morning, and stayed with the poor sick people, comforting them and feeding them, and giving them medicine which Knoal, from his great wisdom, knew would do them good. Thus they saved many precious human lives, and those who were rescued were very thankful, and henceforth ever after lived holier and more unselfish lives.

After a few days, however, they found that the poor sick people needed help even more at night than in the day, and so they came and lived in the city altogether, helping the stricken folk day and night.

At the earliest dawn Zaya would go forth to breathe the morning air; and there, just waked from sleep, would be her feathered friends waiting for her. They sang glad songs of joy, and came and perched on her shoulders and her head, and kissed her. Then, if she went to go towards any place where, during the night, the Plague had laid his deadly hand, they would flutter before her, and try to impede her, and scream out in their own tongue,

'Go back! go back!'

They pecked of her bread and drank of her cup before she touched them; and when there was danger—for the cold hand of the Giant was placed everywhere—they would cry,

'No, no!' and she would not touch the food, or let anyone else do so. Often it happened that, even whilst it pecked at the bread or drank of the cup, a poor little bird would fall down and flutter its wings and die; but all they that died, did so with a chirp of joy, looking at their little mistress, for whom they had gladly perished. Whenever the little birds found that the bread and the cup were pure and free from danger, they would look up at Zaya jauntily, and flap their wings and try to crow, and seemed so saucy that the poor sad little maiden would smile.

There was one old bird that always took a second, and often a great many pecks at the bread when it was good, so that he got quite a hearty meal; and sometimes he would go on feeding till Zaya would shake her finger at him and say,

'Greedy!' and he would hop away as if he had done nothing.

There was one other dear little bird—a robin, with a breast as red as the sunset—that loved Zaya more than one can think. When he tried the food and found that it was safe to eat, he would take a tiny piece in his bill, and fly up and put it in her mouth.

Every little bird that drank from Zaya's cup and found it good raised its head to say grace; and ever since then the little birds do the same, and they never forget to say their grace—as some thankless children do.

Thus Knoal and Zaya lived, although many around them died, and the Giant still remained in the city. So many people died that one began to wonder that so many were left; for it was only when the town began to get thinned that people thought of the vast numbers that had lived in it.

Poor little Zaya had got so pale and thin that she looked a shadow, and Knoal's form was bent more with the sufferings of a few weeks than it had been by his century of age. But although the two were weary and worn, they still kept on their good work of aiding the sick.

Many of the little birds were dead.

One morning the old man was very weak—so weak that he could hardly stand. Zaya got frightened about him, and said,

'Are you ill, father?' for she always called him father now.

He answered her in a voice alas! hoarse and low, but very, very tender:

'My child, I fear the end is coming: take me home, that there I may die.'

At his words Zaya gave a low cry and fell on her knees beside him, and buried her head in his bosom and wept bitterly, whilst she hugged him close. But she had little time for weeping, for the old man struggled up to his feet, and, seeing that he wanted aid, she dried her tears and helped him.

The old man took his staff, and with Zaya helping to support him, got as far as the fountain in the midst of the market-place; and there, on the lowest step, he sank down as though exhausted. Zaya felt him grow cold as ice, and she knew that the chilly hand of the Giant had been laid upon him.

Then, without knowing why, she looked up to where she had last seen the Giant as Knoal and she had stood beside the fountain. And lo! as she looked, holding Knoal's hand, she saw the shadowy form of the terrible Giant who had been so long invisible growing more and more clearly out of the clouds.

His face was stern as ever, and his eyes were still blind.

Zaya cried to the Giant, still holding Knoal tightly by the hand:

'Not him, not him! Oh, mighty Giant! not him! not him!' and she bowed her head and wept.

There was such anguish in her heart that to the blind eyes of the shadowy Giant came tears that fell like dew on the forehead of the old man. Knoal spake to Zaya:

'Grieve not, my child. I am glad that you see the Giant again, for I have hope that he will leave our city free from woe. I am the last victim, and I gladly die.'

Then Zaya knelt to the Giant, and said:

'Spare him! oh! spare him and take me! but spare him! spare him!

The old man raised himself upon his elbow as he lay, and spake to her:

'Grieve not, little one, and repine not. Sooth I know that you would gladly give your life for mine. But we must give for the good of others that which is dearer to us than our lives. Bless you, my little one, and be good. Farewell! farewell!'

As he spake the last word he grew cold as death, and his spirit passed away.

Zaya knelt down and prayed; and when she looked up she saw the shadowy Giant moving away.

The Giant turned as he passed on, and Zaya saw that his blind eyes looked towards her as though he were trying to see. He raised the great shadowy arms, draped still in his shroud of mist, as though blessing her; and she thought that the wind that came by her moaning bore the echo of the words:

'Innocence and devotion save the land.'

Presently she saw far off the great shadowy Giant Plague moving away to the border of the Land, and passing between the Guardian Spirits out through the Portal into the deserts beyond—for ever.

THE JUDGE'S HOUSE

When the time for his examination drew near Malcolm Malcolmson made up his mind to go somewhere to read by himself. He feared the attractions of the seaside, and also he feared completely rural isolation, for of old he knew its charms, and so he determined to find some unpretentious little town where there would be nothing to distract him. He refrained from asking suggestions from any of his friends, for he argued that each would recommend some place of which he had knowledge, and where he had already acquaintances. As Malcolmson wished to avoid friends he had no wish to encumber himself with the attention of friends' friends, and so he determined to look out for a place for himself. He packed a portmanteau with some clothes and all the books he required, and then took ticket for the first name on the local timetable which he did not know.

When at the end of three hours' journey he alighted at Benchurch, he felt satisfied that he had so far obliterated his tracks as to be sure of having a peaceful opportunity of pursuing his studies. He went straight to the one inn which the sleepy little place contained, and put up for the night. Benchurch was a market town, and once in three weeks was crowded to excess, but for the remainder of the twenty-one days it was as attractive as a desert. Malcolmson looked around the day after his arrival to try to find quarters more isolated than even so quiet an inn as The Good Traveller afforded. There was only one place which took his fancy, and it certainly satisfied his wildest ideas regarding quiet; in fact, quiet was not the proper word to apply to it—desolation was the only term conveying any suitable idea of its isolation. It was an old rambling, heavy-built house of the Jacobean style, with heavy gables and windows, unusually small, and set higher than was customary in such houses, and was surrounded with a high brick wall massively built. Indeed, on examination, it looked more like a fortified house than an ordinary dwelling. But all these things pleased Malcolmson. 'Here', he thought' 'is the very spot I have been looking for, and if I can get opportunity of using it I shall be happy.' His joy was increased when he realised beyond doubt that it was not at present inhabited.

From the post-office he got the name of the agent, who was rarely surprised at the application to rent a part of the old house. Mr. Carnford, the local lawyer and agent, was a genial old gentleman, and frankly confessed his delight at anyone being willing to live in the house.

'To tell you the truth,' said he, 'I should be only too happy, on behalf of the owners, to let anyone have the house rent free for a term of years if only to accustom the people here to see it inhabited. It has been so long empty that some kind of absurd prejudice has grown up about it, and this can be best put down by its occupation—if only,' he added with a sly glance at Malcolmson, 'by a scholar like yourself, who wants its quiet for a time.'

Malcolmson thought it needless to ask the agent about the 'absurd prejudice'; he knew he would get more information, if he should require it, on that subject from other quarters. He paid his three months' rent, got a receipt, and the name of an old woman who would probably undertake to 'do' for him, and came away with the keys in his pocket. He then went to the landlady of the inn, who was a cheerful and most kindly person, and asked her advice as to such stores and provisions as he would be likely to require. She threw up her hands in amazement when he told her where he was going to settle himself.

'Not in the Judge's House!' she said, and grew pale as she spoke. He explained the locality of the house, saying that he did not know its name. When he had finished she answered:

'Aye, sure enough—sure enough the very place! It is the Judge's House sure enough.' He asked her to tell him about the place, why so called, and what there was against it. She told him that it was so called locally because it had been many years before —how long she could not say, as she was herself from another part of the country, but she thought it must have been a hundred years or more—the abode of a judge who was held in great terror on account of his harsh sentences and his hostility to prisoners at Assizes. As to what there was against the house itself she could not tell. She had often asked, but no one could inform her; but there was a general feeling that there was *something,* and for her own part she would not take all the money in Drinkwater's Bank and stay in the house an hour by herself. Then she apologised to Malcolmson for her disturbing talk.

'It is too bad of me, sir, and you—and a young gentleman, too—if you will pardon me saying it, going to live there all alone. If you were my boy—and you'll excuse me for saying it—you wouldn't sleep there a night, not if I had to go there myself and pull the big alarm bell that's on the roof!' The good creature was so manifestly in earnest, and was so kindly in her intentions, that Malcolmson, although amused, was touched. He told her kindly how much he appreciated her interest in him, and added:

'But, my dear Mrs. Witham, indeed you need not be concerned about me! A man who is reading for the Mathematical Tripos has too much to think of to be disturbed by any of these mysterious "somethings", and his work is of too exact and prosaic a kind to allow of his having any corner in his mind for mysteries of any kind. Harmonical Progression, Permutations and Combinations, and Elliptic Functions have sufficient mysteries for me!' Mrs. Witham kindly undertook to see after his commissions, and he went himself to look for the old woman who had been recommended to him. When he returned to the Judge's House with her, after an interval of a couple of hours, he found Mrs. Witham herself waiting with several men and boys carrying parcels, and an upholsterer's man with a bed in a car, for she said, though tables and chairs might be all very well, a bed that hadn't been aired for mayhap fifty years was not proper for young bones to lie on. She was evidently curious to see the inside of the house; and though manifestly so afraid of the 'somethings' that at the slightest sound she clutched on to Malcolmson, whom she never left for a moment, went over the whole place.

After his examination of the house, Malcolmson decided to take up his abode in the great dining-room, which was big enough to serve for all his requirements; and Mrs Witham, with the aid of the charwoman, Mrs. Dempster, proceeded to arrange matters. When the hampers were brought in and unpacked, Malcolmson saw that with much kind forethought she had sent from her own kitchen sufficient provisions to last for a few days. Before going she expressed all sorts of kind wishes; and at the door turned and said:

'And perhaps, sir, as the room is big and draughty it might be well to have one of those big screens put round your bed at night—though, truth to tell, I would die myself if I were to be so shut in with all kinds of—of "things", that put their heads round the sides, or over the top, and look on me!' The image which she had called up was too much for her nerves, and she fled incontinently.

Mrs. Dempster sniffed in a superior manner as the landlady disappeared, and remarked that for her own part she wasn't afraid of all the bogies in the kingdom.

'I'll tell you what it is, sir,' she said; 'bogies is all kinds and sorts of things—except bogies! Rats and mice, and beetles; and creaky doors, and loose slates, and broken panes, and stiff drawer handles, that stay out when you pull them and then fall down in the middle of the night. Look at the wainscot of the room! It is old—hundreds of years old! Do you think there's no rats and beetles there! And do you imagine, sir, that you won't see none of them? Rats is bogies, I tell you, and bogies is rats; and don't you get to think anything else!'

'Mrs. Dempster,' said Malcolmson gravely, making her a polite bow, 'you know more than a Senior Wrangler! And let me say that, as a mark of esteem for your indubitable soundness of head and heart, I shall, when I go, give you possession of this house, and let you stay here by yourself for the last two months of my tenancy; for four weeks will serve my purpose.'

'Thank you kindly, sir!' she answered, 'but I couldn't sleep away from home a night. I am in Greenhow's Charity, and if I slept a night away from my rooms I should lose all I have got to live on. The rules is very strict; and there's too many watching for a vacancy for me to run any risks in the matter. Only for that, sir, I'd gladly come here and attend on you altogether during your stay.'

'My good woman,' said Malcolmson hastily, 'I have come here on purpose to obtain solitude; and believe me that I am grateful to the late Greenhow for having so organised his admirable charity—whatever it is—that I am perforce denied the opportunity of suffering from such a form of temptation! Saint Anthony himself could not be more rigid on the point!'

The old woman laughed harshly. 'Ah, you young gentlemen,' she said, 'you don't fear for naught; and belike you'll get all the solitude you want here.' She set to work with her cleaning; and by nightfall, when Malcolmson returned from his walk—he always had one of his books to study as he walked—he found the room swept and tidied, a fire burning in the old hearth, the lamp lit, and the table spread for supper with Mrs. Witham's excellent fare. 'This is comfort, indeed,' he said, as he rubbed his hands.

When he had finished his supper, and lifted the tray to the other end of the great oak dining-table, he got out his books again, put fresh wood on the fire, trimmed his lamp, and set himself down to a spell of real hard work. He went on without pause till about eleven o'clock, when he knocked off for a bit to fix his fire and lamp, and to make himself a cup of tea. He had always been a tea-drinker, and during his college life had sat late at work and had taken tea late. The rest was a great luxury to him, and he enjoyed it with a sense of delicious, voluptuous ease. The renewed fire leaped and sparkled, and threw quaint shadows through the great old room; and as he sipped his hot tea he revelled in the sense of isolation from his kind. Then it was that he began to notice for the first time what a noise the rats were making.

'Surely,' he thought, 'they cannot have been at it all the time I was reading. Had they been, I must have noticed it!' Presently, when the noise increased, he satisfied himself that it was really new. It was evident that at first the rats had been frightened at the presence of a stranger, and the light of fire and lamp; but that as the time went on they had grown bolder and were now disporting themselves as was their wont.

How busy they were! and hark to the strange noises! Up and down behind the old wainscot, over the ceiling and under the floor they raced, and gnawed, and scratched! Malcolmson smiled to himself as he recalled to mind the saying of Mrs. Dempster, 'Bogies is rats, and rats is bogies!' The tea began to have its effect of intellectual and nervous stimulus, he saw with joy another long spell of work to be done before the night was past, and in the sense of security which it gave him, he allowed himself the luxury of a good look around the room. He took his lamp in one hand, and went all around, wondering that so quaint and beautiful an old house had been so long neglected. The carving of the oak on the panels of the wainscot was fine, and on and round the doors and windows it was beautiful and of rare merit. There were some old pictures on the walls, but they were coated so thick with dust and dirt that he could not distinguish any detail of them, though he held his lamp as high as he could over his head. Here and there as he went round he saw some crack or hole blocked for a moment by the face of a rat with its bright eyes glittering in the light, but in an instant it was gone, and a squeak and a scamper followed. The thing that most struck him, however, was the rope of the great alarm bell on the roof, which hung down in a corner of the room on the right-hand side of the fireplace. He pulled up close to the hearth a great high-backed carved oak chair, and sat down to his last cup of tea. When this was done he made up the fire, and went back to his work, sitting at the corner of the table, having the fire to his left. For a little while the rats disturbed him somewhat with their perpetual scampering, but he got accustomed to the noise as one does to the ticking of a clock or to the roar of moving water; and he became so immersed in his work that everything in the world, except the problem which he was trying to solve, passed away from him.

He suddenly looked up, his problem was still unsolved, and there was in the air that sense of the hour before the dawn, which is so dread to doubtful life. The noise of the rats had ceased. Indeed it seemed to him that it must have ceased but lately and that it was the sudden cessation which had disturbed him. The fire had fallen low, but still it threw out a deep red glow. As he looked he started in spite of his *sang froid.*

There on the great high-backed carved oak chair by the right side of the fireplace sat an enormous rat steadily glaring at him with baleful eyes. He made a motion to it as though to hunt it away, but it did not stir. Then he made the motion of throwing something. Still it did not stir, but showed its great white teeth angrily, and its cruel eyes shone in the lamplight with an added vindictiveness.

Malcolmson felt amazed, and seizing the poker from the hearth ran at it to kill it. Before, however, he could strike it, the rat, with a squeak that sounded like the concentration of hate, jumped upon the floor, and, running up the rope of the alarm bell, disappeared in the darkness beyond the range of the green-shaded lamp. Instantly, strange to say, the noisy scampering of the rats in the wainscot began again.

By this time Malcolmson's mind was quite off the problem; and as a shrill cock-crow outside told him of the approach of morning, he went to bed and to sleep.

He slept so sound that he was not even waked by Mrs. Dempster coming in to make up his room. It was only when she had tidied up the place and got his breakfast ready and tapped on the screen which closed in his bed that he woke. He was a little tired still after his night's hard work, but a strong cup of tea soon freshened him up and, taking his book, he went out for his morning walk, bringing with him a few sandwiches lest he should not care to return till dinner time. He found a quiet walk between high elms some way outside the town, and here he spent the greater part of the day studying his Laplace. On his return he looked in to see Mrs. Witham and to thank her for her kindness. When she saw him coming through the diamond-paned bay window of her sanctum she came out to meet him and asked him in. She looked at him searchingly and shook her head as she said:

'You must not overdo it, sir. You are paler this morning than you should be. Too late hours and too hard work on the brain isn't good for any man! But tell me, sir, how did you pass the night? Well, I hope? But my heart! sir, I was glad when Mrs. Dempster told me this morning that you were all right and sleeping sound when she went in.'

'Oh, I was all right,' he answered smiling, 'the "somethings" didn't worry me, as yet. Only the rats; and they had a circus, I tell you, all over the place. There was one wicked looking old devil that sat up on my own chair by the fire, and wouldn't go till I took the poker to him, and then he ran up the rope of the alarm bell and got to somewhere up the wall or the ceiling—I couldn't see where, it was so dark.'

'Mercy on us,' said Mrs. Witham, 'an old devil, and sitting on a chair by the fireside! Take care, sir! take care! There's many a true word spoken in jest.'

'How do you mean? Pon my word I don't understand.'

'An old devil! The old devil, perhaps. There! sir, you needn't laugh,' for Malcolmson had broken into a hearty peal. 'You young folks think it easy to laugh at things that make older ones shudder. Never mind, sir! never mind! Please God, you'll laugh all the time. It's what I wish you myself!' and the good lady beamed all over in sympathy with his enjoyment, her fears gone for a moment.

'Oh, forgive me!' said Malcolmson presently. 'Don't think me rude; but the idea was too much for me—that the old devil himself was on the chair last night!' And at the thought he laughed again. Then he went home to dinner.

This evening the scampering of the rats began earlier; indeed it had been going on before his arrival, and only ceased whilst his presence by its freshness disturbed them. After dinner he sat by the fire for a while and had a smoke; and then, having cleared his table, began to work as before. Tonight the rats disturbed him more than they had done on the previous night. How they scampered up and down and under and over! How they squeaked, and scratched, and gnawed! How they, getting bolder by degrees, came to the mouths of their holes and to the chinks and cracks and crannies in the wainscoting till their eyes shone like tiny lamps as the firelight rose and fell. But to him, now doubtless accustomed to them, their eyes were not wicked; only their playfulness touched him. Sometimes the boldest of them made sallies out on the floor or along the mouldings of the wainscot. Now and again as they disturbed him Malcolmson made a sound to frighten them, smiting the table with his hand or giving a fierce 'Hsh, hsh,' so that they fled straightway to their holes.

And so the early part of the night wore on; and despite the noise Malcolmson got more and more immersed in his work.

All at once he stopped, as on the previous night, being overcome by a sudden sense of silence. There was not the faintest sound of gnaw, or scratch, or squeak. The silence was as of the grave. He remembered the odd occurrence of the previous night, and instinctively he looked at the chair standing close by the fireside. And then a very odd sensation thrilled through him.

There, on the great old high-backed carved oak chair beside the fireplace sat the same enormous rat, steadily glaring at him with baleful eyes.

Instinctively he took the nearest thing to his hand, a book of logarithms, and flung it at it. The book was badly aimed and the rat did not stir, so again the poker performance of the previous night was repeated; and again the rat, being closely pursued, fled up the rope of the alarm bell. Strangely too, the departure of this rat was instantly followed by the renewal of the noise made by the general rat community. On this occasion, as on the previous one, Malcolmson could not see at what part of the room the rat disappeared, for the green shade of his lamp left the upper part of the room in darkness, and the fire had burned low.

On looking at his watch he found it was close on midnight; and, not sorry for the *divertissement,* he made up his fire and made himself his nightly pot of tea. He had got through a good spell of work, and thought himself entitled to a cigarette; and so he sat on the great oak chair before the fire and enjoyed it. Whilst smoking he began to think that he would like to know where the rat disappeared to, for he had certain ideas for the tomorrow not entirely disconnected with a rat-trap. Accordingly he lit another lamp and placed it so that it would shine well into the right-hand corner of the wall by the fireplace. Then he got all the books he had with him, and placed them handy to throw at the vermin. Finally he lifted the rope of the alarm bell and placed the end of it on the table, fixing the extreme end under the lamp. As he handled it he could not help noticing how pliable it was, especially for so strong a rope, and one not in use. 'You could hang a man with it,' he thought to himself. When his preparations were made he looked around, and said complacently:

'There now, my friend, I think we shall learn something of you this time!' He began his work again, and though as before somewhat disturbed at first by the noise of the rats, soon lost himself in his propositions and problems.

Again he was called to his immediate surroundings suddenly. This time it might not have been the sudden silence only which took his attention; there was a slight movement of the rope, and the lamp moved. Without stirring, he looked to see if his pile of books was within range, and then cast his eye along the rope. As he looked he saw the great rat drop from the rope on the oak armchair and sit there glaring at him. He raised a book in his right hand, and taking careful aim, flung it at the rat. The latter, with a quick movement, sprang aside and dodged the missile. He then took another book, and a third, and flung them one after another at the rat, but each time unsuccessfully. At last, as he stood with a book poised in his hand to throw, the rat squeaked and seemed afraid. This made Malcolmson more than ever eager to strike, and the book flew and struck the rat a resounding blow. It gave a terrified squeak, and turning on his pursuer a look of terrible malevolence, ran up the chair-back and made a great jump to the rope of the alarm bell and ran up it like lightning. The lamp rocked under the sudden strain, but it was a heavy one and did not topple over. Malcolmson kept his eyes on the rat, and saw it by the light of the second lamp leap to a moulding of the wainscot and disappear through a hole in one of the great pictures which hung on the wall, obscured and invisible through its coating of dirt and dust.

'I shall look up my friend's habitation in the morning,' said the student, as he went over to collect his books. 'The third picture from the fireplace; I shall not forget.' He picked up the books one by one, commenting on them as he lifted them. '*Conic Sections* he does not mind, nor *Cycloidal Oscillations,* nor the *Principia,* nor *Quaternions,* nor *Thermodynamics.* Now for the book that fetched him!' Malcolmson took it up and looked at it. As he did so he started, and a sudden pallor overspread his face. He looked round uneasily and shivered slightly, as he murmured to himself:

'The Bible my mother gave me! What an odd coincidence.' He sat down to work again, and the rats in the wainscot renewed their gambols. They did not disturb him, however; somehow their presence gave him a sense of companionship. But he could not attend to his work, and after striving to master the subject on which he was engaged gave it up in despair, and went to bed as the first streak of dawn stole in through the eastern window.

He slept heavily but uneasily, and dreamed much; and when Mrs. Dempster woke him late in the morning he seemed ill at ease, and for a few minutes did not seem to realise exactly where he was. His first request rather surprised the servant.

'Mrs. Dempster, when I am out today I wish you would get the steps and dust or wash those pictures—specially that one the third from the fireplace—I want to see what they are.'

Late in the afternoon Malcolmson worked at his books in the shaded walk, and the cheerfulness of the previous day came back to him as the day wore on, and he found that his reading was progressing well. He had worked out to a satisfactory conclusion all the problems which had as yet baffled him, and it was in a state of jubilation that he paid a visit to Mrs. Witham at 'The Good Traveller'. He found a stranger in the cosy sitting-room with the landlady, who was introduced to him as Dr. Thornhill. She was not quite at ease, and this, combined with the doctor's plunging at once into a series of questions, made Malcolmson come to the conclusion that his presence was not an accident, so without preliminary he said:

'Dr. Thornhill, I shall with pleasure answer you any question you may choose to ask me if you will answer me one question first.'

The doctor seemed surprised, but he smiled and answered at once, 'Done! What is it?'

'Did Mrs. Witham ask you to come here and see me and advise me?'

Dr. Thornhill for a moment was taken aback, and Mrs. Witham got fiery red and turned away; but the doctor was a frank and ready man, and he answered at once and openly.

'She did: but she didn't intend you to know it. I suppose it was my clumsy haste that made you suspect. She told me that she did not like the idea of your being in that house all by yourself, and that she thought you took too much strong tea. In fact, she wants me to advise you if possible to give up the tea and the very late hours. I was a keen student in my time, so I suppose I may take the liberty of a college man, and without offence, advise you not quite as a stranger.'

Malcolmson with a bright smile held out his hand. 'Shake! as they say in America,' he said. 'I must thank you for your kindness and Mrs. Witham too, and your kindness deserves a return on my part. I promise to take no more strong tea—no tea at all till you let me—and I shall go to bed tonight at one o'clock at latest. Will that do?'

'Capital,' said the doctor. 'Now tell us all that you noticed in the old house,' and so Malcolmson then and there told in minute detail all that had happened in the last two nights. He was interrupted every now and then by some exclamation from Mrs. Witham, till finally when he told of the episode of the Bible the landlady's pent-up emotions found vent in a shriek; and it was not till a stiff glass of brandy and water had been administered that she grew composed again. Dr. Thornhill listened with a face of growing gravity, and when the narrative was complete and Mrs. Witham had been restored he asked:

'The rat always went up the rope of the alarm bell?'

'Always.'

'I suppose you know,' said the Doctor after a pause, 'what the rope is?'

'No!'

'It is,' said the Doctor slowly, 'the very rope which the hangman used for all the victims of the Judge's judicial rancour!' Here he was interrupted by another scream from Mrs. Witham, and steps had to be taken for her recovery. Malcolmson having looked at his watch, and found that it was close to his dinner hour, had gone home before her complete recovery.

When Mrs. Witham was herself again she almost assailed the Doctor with angry questions as to what he meant by putting such horrible ideas into the poor young man's mind. 'He has quite enough there already to upset him,' she added. Dr. Thornhill replied:

'My dear madam, I had a distinct purpose in it! I wanted to draw his attention to the bell rope, and to fix it there. It may be that he is in a highly overwrought state, and has been studying too much, although I am bound to say that he seems as sound and healthy a young man, mentally and bodily, as ever I saw—but then the rats—and that suggestion of the devil.' The doctor shook his head and went on. 'I would have offered to go and stay the first night with him but that I felt sure it would have been a cause of offence. He may get in the night some strange fright or hallucination; and if he does I want him to pull that rope. All alone as he is it will give us warning, and we may reach him in time to be of service. I shall be sitting up pretty late tonight and shall keep my ears open. Do not be alarmed if Benchurch gets a surprise before morning.'

'Oh, Doctor, what do you mean? What do you mean?'

'I mean this; that possibly—nay, more probably—we shall hear the great alarm bell from the Judge's House tonight,' and the Doctor made about as effective an exit as could be thought of.

When Malcolmson arrived home he found that it was a little after his usual time, and Mrs. Dempster had gone away—the rules of Greenhow's Charity were not to be neglected. He was glad to see that the place was bright and tidy with a cheerful fire and a well-trimmed lamp. The evening was colder than might have been expected in April, and a heavy wind was blowing with such rapidly-increasing strength that there was every promise of a storm during the night. For a few minutes after his entrance the noise of the rats ceased; but so soon as they became accustomed to his presence they began again. He was glad to hear them, for he felt once more the feeling of companionship in their noise, and his mind ran back to the strange fact that they only ceased to manifest themselves when that other—the great rat with the baleful eyes—came upon the scene. The reading-lamp only was lit and its green shade kept the ceiling and the upper part of the room in darkness, so that the cheerful light from the hearth spreading over the floor and shining on the white cloth laid over the end of the table was warm and cheery. Malcolmson sat down to his dinner with a good appetite and a buoyant spirit. After his dinner and a cigarette he sat steadily down to work, determined not to let anything disturb him, for he remembered his promise to the doctor, and made up his mind to make the best of the time at his disposal.

For an hour or so he worked all right, and then his thoughts began to wander from his books. The actual circumstances around him, the calls on his physical attention, and his nervous susceptibility were not to be denied. By this time the wind had become a gale, and the gale a storm. The old house, solid though it was, seemed to shake to its foundations, and the storm roared and raged through its many chimneys and its queer old gables, producing strange, unearthly sounds in the empty rooms and corridors. Even the great alarm bell on the roof must have felt the force of the wind, for the rope rose and fell slightly, as though the bell were moved a little from time to time, and the limber rope fell on the oak floor with a hard and hollow sound.

As Malcolmson listened to it he bethought himself of the doctor's words, 'It is the rope which the hangman used for the victims of the judge's judicial rancour,' and he went over to the corner of the fireplace and took it in his hand to look at it. There seemed a sort of deadly interest in it, and as he stood there he lost himself for a moment in speculation as to who these victims were, and the grim wish of the Judge to have such a ghastly relic ever under his eyes. As he stood there the swaying of the bell on the roof still lifted the rope now and again; but presently there came a new sensation—a sort of tremor in the rope, as though something was moving along it.

Looking up instinctively Malcolmson saw the great rat coming slowly down towards him, glaring at him steadily. He dropped the rope and started back with a muttered curse, and the rat, turning, ran up the rope again and disappeared, and at the same instant Malcolmson became conscious that the noise of the rats, which had ceased for a while, began again.

All this set him thinking, and it occurred to him that he had not investigated the lair of the rat or looked at the pictures, as he had intended. He lit the other lamp without the shade, and, holding it up, went and stood opposite the third picture from the fireplace on the right-hand side where he had seen the rat disappear on the previous night.

At the first glance he started back so suddenly that he almost dropped the lamp, and a deadly pallor overspread his face. His knees shook, and heavy drops of sweat came on his forehead, and he trembled like an aspen. But he was young and plucky, and pulled himself together, and after the pause of a few seconds stepped forward again, raised the lamp, and examined the picture which had been dusted and washed, and now stood out clearly.

It was of a judge dressed in his robes of scarlet and ermine. His face was strong and merciless, evil, crafty, and vindictive, with a sensual mouth, hooked nose of ruddy colour, and shaped like the beak of a bird of prey. The rest of the face was of a cadaverous colour. The eyes were of peculiar brilliance and with a terribly malignant expression. As he looked at them, Malcolmson grew cold, for he saw there the very counterpart of the eyes of the great rat. The lamp almost fell from his hand, he saw the rat with its baleful eyes peering out through the hole in the corner of the picture, and noted the sudden cessation of the noise of the other rats. However, he pulled himself together, and went on with his examination of the picture.

The Judge was seated in a great high-backed carved oak chair, on the right-hand side of a great stone fireplace where, in the corner, a rope hung down from the ceiling, its end lying coiled on the floor. With a feeling of something like horror, Malcolmson recognised the scene of the room as it stood, and gazed around him in an awestruck manner as though he expected to find some strange presence behind him. Then he looked over to the corner of the fireplace—and with a loud cry he let the lamp fall from his hand.

There, in the Judge's arm-chair, with the rope ranging behind, sat the rat with the Judge's baleful eyes, now intensified and with a fiendish leer. Save for the howling of the storm without there was silence.

The fallen lamp recalled Malcolmson to himself. Fortunately it was of metal, and so the oil was not spilt. However, the practical need of attending to it settled at once his nervous apprehensions. When he had turned it out, he wiped his brow and thought for a moment.

'This will not do,' he said to himself. 'If I go on like this I shall become a crazy fool. This must stop! I promised the doctor I would not take tea. Faith, he was pretty right! My nerves must have been getting into a queer state. Funny I did not notice it. I never felt better in my life. However, it is all right now, and I shall not be such a fool again.'

Then he mixed himself a good stiff glass of brandy and water and resolutely sat down to his work.

It was nearly an hour when he looked up from his book, disturbed by the sudden stillness. Without, the wind howled and roared louder than ever, and the rain drove in sheets against the windows, beating like hail on the glass; but within there was no sound whatever save the echo of the wind as it roared in the great chimney, and now and then a hiss as a few raindrops found their way down the chimney in a lull of the storm. The fire had fallen low and had ceased to flame, though it threw out a red glow. Malcolmson listened attentively, and presently heard a thin, squeaking noise, very faint. It came from the corner of the room where the rope hung down, and he thought it was the creaking of the rope on the floor as the swaying of the bell raised and lowered it. Looking up, however, he saw in the dim light the great rat clinging to the rope and gnawing it. The rope was already nearly gnawed through—he could see the lighter colour where the strands were laid bare. As he looked the job was completed, and the severed end of the rope fell clattering on the oaken floor, whilst for an instant the great rat remained like a knob or tassel at the end of the rope, which now began to sway to and fro. Malcolmson felt for a moment another pang of terror as he thought that now the possibility of calling the outer world to his assistance was cut off, but an intense anger took its place, and seizing the book he was reading he hurled it at the rat. The blow was well aimed, but before the missile could reach him the rat dropped off and struck the floor with a soft thud. Malcolmson instantly rushed over towards him, but it darted away and disappeared in the darkness of the shadows of the room. Malcolmson felt that his work was over for the night, and determined then and there to vary the monotony of the proceedings by a hunt for the rat, and took off the green shade of the lamp so as to insure a wider spreading light. As he did so the gloom of the upper part of the room was relieved, and in the new flood of light, great by comparison with the previous darkness, the pictures on the wall stood out boldly. From where he stood, Malcolmson saw right opposite to him the third picture on the wall from the right of the fireplace. He rubbed his eyes in surprise, and then a great fear began to come upon him.

In the centre of the picture was a great irregular patch of brown canvas, as fresh as when it was stretched on the frame. The background was as before, with chair and chimney-corner and rope, but the figure of the Judge had disappeared.

Malcolmson, almost in a chill of horror, turned slowly round, and then he began to shake and tremble like a man in a palsy. His strength seemed to have left him, and he was incapable of action or movement, hardly even of thought. He could only see and hear.

There, on the great high-backed carved oak chair sat the Judge in his robes of scarlet and ermine, with his baleful eyes glaring vindictively, and a smile of triumph on the resolute, cruel mouth, as he lifted with his hands a *black cap*. Malcolmson felt as if the blood was running from his heart, as one does in moments of prolonged suspense. There was a singing in his ears. Without, he could hear the roar and howl of the tempest, and through it, swept on the storm, came the striking of midnight by the great chimes in the market place. He stood for a space of time that seemed to him endless still as a statue, and with wide-open, horror-struck eyes, breathless. As the clock struck, so the smile of triumph on the Judge's face intensified, and at the last stroke of midnight he placed the black cap on his head.

Slowly and deliberately the Judge rose from his chair and picked up the piece of the rope of the alarm bell which lay on the floor, drew it through his hands as if he enjoyed its touch, and then deliberately began to knot one end of it, fashioning it into a noose. This he tightened and tested with his foot, pulling hard at it till he was satisfied and then making a running noose of it, which he held in his hand. Then he began to move along the table on the opposite side to Malcolmson keeping his eyes on him until he had passed him, when with a quick movement he stood in front of the door. Malcolmson then began to feel that he was trapped, and tried to think of what he should do. There was some fascination in the Judge's eyes, which he never took off him, and he had, perforce, to look. He saw the Judge approach—still keeping between him and the door—and raise the noose and throw it towards him as if to entangle him. With a great effort he made a quick movement to one side, and saw the rope fall beside him, and heard it strike the oaken floor. Again the Judge raised the noose and tried to ensnare him, ever keeping his baleful eyes fixed on him, and each time by a mighty effort the student just managed to evade it. So this went on for many times, the Judge seeming never discouraged nor discomposed at failure, but playing as a cat does with a mouse. At last in despair, which had reached its climax, Malcolmson cast a quick glance round him. The lamp seemed to have blazed up, and there was a fairly good light in the room. At the many rat-holes and in the chinks and crannies of the wainscot he saw the rats' eyes; and this aspect, that was purely physical, gave him a gleam of comfort. He looked around and saw that the rope of the great alarm bell was laden with rats. Every inch of it was covered with them, and more and more were pouring through the small circular hole in the ceiling whence it emerged, so that with their weight the bell was beginning to sway.

Hark! It had swayed till the clapper had touched the bell. The sound was but a tiny one, but the bell was only beginning to sway, and it would increase.

At the sound the Judge, who had been keeping his eyes fixed on Malcolmson, looked up, and a scowl of diabolical anger overspread his face. His eyes fairly glowed like hot coals, and he stamped his foot with a sound that seemed to make the house shake. A dreadful peal of thunder broke overhead as he raised the rope again, whilst the rats kept running up and down the rope as though working against time. This time, instead of throwing it, he drew close to his victim, and held open the noose as he approached. As he came closer there seemed something paralysing in his very presence, and Malcolmson stood rigid as a corpse. He felt the Judge's icy fingers touch his throat as he adjusted the rope. The noose tightened—tightened. Then the Judge, taking the rigid form of the student in his arms, carried him over and placed him standing in the oak chair, and stepping up beside him, put his hand up and caught the end of the swaying rope of the alarm bell. As he raised his hand the rats fled squeaking, and disappeared through the hole in the ceiling. Taking the end of the noose which was round Malcolmson's neck he tied it to the hanging-bell rope, and then descending, pulled away the chair.

When the alarm bell of the Judge's House began to sound a crowd soon assembled. Lights and torches of various kinds appeared, and soon a silent crowd was hurrying to the spot. They knocked loudly at the door, but there was no reply. Then they burst in the door, and poured into the great dining-room, the doctor at the head.

There at the end of the rope of the great alarm bell hung the body of the student, and on the face of the Judge in the picture was a malignant smile.

THE BURIAL OF THE RATS

LEAVING PARIS BY the Orleans road, cross the Enceinte, and, turning to the right, you find yourself in a somewhat wild and not at all savoury district. Right and left, before and behind, on every side rise great heaps of dust and waste accumulated by the process of time.

Paris has its night as well as its day life, and the sojourner who enters his hotel in the Rue de Rivoli or the Rue St. Honoré late at night or leaves it early in the morning, can guess, in coming near Montrouge—if he has not done so already—the purpose of those great wagons that look like boilers on wheels which he finds halting everywhere as he passes.

Every city has its peculiar institutions created out of its own needs; and one of the most notable institutions of Paris is its rag-picking population. In the early morning—and Parisian life commences at an early hour—may be seen in most streets standing on the pathway opposite every court and alley and between every few houses, as still in some American cities, even in parts of New York, large wooden boxes into which the domestics or tenement-holders empty the accumulated dust of the past day. Round these boxes gather and pass on, when the work is done, to fresh fields of labour and pastures new, squalid hungry-looking men and women, the implements of whose craft consist of a coarse bag or basket slung over the shoulder and a little rake with which they turn over and probe and examine in the minutest manner the dustbins. They pick up and deposit in their baskets, by aid of their rakes, whatever they may find, with the same facility as a Chinaman uses his chopsticks.

Paris is a city of centralisation—and centralisation and classification are closely allied. In the early times, when centralisation is becoming a fact, its forerunner is classification. All things which are similar or analogous become grouped together, and from the grouping of groups rises one whole or central point. We see radiating many long arms with innumerable tentaculae, and in the centre rises a gigantic head with a comprehensive brain and keen eyes to look on every side and ears sensitive to hear—and a voracious mouth to swallow.

Other cities resemble all the birds and beasts and fishes whose appetites and digestions are normal. Paris alone is the analogical apotheosis of the octopus. Product of centralisation carried to an *ad absurdum,* it fairly represents the devil fish; and in no respects is the resemblance more curious than in the similarity of the digestive apparatus.

Those intelligent tourists who, having surrendered their individuality into the hands of Messrs. Cook or Gaze, 'do' Paris in three days, are often puzzled to know how it is that the dinner which in London would cost about six shillings, can be had for three francs in a café in the Palais Royal. They need have no more wonder if they will but consider the classification which is a theoretic speciality of Parisian life, and adopt all round the fact from which the chiffonnier has his genesis.

The Paris of 1850 was not like the Paris of today, and those who see the Paris of Napoleon and Baron Hausmann can hardly realise the existence of the state of things forty-five years ago.

Amongst other things, however, which have not changed are those districts where the waste is gathered. Dust is dust all the world over, in every age, and the family likeness of dust-heaps is perfect. The traveller, therefore, who visits the environs of Montrouge can go back in fancy without difficulty to the year 1850.

In this year I was making a prolonged stay in Paris. I was very much in love with a young lady who, though she returned my passion, so far yielded to the wishes of her parents that she had promised not to see me or to correspond with me for a year. I, too, had been compelled to accede to these conditions under a vague hope of parental approval. During the term of probation I had promised to remain out of the country and not to write to my dear one until the expiration of the year.

Naturally the time went heavily with me. There was not one of my own family or circle who could tell me of Alice, and none of her own folk had, I am sorry to say, sufficient generosity to send me even an occasional word of comfort regarding her health and well-being. I spent six months wandering about Europe, but as I could find no satisfactory distraction in travel, I determined to come to Paris, where, at least, I would be within easy hail of London in case any good fortune should call me thither before the appointed time. That 'hope deferred maketh the heart sick' was never better exemplified than in my case, for in addition to the perpetual longing to see the face I loved there was always with me a harrowing anxiety lest some accident should prevent me showing Alice in due time that I had, throughout the long period of probation, been faithful to her trust and my own love. Thus, every adventure which I undertook had a fierce pleasure of its own, for it was fraught with possible consequences greater than it would have ordinarily borne.

Like all travellers I exhausted the places of most interest in the first month of my stay, and was driven in the second month to look for amusement whithersoever I might. Having made sundry journeys to the better-known suburbs, I began to see that there was a *terra incognita,* in so far as the guide book was concerned, in the social wilderness lying between these attractive points. Accordingly I began to systematise my researches, and each day took up the thread of my exploration at the place where I had on the previous day dropped it.

In the process of time my wanderings led me near Montrouge, and I saw that hereabouts lay the Ultima Thule of social exploration—a country as little known as that round the source of the White Nile. And so I determined to investigate philosophically the chiffonnier—his habitat, his life, and his means of life.

The job was an unsavoury one, difficult of accomplishment, and with little hope of adequate reward. However, despite reason, obstinacy prevailed, and I entered into my new investigation with a keener energy than I could have summoned to aid me in any investigation leading to any end, valuable or worthy.

One day, late in a fine afternoon, toward the end of September, I entered the holy of holies of the city of dust. The place was evidently the recognised abode of a number of chiffonniers, for some sort of arrangement was manifested in the formation of the dust heaps near the road. I passed amongst these heaps, which stood like orderly sentries, determined to penetrate farther and trace dust to its ultimate location.

As I passed along I saw behind the dust heaps a few forms that flitted to and fro, evidently watching with interest the advent of any stranger to such a place. The district was like a small Switzerland, and as I went forward my tortuous course shut out the path behind me.

Presently I got into what seemed a small city or community of chiffonniers. There were a number of shanties or huts, such as may be met with in the remote parts of the Bog of Allan—rude places with wattled walls, plastered with mud and roofs of rude thatch made from stable refuse—such places as one would not like to enter for any consideration, and which even in water-colour could only look picturesque if judiciously treated. In the midst of these huts was one of the strangest adaptations—I cannot say habitations—I had ever seen. An immense old wardrobe, the colossal remnant of some boudoir of Charles VII, or Henry II, had been converted into a dwelling-house. The double doors lay open, so that the entire ménage was open to public view. In the open half of the wardrobe was a common sitting-room of some four feet by six, in which sat, smoking their pipes round a charcoal brazier, no fewer than six old soldiers of the First Republic, with their uniforms torn and worn threadbare. Evidently they were of the *mauvais sujet* class; their bleary eyes and limp jaws told plainly of a common love of absinthe; and their eyes had that haggard, worn look of slumbering ferocity which follows hard in the wake of drink. The other side stood as of old, with its shelves intact, save that they were cut to half their depth, and in each shelf of which there were six, was a bed made with rags and straw. The half-dozen of worthies who inhabited this structure looked at me curiously as I passed; and when I looked back after going a little way I saw their heads together in a whispered conference. I did not like the look of this at all, for the place was very lonely, and the men looked very villainous. However, I did not see any cause for fear, and went on my way, penetrating farther and farther into the Sahara. The way was tortuous to a degree, and from going round in a series of semi-circles, as one goes in skating with the Dutch roll, I got rather confused with regard to the points of the compass.

When I had penetrated a little way I saw, as I turned the corner of a half-made heap, sitting on a heap of straw an old soldier with threadbare coat.

'Hallo!' said I to myself; 'the First Republic is well represented here in its soldiery.'

As I passed him the old man never even looked up at me, but gazed on the ground with stolid persistency. Again I remarked to myself: 'See what a life of rude warfare can do! This old man's curiosity is a thing of the past.'

When I had gone a few steps, however, I looked back suddenly, and saw that curiosity was not dead, for the veteran had raised his head and was regarding me with a very queer expression. He seemed to me to look very like one of the six worthies in the press. When he saw me looking he dropped his head; and without thinking further of him I went on my way, satisfied that there was a strange likeness between these old warriors.

Presently I met another old soldier in a similar manner. He, too, did not notice me whilst I was passing.

By this time it was getting late in the afternoon, and I began to think of retracing my steps. Accordingly I turned to go back, but could see a number of tracks leading between different mounds and could not ascertain which of them I should take. In my perplexity I wanted to see someone of whom to ask the way, but could see no one. I determined to go on a few mounds further and so try to see someone—not a veteran.

I gained my object, for after going a couple of hundred yards I saw before me a single shanty such as I had seen before—with, however, the difference that this was not one for living in, but merely a roof with three walls, open in front. From the evidences which the neighbourhood exhibited I took it to be a place for sorting. Within it was an old woman wrinkled and bent with age; I approached her to ask the way.

She rose as I came close and I asked her my way. She immediately commenced a conversation; and it occurred to me that here in the very centre of the Kingdom of Dust was the place to gather details of the history of Parisian rag-picking—particularly as I could do so from the lips of one who looked like the oldest inhabitant.

I began my inquiries, and the old woman gave me most interesting answers—she had been one of the ceteuces who sat daily before the guillotine and had taken an active part among the women who signalised themselves by their violence in the revolution. While we were talking she said suddenly: 'But m'sieur must be tired standing,' and dusted a rickety old stool for me to sit down. I hardly liked to do so for many reasons; but the poor old woman was so civil that I did not like to run the risk of hurting her by refusing, and moreover the conversation of one who had been at the taking of the Bastille was so interesting that I sat down and so our conversation went on.

While we were talking an old man—older and more bent and wrinkled even than the woman—appeared from behind the shanty. 'Here is Pierre,' said she. 'M'sieur can hear stories now if he wishes, for Pierre was in everything, from the Bastille to Waterloo.' The old man took another stool at my request and we plunged into a sea of revolutionary reminiscences. This old man, albeit clothed like a scarecrow, was like any one of the six veterans.

I was now sitting in the centre of the low hut with the woman on my left hand and the man on my right, each of them being somewhat in front of me. The place was full of all sorts of curious objects of lumber, and of many things that I wished far away. In one corner was a heap of rags which seemed to move from the number of vermin it contained, and in the other a heap of bones whose odour was something shocking. Every now and then, glancing at the heaps, I could see the gleaming eyes of some of the rats which infested the place. These loathsome objects were bad enough, but what looked even more dreadful was an old butcher's axe with an iron handle stained with clots of blood leaning up against the wall on the right hand side. Still, these things did not give me much concern. The talk of the two old people was so fascinating that I stayed on and on, till the evening came and the dust heaps threw dark shadows over the vales between them.

After a time I began to grow uneasy. I could not tell how or why, but somehow I did not feel satisfied. Uneasiness is an instinct and means warning. The psychic faculties are often the sentries of the intellect, and when they sound alarm the reason begins to act, although perhaps not consciously.

This was so with me. I began to bethink me where I was and by what surrounded, and to wonder how I should fare in case I should be attacked; and then the thought suddenly burst upon me, although without any overt cause, that I was in danger. Prudence whispered: 'Be still and make no sign,' and so I was still and made no sign, for I knew that four cunning eyes were on me. 'Four eyes—if not more.' My God, what a horrible thought! The whole shanty might be surrounded on three sides with villains! I might be in the midst of a band of such desperadoes as only half a century of periodic revolution can produce.

With a sense of danger my intellect and observation quickened, and I grew more watchful than was my wont. I noticed that the old woman's eyes were constantly wandering towards my hands. I looked at them too, and saw the cause—my rings. On my left little finger I had a large signet and on the right a good diamond.

I thought that if there was any danger my first care was to avert suspicion. Accordingly I began to work the conversation round to rag-picking—to the drains—of the things found there; and so by easy stages to jewels. Then, seizing a favourable opportunity, I asked the old woman if she knew anything of such things. She answered that she did, a little. I held out my right hand, and, showing her the diamond, asked her what she thought of that. She answered that her eyes were bad, and stooped over my hand. I said as nonchalantly as I could: 'Pardon me! You will see better thus!' and taking it off handed it to her. An unholy light came into her withered old face, as she touched it. She stole one glance at me swift and keen as a flash of lightning.

She bent over the ring for a moment, her face quite concealed as though examining it. The old man looked straight out of the front of the shanty before him, at the same time fumbling in his pockets and producing a screw of tobacco in a paper and a pipe, which he proceeded to fill. I took advantage of the pause and the momentary rest from the searching eyes on my face to look carefully round the place, now dim and shadowy in the gloaming. There still lay all the heaps of varied reeking foulness; there the terrible blood-stained axe leaning against the wall in the right hand corner, and everywhere, despite the gloom, the baleful glitter of the eyes of the rats. I could see them even through some of the chinks of the boards at the back low down close to the ground. But stay! these latter eyes seemed more than usually large and bright and baleful!

For an instant my heart stood still, and I felt in that whirling condition of mind in which one feels a sort of spiritual drunkenness, and as though the body is only maintained erect in that there is no time for it to fall before recovery. Then, in another second, I was calm—coldly calm, with all my energies in full vigour, with a self-control which I felt to be perfect and with all my feelings and instincts alert.

Now I knew the full extent of my danger: I was watched and surrounded by desperate people! I could not even guess at how many of them were lying there on the ground behind the shanty, waiting for the moment to strike. I knew that I was big and strong, and they knew it, too. They knew also, as I did, that I was an Englishman and would make a fight for it; and so we waited. I had, I felt, gained an advantage in the last few seconds, for I knew my danger and understood the situation. Now, I thought, is the test of my courage—the enduring test: the fighting test may come later!

The old woman raised her head and said to me in a satisfied kind of way:

'A very fine ring, indeed—a beautiful ring! Oh, me! I once had such rings, plenty of them, and bracelets and earrings! Oh! for in those fine days I led the town a dance! But they have forgotten me now! They've forgotten me! They? Why they never heard of me! Perhaps their grandfathers remember me, some of them!' and she laughed a harsh, croaking laugh. And then I am bound to say that she astonished me, for she handed me back the ring with a certain suggestion of old-fashioned grace which was not without its pathos.

The old man eyed her with a sort of sudden ferocity, half rising from his stool, and said to me suddenly and hoarsely:

'Let me see!'

I was about to hand the ring when the old woman said:

'No! no, do not give it to Pierre! Pierre is eccentric. He loses things; and such a pretty ring!'

'Cat!' said the old man, savagely. Suddenly the old woman said, rather more loudly than was necessary:

'Wait! I shall tell you something about a ring.' There was something in the sound of her voice that jarred upon me. Perhaps it was my hyper-sensitiveness, wrought up as I was to such a pitch of nervous excitement, but I seemed to think that she was not addressing me. As I stole a glance round the place I saw the eyes of the rats in the bone heaps, but missed the eyes along the back. But even as I looked I saw them again appear. The old woman's 'Wait!' had given me a respite from attack, and the men had sunk back to their reclining posture.

'I once lost a ring—a beautiful diamond hoop that had belonged to a queen, and which was given to me by a farmer of the taxes, who afterwards cut his throat because I sent him away. I thought it must have been stolen, and taxed my people; but I could get no trace. The police came and suggested that it had found its way to the drain. We descended—I in my fine clothes, for I would not trust them with my beautiful ring! I know more of the drains since then, and of rats, too! but I shall never forget the horror of that place—alive with blazing eyes, a wall of them just outside the light of our torches. Well, we got beneath my house. We searched the outlet of the drain, and there in the filth found my ring, and we came out.

'But we found something else also before we came! As we were coming toward the opening a lot of sewer rats—human ones this time—came towards us. They told the police that one of their number had gone into the drain, but had not returned. He had gone in only shortly before we had, and, if lost, could hardly be far off. They asked help to seek him, so we turned back. They tried to prevent me going, but I insisted. It was a new excitement, and had I not recovered my ring? Not far did we go till we came on something. There was but little water, and the bottom of the drain was raised with brick, rubbish, and much matter of the kind. He had made a fight for it, even when his torch had gone out. But there were too many for him! They had not been long about it! The bones were still warm; but they were picked clean. They had even eaten their own dead ones and there were bones of rats as well as of the man. They took it cool enough those other—the human ones—and joked of their comrade when they found him dead, though they would have helped him living. Bah! what matters it—life or death?'

'And you had no fear?' I asked her.

'Fear!' she said with a laugh. 'Me have fear? Ask Pierre! But I was younger then, and, as I came through that horrible drain with its wall of greedy eyes, always moving with the circle of the light from the torches, I did not feel easy. I kept on before the men, though! It is a way I have! I never let the men get it before me. All I want is a chance and a means! And they ate him up—took every trace away except the bones; and no one knew it, nor no sound of him was ever heard!' Here she broke into a chuckling fit of the ghastliest merriment which it was ever my lot to hear and see. A great poetess describes her heroine singing: 'Oh! to see or hear her singing! Scarce I know which is the divinest.'

And I can apply the same idea to the old crone—in all save the divinity, for I scarce could tell which was the most hellish—the harsh, malicious, satisfied, cruel laugh, or the leering grin, and the horrible square opening of the mouth like a tragic mask, and the yellow gleam of the few discoloured teeth in the shapeless gums. In that laugh and with that grin and the chuckling satisfaction I knew as well as if it had been spoken to me in words of thunder that my murder was settled, and the murderers only bided the proper time for its accomplishment. I could read between the lines of her gruesome story the commands to her accomplices. 'Wait,' she seemed to say, 'bide your time. I shall strike the first blow. Find the weapon for me, and I shall make the opportunity! He shall not escape! Keep him quiet, and then no one will be wiser. There will be no outcry, and the rats will do their work!'

It was growing darker and darker; the night was coming. I stole a glance round the shanty, still all the same! The bloody axe in the corner, the heaps of filth, and the eyes on the bone heaps and in the crannies of the floor.

Pierre had been still ostensibly filling his pipe; he now struck a light and began to puff away at it. The old woman said:

'Dear heart, how dark it is! Pierre, like a good lad, light the lamp!'

Pierre got up and with the lighted match in his hand touched the wick of a lamp which hung at one side of the entrance to the shanty, and which had a reflector that threw the light all over the place. It was evidently that which was used for their sorting at night.

'Not that, stupid! Not that! The lantern!' she called out to him.

He immediately blew it out, saying: 'All right, mother, I'll find it,' and he hustled about the left corner of the room—the old woman saying through the darkness:

'The lantern! the lantern! Oh! That is the light that is most useful to us poor folks. The lantern was the friend of the revolution! It is the friend of the chiffonier! It helps us when all else fails.'

Hardly had she said the word when there was a kind of creaking of the whole place, and something was steadily dragged over the roof.

Again I seemed to read between the lines of her words. I knew the lesson of the lantern.

'One of you get on the roof with a noose and strangle him as he passes out if we fail within.'

As I looked out of the opening I saw the loop of a rope outlined black against the lurid sky. I was now, indeed, beset!

Pierre was not long in finding the lantern. I kept my eyes fixed through the darkness on the old woman. Pierre struck his light, and by its flash I saw the old woman raise from the ground beside her where it had mysteriously appeared, and then hide in the folds of her gown, a long sharp knife or dagger. It seemed to be like a butcher's sharpening iron fined to a keen point.

The lantern was lit.

'Bring it here, Pierre,' she said. 'Place it in the doorway where we can see it. See how nice it is! It shuts out the darkness from us; it is just right!'

Just right for her and her purposes! It threw all its light on my face, leaving in gloom the faces of both Pierre and the woman, who sat outside of me on each side.

I felt that the time of action was approaching; but I knew now that the first signal and movement would come from the woman, and so watched her.

I was all unarmed, but I had made up my mind what to do. At the first movement I would seize the butcher's axe in the right-hand corner and fight my way out. At least, I would die hard. I stole a glance round to fix its exact locality so that I could not fail to seize it at the first effort, for then, if ever, time and accuracy would be precious.

Good God! It was gone! All the horror of the situation burst upon me; but the bitterest thought of all was that if the issue of the terrible position should be against me Alice would infallibly suffer. Either she would believe me false—and any lover, or any one who has ever been one, can imagine the bitterness of the thought—or else she would go on loving long after I had been lost to her and to the world, so that her life would be broken and embittered, shattered with disappointment and despair. The very magnitude of the pain braced me up and nerved me to bear the dread scrutiny of the plotters.

I think I did not betray myself. The old woman was watching me as a cat does a mouse; she had her right hand hidden in the folds of her gown, clutching, I knew, that long, cruel-looking dagger. Had she seen any disappointment in my face she would, I felt, have known that the moment had come, and would have sprung on me like a tigress, certain of taking me unprepared.

I looked out into the night, and there I saw new cause for danger. Before and around the hut were at a little distance some shadowy forms; they were quite still, but I knew that they were all alert and on guard. Small chance for me now in that direction.

Again I stole a glance round the place. In moments of great excitement and of great danger, which is excitement, the mind works very quickly, and the keenness of the faculties which depend on the mind grows in proportion. I now felt this. In an instant I took in the whole situation. I saw that the axe had been taken through a small hole made in one of the rotten boards. How rotten they must be to allow of such a thing being done without a particle of noise.

The hut was a regular murder-trap, and was guarded all around. A garrotter lay on the roof ready to entangle me with his noose if I should escape the dagger of the old hag. In front the way was guarded by I know not how many watchers. And at the back was a row of desperate men—I had seen their eyes still through the crack in the boards of the floor, when last I looked—as they lay prone waiting for the signal to start erect. If it was to be ever, now for it!

As nonchalantly as I could I turned slightly on my stool so as to get my right leg well under me. Then with a sudden jump, turning my head, and guarding it with my hands, and with the fighting instinct of the knights of old, I breathed my lady's name, and hurled myself against the back wall of the hut.

Watchful as they were, the suddenness of my movement surprised both Pierre and the old woman. As I crashed through the rotten timbers I saw the old woman rise with a leap like a tiger and heard her low gasp of baffled rage. My feet lit on something that moved, and as I jumped away I knew that I had stepped on the back of one of the row of men lying on their faces outside the hut. I was torn with nails and splinters, but otherwise unhurt. Breathless I rushed up the mound in front of me, hearing as I went the dull crash of the shanty as it collapsed into a mass.

It was a nightmare climb. The mound, though but low, was awfully steep, and with each step I took the mass of dust and cinders tore down with me and gave way under my feet. The dust rose and choked me; it was sickening, fœtid, awful; but my climb was, I felt, for life or death, and I struggled on. The seconds seemed hours; but the few moments I had in starting, combined with my youth and strength, gave me a great advantage, and, though several forms struggled after me in deadly silence which was more dreadful than any sound, I easily reached the top. Since then I have climbed the cone of Vesuvius, and as I struggled up that dreary steep amid the sulphurous fumes the memory of that awful night at Montrouge came back to me so vividly that I almost grew faint.

The mound was one of the tallest in the region of dust, and as I struggled to the top, panting for breath and with my heart beating like a sledge-hammer, I saw away to my left the dull red gleam of the sky, and nearer still the flashing of lights. Thank God! I knew where I was now and where lay the road to Paris!

For two or three seconds I paused and looked back. My pursuers were still well behind me, but struggling up resolutely, and in deadly silence. Beyond, the shanty was a wreck—a mass of timber and moving forms. I could see it well, for flames were already bursting out; the rags and straw had evidently caught fire from the lantern. Still silence there! Not a sound! These old wretches could die game, anyhow.

I had no time for more than a passing glance, for as I cast an eye round the mound preparatory to making my descent I saw several dark forms rushing round on either side to cut me off on my way. It was now a race for life. They were trying to head me on my way to Paris, and with the instinct of the moment I dashed down to the right-hand side. I was just in time, for, though I came as it seemed to me down the steep in a few steps, the wary old men who were watching me turned back, and one, as I rushed by into the opening between the two mounds in front, almost struck me a blow with that terrible butcher's axe. There could surely not be two such weapons about!

Then began a really horrible chase. I easily ran ahead of the old men, and even when some younger ones and a few women joined in the hunt I easily distanced them. But I did not know the way, and I could not even guide myself by the light in the sky, for I was running away from it. I had heard that, unless of conscious purpose, hunted men turn always to the left, and so I found it now; and so, I suppose, knew also my pursuers, who were more animals than men, and with cunning or instinct had found out such secrets for themselves: for on finishing a quick spurt, after which I intended to take a moment's breathing space, I suddenly saw ahead of me two or three forms swiftly passing behind a mound to the right.

I was in the spider's web now indeed! But with the thought of this new danger came the resource of the hunted, and so I darted down the next turning to the right. I continued in this direction for some hundred yards, and then, making a turn to the left again, felt certain that I had, at any rate, avoided the danger of being surrounded.

But not of pursuit, for on came the rabble after me, steady, dogged, relentless, and still in grim silence.

In the greater darkness the mounds seemed now to be somewhat smaller than before, although—for the night was closing—they looked bigger in proportion. I was now well ahead of my pursuers, so I made a dart up the mound in front.

Oh joy of joys! I was close to the edge of this inferno of dust-heaps. Away behind me the red light of Paris was in the sky, and towering up behind rose the heights of Montmartre—a dim light, with here and there brilliant points like stars.

Restored to vigour in a moment, I ran over the few remaining mounds of decreasing size, and found myself on the level land beyond. Even then, however, the prospect was not inviting. All before me was dark and dismal, and I had evidently come on one of those dank, low-lying waste places which are found here and there in the neighbourhood of great cities. Places of waste and desolation, where the space is required for the ultimate agglomeration of all that is noxious, and the ground is so poor as to create no desire of occupancy even in the lowest squatter. With eyes accustomed to the gloom of the evening, and away now from the shadows of those dreadful dustheaps, I could see much more easily than I could a little while ago. It might have been, of course, that the glare in the sky of the lights of Paris, though the city was some miles away, was reflected here. Howsoever it was, I saw well enough to take bearings for certainly some little distance around me.

In front was a bleak, flat waste that seemed almost dead level, with here and there the dark shimmering of stagnant pools. Seemingly far off on the right, amid a small cluster of scattered lights, rose the dark mass of Fort Montrouge, and away to the left in the dim distance, pointed with stray gleams from cottage windows, the lights in the sky showed the locality of Bicêtre. A moment's thought decided me to take to the right and try to reach Montrouge. There at least would be some sort of safety, and I might possibly long before come on some of the cross roads which I knew. Somewhere, not far off, must lie the strategic road made to connect the outlying chain of forts circling the city.

Then I looked back. Coming over the mounds, and outlined black against the glare of the Parisian horizon, I saw several moving figures, and still away to the right several more deploying out between me and my destination. They evidently meant to cut me off in this direction, and so my choice became constricted; it lay now between going straight ahead or turning to the left. Stooping to the ground, so as to get the advantage of the horizon as a line of sight, I looked carefully in this direction, but could detect no sign of my enemies. I argued that as they had not guarded or were not trying to guard that point, there was evidently danger to me there already. So I made up my mind to go straight on before me.

It was not an inviting prospect, and as I went on the reality grew worse. The ground became soft and oozy, and now and again gave way beneath me in a sickening kind of way. I seemed somehow to be going down, for I saw round me places seemingly more elevated than where I was, and this in a place which from a little way back seemed dead level. I looked around, but could see none of my pursuers. This was strange, for all along these birds of the night had followed me through the darkness as well as though it was broad daylight. How I blamed myself for coming out in my light-coloured tourist suit of tweed. The silence, and my not being able to see my enemies, whilst I felt that they were watching me, grew appalling, and in the hope of some one not of this ghastly crew hearing me I raised my voice and shouted several times. There was not the slightest response; not even an echo rewarded my efforts. For a while I stood stock still and kept my eyes in one direction. On one of the rising places around me I saw something dark move along, then another, and another. This was to my left, and seemingly moving to head me off.

I thought that again I might with my skill as a runner elude my enemies at this game, and so with all my speed darted forward.

Splash!

My feet had given way in a mass of slimy rubbish, and I had fallen headlong into a reeking, stagnant pool. The water and the mud in which my arms sank up to the elbows was filthy and nauseous beyond description, and in the suddenness of my fall I had actually swallowed some of the filthy stuff, which nearly choked me, and made me gasp for breath. Never shall I forget the moments during which I stood, trying to recover myself almost fainting from the fœtid odour of the filthy pool, whose white mist rose ghostlike around. Worst of all, with the acute despair of the hunted animal when he sees the pursuing pack closing on him, I saw before my eyes whilst I stood helpless the dark forms of my pursuers moving swiftly to surround me.

It is curious how our minds work on odd matters even when the energies of thought are seemingly concentrated on some terrible and pressing need. I was in momentary peril of my life: my safety depended on my action, and my choice of alternatives coming now with almost every step I took, and yet I could not but think of the strange dogged persistency of these old men. Their silent resolution, their steadfast, grim, persistency even in such a cause commanded, as well as fear, even a measure of respect. What must they have been in the vigour of their youth. I could understand now that whirlwind rush on the bridge of Arcola, that scornful exclamation of the Old Guard at Waterloo! Unconscious cerebration has its own pleasures, even at such moments; but fortunately it does not in any way clash with the thought from which action springs.

I realised at a glance that so far I was defeated in my object, my enemies as yet had won. They had succeeded in surrounding me on three sides, and were bent on driving me off to the left-hand, where there was already some danger for me, for they had left no guard. I accepted the alternative—it was a case of Hobson's choice and run. I had to keep the lower ground, for my pursuers were on the higher places. However, though the ooze and broken ground impeded me my youth and training made me able to hold my ground, and by keeping a diagonal line I not only kept them from gaining on me but even began to distance them. This gave me new heart and strength, and by this time habitual training was beginning to tell and my second wind had come. Before me the ground rose slightly. I rushed up the slope and found before me a waste of watery slime, with a low dyke or bank looking black and grim beyond. I felt that if I could but reach that dyke in safety I could there, with solid ground under my feet and some kind of path to guide me, find with comparative ease a way out of my troubles. After a glance right and left and seeing no one near, I kept my eyes for a few minutes to their rightful work of aiding my feet whilst I crossed the swamp. It was rough, hard work, but there was little danger, merely toil; and a short time took me to the dyke. I rushed up the slope exulting; but here again I met a new shock. On either side of me rose a number of crouching figures. From right and left they rushed at me. Each body held a rope.

The cordon was nearly complete. I could pass on neither side, and the end was near.

There was only one chance, and I took it. I hurled myself across the dyke, and escaping out of the very clutches of my foes threw myself into the stream.

At any other time I should have thought that water foul and filthy, but now it was as welcome as the most crystal stream to the parched traveller. It was a highway of safety!

My pursuers rushed after me. Had only one of them held the rope it would have been all up with me, for he could have entangled me before I had time to swim a stroke; but the many hands holding it embarrassed and delayed them, and when the rope struck the water I heard the splash well behind me. A few minutes' hard swimming took me across the stream. Refreshed with the immersion and encouraged by the escape, I climbed the dyke in comparative gaiety of spirits.

From the top I looked back. Through the darkness I saw my assailants scattering up and down along the dyke. The pursuit was evidently not ended, and again I had to choose my course. Beyond the dyke where I stood was a wild, swampy space very similar to that which I had crossed. I determined to shun such a place, and thought for a moment whether I would take up or down the dyke. I thought I heard a sound—the muffled sound of oars, so I listened, and then shouted.

No response; but the sound ceased. My enemies had evidently got a boat of some kind. As they were on the up side of me I took the down path and began to run. As I passed to the left of where I had entered the water I heard several splashes, soft and stealthy, like the sound a rat makes as he plunges into the stream, but vastly greater; and as I looked I saw the dark sheen of the water broken by the ripples of several advancing heads. Some of my enemies were swimming the stream also.

And now behind me, up the stream, the silence was broken by the quick rattle and creak of oars; my enemies were in hot pursuit.

I put my best leg foremost and ran on. After a break of a couple of minutes I looked back, and by a gleam of light through the ragged clouds I saw several dark forms climbing the bank behind me. The wind had now begun to rise, and the water beside me was ruffled and beginning to break in tiny waves on the bank. I had to keep my eyes pretty well on the ground before me, lest I should stumble, for I knew that to stumble was death. After a few minutes I looked back behind me. On the dyke were only a few dark figures, but crossing the waste, swampy ground were many more. What new danger this portended I did not know—could only guess. Then as I ran it seemed to me that my track kept ever sloping away to the right. I looked up ahead and saw that the river was much wider than before, and that the dyke on which I stood fell quite away, and beyond it was another stream on whose near bank I saw some of the dark forms now across the marsh. I was on an island of some kind.

My situation was now indeed terrible, for my enemies had hemmed me in on every side. Behind came the quickening roll of the oars, as though my pursuers knew that the end was close. Around me on every side was desolation; there was not a roof or light, as far as I could see. Far off to the right rose some dark mass, but what it was I knew not. For a moment I paused to think what I should do, not for more, for my pursuers were drawing closer. Then my mind was made up. I slipped down the bank and took to the water. I struck out straight ahead so as to gain the current by clearing the backwater of the island, for such I presume it was, when I had passed into the stream. I waited till a cloud came driving across the moon and leaving all in darkness. Then I took off my hat and laid it softly on the water floating with the stream, and a second after dived to the right and struck out under water with all my might. I was, I suppose, half a minute under water, and when I rose came up as softly as I could, and turning, looked back. There went my light brown hat floating merrily away. Close behind it came a rickety old boat, driven furiously by a pair of oars. The moon was still partly obscured by the drifting clouds, but in the partial light I could see a man in the bows holding aloft ready to strike what appeared to me to be that same dreadful pole-axe which I had before escaped. As I looked the boat drew closer, closer, and the man struck savagely. The hat disappeared. The man fell forward, almost out of the boat. His comrades dragged him in but without the axe, and then as I turned with all my energies bent on reaching the further bank, I heard the fierce whirr of the muttered 'Sacré!' which marked the anger of my baffled pursuers.

That was the first sound I had heard from human lips during all this dreadful chase, and full as it was of menace and danger to me it was a welcome sound for it broke that awful silence which shrouded and appalled me. It was as though an overt sign that my opponents were men and not ghosts, and that with them I had, at least, the chance of a man, though but one against many.

But now that the spell of silence was broken the sounds came thick and fast. From boat to shore and back from shore to boat came quick question and answer, all in the fiercest whispers. I looked back—a fatal thing to do—for in the instant someone caught sight of my face, which showed white on the dark water, and shouted. Hands pointed to me, and in a moment or two the boat was under weigh, and following hard after me. I had but a little way to go, but quick and quicker came the boat after me. A few more strokes and I would be on the shore, but I felt the oncoming of the boat, and expected each second to feel the crash of an oar or other weapon on my head. Had I not seen that dreadful axe disappear in the water I do not think that I could have won the shore. I heard the muttered curses of those not rowing and the laboured breath of the rowers. With one supreme effort for life or liberty I touched the bank and sprang up it. There was not a single second to spare, for hard behind me the boat grounded and several dark forms sprang after me. I gained the top of the dyke, and keeping to the left ran on again. The boat put off and followed down the stream. Seeing this I feared danger in this direction, and quickly turning, ran down the dyke on the other side, and after passing a short stretch of marshy ground gained a wild, open flat country and sped on.

Still behind me came on my relentless pursuers. Far away, below me, I saw the same dark mass as before, but now grown closer and greater. My heart gave a great thrill of delight, for I knew that it must be the fortress of Bicêtre, and with new courage I ran on. I had heard that between each and all of the protecting forts of Paris there are strategic ways, deep sunk roads, where soldiers marching should be sheltered from an enemy. I knew that if I could gain this road I would be safe, but in the darkness I could not see any sign of it, so, in blind hope of striking it, I ran on.

Presently I came to the edge of a deep cut, and found that down below me ran a road guarded on each side by a ditch of water fenced on either side by a straight, high wall.

Getting fainter and dizzier, I ran on; the ground got more broken—more and more still, till I staggered and fell, and rose again, and ran on in the blind anguish of the hunted. Again the thought of Alice nerved me. I would not be lost and wreck her life: I would fight and struggle for life to the bitter end. With a great effort I caught the top of the wall. As, scrambling like a catamount, I drew myself up, I actually felt a hand touch the sole of my foot. I was now on a sort of causeway, and before me I saw a dim light. Blind and dizzy, I ran on, staggered, and fell, rising, covered with dust and blood.

'Halt la!'

The words sounded like a voice from heaven. A blaze of light seemed to enwrap me, and I shouted with joy.

'Qui va la?' The rattle of musketry, the flash of steel before my eyes. Instinctively I stopped, though close behind me came a rush of my pursuers.

Another word or two, and out from a gateway poured, as it seemed to me, a tide of red and blue, as the guard turned out. All around seemed blazing with light, and the flash of steel, the clink and rattle of arms, and the loud, harsh voices of command. As I fell forward, utterly exhausted, a soldier caught me. I looked back in dreadful expectation, and saw the mass of dark forms disappearing into the night. Then I must have fainted. When I recovered my senses I was in the guard room. They gave me brandy, and after a while I was able to tell them something of what had passed. Then a commissary of police appeared, apparently out of the empty air, as is the way of the Parisian police officer. He listened attentively, and then had a moment's consultation with the officer in command. Apparently they were agreed, for they asked me if I were ready now to come with them.

'Where to?' I asked, rising to go.

'Back to the dust heaps. We shall perhaps, catch them yet!'

'I shall try!' said I.

He eyed me for a moment keenly and said suddenly:

'Would you like to wait a while or till tomorrow, young Englishman?' This touched me to the quick, as, perhaps, he intended, and I jumped to my feet.

'Come now!' I said; 'now! now! An Englishman is always ready for his duty!'

The commissary was a good fellow, as well as a shrewd one; he slapped my shoulder kindly. 'Brave garçon!' he said. 'Forgive me, but I knew what would do you most good. The guard is ready. Come!'

And so, passing right through the guard room, and through a long vaulted passage, we were out into the night. A few of the men in front had powerful lanterns. Through courtyards and down a sloping way we passed out through a low archway to a sunken road, the same that I had seen in my flight. The order was given to get at the double, and with a quick, springing stride, half run, half walk, the soldiers went swiftly along. I felt my strength renewed again—such is the difference between hunter and hunted. A very short distance took us to a low-lying pontoon bridge across the stream, and evidently very little higher up than I had struck it. Some effort had evidently been made to damage it, for the ropes had all been cut, and one of the chains had been broken. I heard the officer say to the commissary:

'We are just in time! A few more minutes, and they would have destroyed the bridge. Forward, quicker still!' and on we went. Again we reached a pontoon on the winding stream; as we came up we heard the hollow boom of the metal drums as the efforts to destroy the bridge were again renewed. A word of command was given, and several men raised their rifles.

'Fire!' A volley rang out. There was a muffled cry, and the dark forms dispersed. But the evil was done, and we saw the far end of the pontoon swing into the stream. This was a serious delay, and it was nearly an hour before we had renewed ropes and restored the bridge sufficiently to allow us to cross.

We renewed the chase. Quicker, quicker we went towards the dust heaps.

After a time we came to a place that I knew. There were the remains of a fire—a few smouldering wood ashes still cast a red glow, but the bulk of the ashes were cold. I knew the site of the hut and the hill behind it up which I had rushed, and in the flickering glow the eyes of the rats still shone with a sort of phosphorescence. The commissary spoke a word to the officer, and he cried:

'Halt!'

The soldiers were ordered to spread around and watch, and then we commenced to examine the ruins. The commissary himself began to lift away the charred boards and rubbish. These the soldiers took and piled together. Presently he started back, then bent down and rising beckoned me.

'See!' he said.

It was a gruesome sight. There lay a skeleton face downwards, a woman by the lines—an old woman by the coarse fibre of the bone. Between the ribs rose a long spike-like dagger made from a butcher's sharpening knife, its keen point buried in the spine.

'You will observe,' said the commissary to the officer and to me as he took out his note book, 'that the woman must have fallen on her dagger. The rats are many here—see their eyes glistening among that heap of bones—and you will also notice'—I shuddered as he placed his hand on the skeleton—'that but little time was lost by them, for the bones are scarcely cold!'

There was no other sign of any one near, living or dead; and so deploying again into line the soldiers passed on. Presently we came to the hut made of the old wardrobe. We approached. In five of the six compartments was an old man sleeping—sleeping so soundly that even the glare of the lanterns did not wake them. Old and grim and grizzled they looked, with their gaunt, wrinkled, bronzed faces and their white moustaches.

The officer called out harshly and loudly a word of command, and in an instant each one of them was on his feet before us and standing at 'attention!'

'What do you here?'

'We sleep,' was the answer.

'Where are the other chiffoniers?' asked the commissary.

'Gone to work.'

'And you?'

'We are on guard!'

'Peste!' laughed the officer grimly, as he looked at the old men one after the other in the face and added with cool deliberate cruelty: 'Asleep on duty! Is this the manner of the Old Guard? No wonder, then, a Waterloo!'

By the gleam of the lantern I saw the grim old faces grow deadly pale, and almost shuddered at the look in the eyes of the old men as the laugh of the soldiers echoed the grim pleasantry of the officer.

I felt in that moment that I was in some measure avenged.

For a moment they looked as if they would throw themselves on the taunter, but years of their life had schooled them and they remained still.

'You are but five,' said the commissary; 'where is the sixth?' The answer came with a grim chuckle.

'He is there!' and the speaker pointed to the bottom of the wardrobe. 'He died last night. You won't find much of him. The burial of the rats is quick!'

The commissary stooped and looked in. Then he turned to the officer and said calmly:

'We may as well go back. No trace here now; nothing to prove that man was the one wounded by your soldiers' bullets! Probably they murdered him to cover up the trace. See!' again he stooped and placed his hands on the skeleton. 'The rats work quickly and they are many. These bones are warm!'

I shuddered, and so did many more of those around me.

'Form!' said the officer, and so in marching order, with the lanterns swinging in front and the manacled veterans in the midst, with steady tramp we took ourselves out of the dustheaps and turned backward to the fortress of Bicêtre.

My year of probation has long since ended, and Alice is my wife. But when I look back upon that trying twelvemonth one of the most vivid incidents that memory recalls is that associated with my visit to the City of Dust.

A STAR TRAP

'WHEN I WAS apprenticed to theatrical carpentering my master was John Haliday, who was Master Machinist—we called men in his post "Master Carpenter" in those days—of the old Victoria Theatre, Hulme. It wasn't called Hulme; but that name will do. It would only stir up painful memories if I were to give the real name. I daresay some of you—not the Ladies (this with a gallant bow all round)—will remember the case of a Harlequin as was killed in an accident in the pantomime. We needn't mention names; Mortimer will do for a name to call him by—Henry Mortimer. The cause of it was never found out. But I knew it; and I've kept silence for so long that I may speak now without hurting anyone. They're all dead long ago that was interested in the death of Henry Mortimer or the man who wrought that death.

'Any of you who know of the case will remember what a handsome, dapper, well-built man Mortimer was. To my own mind he was the handsomest man I ever saw.'

The Tragedian's low, grumbling whisper, 'That's a large order,' sounded a warning note. Hempitch, however, did not seem to hear it, but went on:

'Of course, I was only a boy then, and I hadn't seen any of you gentlemen—Yer very good health, Mr. Wellesley Dovercourt, sir, and cettera. I needn't tell you, Ladies, how well a harlequin's dress sets off a nice slim figure. No wonder that in these days of suffragettes, women wants to be harlequins as well as columbines. Though I hope they won't make the columbine a man's part!

'Mortimer was the nimblest chap at the traps I ever see. He was so sure of hisself that he would have extra weight put on so that when the counter weights fell he'd shoot up five or six feet higher than anyone else could even try to. Moreover, he had a way of drawing up his legs when in the air—the way a frog does when he is swimming—that made his jump look ever so much higher.

'I think the girls were all in love with him, the way they used to stand in the wings when the time was comin' for his entrance. That wouldn't have mattered much, for girls are always falling in love with some man or other, but it made trouble, as it always does when the married ones take the same start. There were several of these that were always after him, more shame for them, with husbands of their own. That was dangerous enough, and hard to stand for a man who might mean to be decent in any way. But the real trial—and the real trouble, too—was none other than the young wife of my own master, and she was more than flesh and blood could stand. She had come into the panto. the season before as a high-kicker—and she could! She could kick higher than girls that was more than a foot taller than her; for she was a wee bit of a thing and as pretty as pie; a gold-haired, blue-eyed, slim thing with much the figure of a boy, except for . . . and they saved her from any mistaken idea of that kind. Jack Haliday went crazy over her, and when the notice was up, and there was no young spark with plenty of oof coming along to do the proper thing by her, she married him. It was, when they was joined, what you Ladies call a marriage of convenience; but after a bit they two got on very well, and we all thought she was beginning to like the old man—for Jack was old enough to be her father, with a bit to spare. In the summer, when the house was closed, he took her to the Isle of Man; and when they came back he made no secret of it that he'd had the happiest time of his life. She looked quite happy, too, and treated him affectionate; and we all began to think that *that* marriage had not been a failure at any rate.

'Things began to change, however, when the panto. rehearsals began next year. Old Jack began to look unhappy, and didn't take no interest in his work. Loo—that was Mrs. Haliday's name—didn't seem over fond of him now, and was generally impatient when he was by. Nobody said anything about this, however, to us men; but the married women smiled and nodded their heads and whispered that perhaps there were reasons. One day on the stage, when the harlequinade rehearsal was beginning, someone mentioned as how perhaps Mrs. Haliday wouldn't be dancing that year, and they smiled as if they was all in the secret. Then Mrs. Jack ups and gives them Johnny-up-the-orchard for not minding their own business and telling a pack of lies, and such like as you Ladies like to express in your own ways when you get your back hair down. The rest of us tried to soothe her all we could, and she went off home.

'It wasn't long after that that she and Henry Mortimer left together after rehearsal was over, he saying he'd leave her at home. She didn't make no objections—I told you he was a very handsome man.

'Well, from that on she never seemed to take her eyes from him during every rehearsal, right up to the night of the last rehearsal, which, of course, was full dress—"Everybody and Everything."

"Jack Haliday never seemed to notice anything that was going on, like the rest of them did. True, his time was taken up with his own work, for I'm telling you that a Master Machinist hasn't got no loose time on his hands at the first dress rehearsal of a panto. And, of course, none of the company ever said a word or gave a look that would call his attention to it. Men and women are queer beings. They will be blind and deaf whilst danger is being run; and it's only after the scandal is beyond repair that they begin to talk—just the very time when most of all they should be silent.

'I saw all that went on, but I didn't understand it. I liked Mortimer myself and admired him—like I did Mrs. Haliday, too —and I thought he was a very fine fellow. I was only a boy, you know, and Haliday's apprentice, so naturally I wasn't looking for any trouble I could help, even if I'd seen it coming. It was when I looked back afterwards at the whole thing that I began to comprehend; so you will all understand now, I hope, that what I tell you is the result of much knowledge of what I saw and heard and was told of afterwards—all morticed and clamped up by thinking.

'The panto. had been on about three weeks when one Saturday, between the shows, I heard two of our company talking. Both of them was among the extra girls that both sang and danced and had to make theirselves useful. I don't think either of them was better than she should be; they went out to too many champagne suppers with young men that had money to burn. That part doesn't matter in this affair—except that they was naturally enough jealous of women who was married—which was what they was aiming at—and what lived straighter than they did. Women of that kind like to see a good woman tumble down; it seems to make them all more even. Now real bad girls what have gone under altogether will try to save a decent one from following their road. That is, so long as they're young; for a bad one what is long in the tooth is the limit. They'll help anyone down hill—so long as they get anything out of it.

'Well—no offence, you Ladies, as has growed up!—these two girls was enjoyin' themselves over Mrs Haliday and the mash she had set up on Mortimer. They didn't see that I was sitting on a stage box behind a built-out piece of the Prologue of the panto., which was set ready for night. They were both in love with Mortimer, who wouldn't look at either of them, so they was miaw'n cruel, like cats on the tiles. Says one:

'"The Old Man seems worse than blind; he *won't* see."

'"Don't you be too sure of that," says the other. "He don't mean to take no chances. I think you must be blind, too, Kissie." That was her name—on the bills anyhow, Kissie Mountpelier. "Don't he make a point of taking her home hisself every night after the play. You should know, for you're in the hall yourself waiting for your young man till he comes from his club."

'"Wot-ho, you bally geeser," says the other—which her language was mostly coarse—"don't you know there's two ends to everything? The Old Man looks to one end only!" Then they began to snigger and whisper; and presently the other one says:

'"Then he thinks harm can be only done when work is over!"

'"Jest so," she answers. "Her and him knows that the old man has to be down long before the risin' of the rag; but she doesn't come in till the Vision of Venus dance after half time; and he not till the harlequinade!"

'Then I quit. I didn't want to hear any more of that sort.

'All that week things went on as usual. Poor old Haliday wasn't well. He looked worried and had a devil of a temper. I had reason to know that, for what worried him was his work. He was always a hard worker, and the panto. season was a terror with him. He didn't ever seem to mind anything else outside his work. I thought at the time that that was how those two chattering girls made up their slanderous story; for, after all, a slander, no matter how false it may be, must have some sort of beginning. Something that seems, if there isn't something that is! But no matter how busy he might be, old Jack always made time to leave the wife at home.

'As the week went on he got more and more pale; and I began to think he was in for some sickness. He generally remained in the theatre between the shows on Saturday; that is, he didn't go home, but took a high tea in the coffee shop close to the theatre, so as to be handy in case there might be a hitch anywhere in the preparation for night. On that Saturday he went out as usual when the first scene was set, and the men were getting ready the packs for the rest of the scenes. By and bye there was some trouble—the usual Saturday kind—and I went off to tell him. When I went into the coffee shop I couldn't see him. I thought it best not to ask or to seem to take any notice, so I came back to the theatre, and heard that the trouble had settled itself as usual, by the men who had been quarrelling going off to have another drink. I hustled up those who remained, and we got things smoothed out in time for them all to have their tea. Then I had my own. I was just then beginning to feel the responsibility of my business, so I wasn't long over my food, but came back to look things over and see that all was right, especially the trap, for that was a thing Jack Haliday was most particular about. He would overlook a fault for anything else; but if it was along of a trap, the man had to go. He always told the men that that wasn't ordinary work; it was life or death.

'I had just got through my inspection when I saw old Jack coming in from the hall. There was no one about at that hour, and the stage was dark. But dark as it was I could see that the old man was ghastly pale. I didn't speak, for I wasn't near enough, and as he was moving very silently behind the scenes I thought that perhaps he wouldn't like anyone to notice that he had been away. I thought the best thing I could do would be to clear out of the way, so I went back and had another cup of tea.

'I came away a little before the men, who had nothing to think of except to be in their places when Haliday's whistle sounded. I went to report myself to my master, who was in his own little glass-partitioned den at the back of the carpenter's shop. He was there bent over his own bench, and was filing away at something so intently that he did not seem to hear me; so I cleared out. I tell you, Ladies and Gents., that from an apprentice point of view it is not wise to be too obtrusive when your master is attending to some private matter of his own!

'When the "get-ready" time came and the lights went up, there was Haliday as usual at his post. He looked very white and ill—so ill that the stage manager, when he came in, said to him that if he liked to go home and rest he would see that all his work would be attended to. He thanked him, and said that he thought he would be able to stay. "I do feel a little weak and ill, sir," he said. "I felt just now for a few moments as if I was going to faint. But that's gone by already, and I'm sure I shall be able to get through the work before us all right."

'Then the doors was opened, and the Saturday night audience came rushing and tumbling in. The Victoria was a great Saturday night house. No matter what other nights might be, *that* was sure to be good. They used to say in the perfesh that the Victoria lived on it, and that the management was on holiday for the rest of the week. The actors knew it, and no matter how slack they might be from Monday to Friday they was all taut and trim then. There was no walking through and no fluffing on Saturday nights—or else they'd have had the bird.

'Mortimer was one of the most particular of the lot in this way. He never was slack at any time—indeed, slackness is not a harlequin's fault, for if there's slackness there's no harlequin, that's all. But Mortimer always put on an extra bit on the Saturday night. When he jumped up through the star trap he always went then a couple of feet higher. To do this we had always to put on a lot more weight. This he always saw to himself; for, mind you, it's no joke being driven up through the trap as if you was shot out of a gun. The points of the star had to be kept free, and the hinges at their bases must be well oiled, or else there can be a disaster at any time. Moreover, 'tis the duty of someone appointed for the purpose to see that all is clear upon the stage. I remember hearing that once at New York, many years ago now, a harlequin was killed by a "grip"—as the Yankees call a carpenter—what outsiders here call a scene-shifter—walking over the trap just as the stroke had been given to let go the counter-weights. It wasn't much satisfaction to the widow to know that the "grip" was killed too.

'That night Mrs. Haliday looked prettier than ever, and kicked even higher than I had ever seen her do. Then, when she got dressed for home, she came as usual and stood in the wings for the beginning of the harlequinade. Old Jack came across the stage and stood beside her; I saw him from the back follow up the sliding ground-row that closed in on the Realms of Delight. I couldn't help noticing that he still looked ghastly pale. He kept turning his eyes on the star trap. Seeing this, I naturally looked at it too, for I feared lest something might have gone wrong. I had seen that it was in good order, and that the joints were properly oiled when the stage was set for the evening show, and as it wasn't used all night for anything else I was reassured. Indeed, I thought I could see it shine a bit as the limelight caught the brass hinges. There was a spot light just above it on the bridge, which was intended to make a good show of harlequin and his big jump. The people used to howl with delight as he came rushing up through the trap and when in the air drew up his legs and spread them wide for an instant and then straightened them again as he came down—only bending his knees just as he touched the stage.

'When the signal was given the counterweight worked properly. I knew, for the sound of it at that part was all right.

'But something was wrong. The trap didn't work smooth, and

open at once as the harlequin's head touched it. There was a shock and a tearing sound, and the pieces of the star seemed torn about, and some of them were thrown about the stage. And in the middle of them came the coloured and spangled figure that we knew.

'But somehow it didn't come up in the usual way. It was erect enough, but there was not the usual elasticity. The legs never moved; and when it went up a fair height—though nothing like usual—it seemed to topple over and fall on the stage on its side. The audience shrieked, and the people in the wings—actors and staff all the same—closed in, some of them in their stage clothes, others dressed for going home. But the man in the spangles lay quite still.

'The loudest shriek of all was from Mrs. Haliday; and she was the first to reach the spot where he—it—lay. Old Jack was close behind her, and caught her as she fell. I had just time to see that, for I made it my business to look after the pieces of the trap; there was plenty of people to look after the corpse. And the pit was by now crossing the orchestra and climbing up on the stage.

'I managed to get the bits together before the rush came. I noticed that there were deep scratches on some of them, but I didn't have time for more than a glance. I put a stage box over the hole lest anyone should put a foot through it. Such would mean a broken leg at least; and if one fell through, it might mean worse. Amongst other things I found a queer-looking piece of flat steel with some bent points on it. I knew it didn't belong to the trap; but it came from *somewhere*, so I put it in my pocket.

'By this time there was a crowd where Mortimer's body lay. That he was stone dead nobody could doubt. The very attitude was enough. He was all straggled about in queer positions; one of the legs was doubled under him with the toes sticking out in the wrong way. But let that suffice! It doesn't do to go into details of a dead body . . . I wish someone would give me a drop of punch.

'There was another crowd round Mrs. Haliday, who was lying a little on one side nearer the wings where her husband had carried her and laid her down. She, too, looked like a corpse;

for she was as white as one and as still, and looked as cold. Old Jack was kneeling beside her, chafing her hands. He was evidently frightened about her, for he, too, was deathly white. However, he kept his head, and called his men round him. He left his wife in care of Mrs. Homcroft, the Wardrobe Mistress, who had by this time hurried down. She was a capable woman, and knew how to act promptly. She got one of the men to lift Mrs. Haliday and carry her up to the wardrobe. I heard afterwards that when she got her there she turned out all the rest of them that followed up—the women as well as the men—and looked after her herself.

'I put the pieces of the broken trap on the top of the stage box, and told one of our chaps to mind them, and see that no one touched them, as they might be wanted. By this time the police who had been on duty in front had come round, and as they had at once telephoned to headquarters, more police kept coming in all the time. One of them took charge of the place where the broken trap was; and when he heard who put the box and the broken pieces there, sent for me. More of them took the body away to the property room, which was a large room with benches in it, and which could be locked up. Two of them stood at the door, and wouldn't let anyone go in without permission.

'The man who was in charge of the trap asked me if I had seen the accident. When I said I had, he asked me to describe it. I don't think he had much opinion of my powers of description, for he soon dropped that part of his questioning. Then he asked me to point out where I found the bits of the broken trap. I simply said:

' "Lord bless you, sir, I couldn't tell. They was scattered all over the place. I had to pick them up between people's feet as they were rushing in from all sides."

' "All right, my boy," he said, in quite a kindly way, for a policeman, "I don't think they'll want to worry you. There are lots of men and women, I am told, who were standing by and saw the whole thing. They will be all subpœnaed." I was a small-made lad in those days—I ain't a giant now!—and I suppose he thought it was no use having children for witnesses when they had plenty of grown-ups. Then he said something about me and an idiot asylum that was not kind—no, nor wise either, for I dried up and did not say another word.

'Gradually the public was got rid of. Some strolled off by degrees, going off to have a glass before the pubs. closed, and talk it all over. The rest of us and the police ballooned out. Then, when the police had taken charge of everything and put in men to stay all night, the coroner's officer came and took off the body to the city mortuary, where the police doctor made a post mortem. I was allowed to go home. I did so—and gladly—when I had seen the place settling down. Mr. Haliday took his wife home in a four-wheeler. It was perhaps just as well, for Mrs. Homcroft and some other kindly souls had poured so much whisky and brandy and rum and gin and beer and peppermint into her that I don't believe she could have walked if she had tried.

'When I was undressing myself something scratched my leg as I was taking off my trousers. I found it was the piece of flat steel which I had picked up on the stage. It was in the shape of a star fish, but the spikes of it were short. Some of the points were turned down, the rest were pulled out straight again. I stood with it in my hand wondering where it had come from and what it was for, but I couldn't remember anything in the whole theatre that it could have belonged to. I looked at it closely again, and saw that the edges were all filed and quite bright. But that did not help me, so I put it on the table and thought I would take it with me in the morning; perhaps one of the chaps might know. I turned out the gas and went to bed—and to sleep.

'I must have begun to dream at once, and it was, naturally enough, all about the terrible thing that had occurred. But, like all dreams, it was a bit mixed. They were all mixed. Mortimer with his spangles flying up the trap, it breaking, and the pieces scattering round. Old Jack Haliday looking on at one side of the stage with his wife beside him—he as pale as death, and she looking prettier than ever. And then Mortimer coming down all crooked and falling on the stage, Mrs. Haliday shrieking, and her and Jack running forward, and me picking up the pieces of the broken trap from between people's legs, and finding the steel star with the bent points.

'I woke in a cold sweat, saying to myself as I sat up in bed in the dark:

' "That's it!"

'And then my head began to reel about so that I lay down again and began to think it all over. And it all seemed clear enough then. It was Mr. Haliday who made that star and put it over the star trap where the points joined! That was what Jack Haliday was filing at when I saw him at his bench; and he had done it because Mortimer and his wife had been making love to each other. Those girls were right, after all. Of course, the steel points had prevented the trap opening, and when Mortimer was driven up against it his neck was broken.

'But then came the horrible thought that if Jack did it, it was murder, and he would be hung. And, after all, it was his wife that the harlequin had made love to—and old Jack loved her very much indeed himself and had been good to her—and she was his wife. And that bit of steel would hang him if it should be known. But no one but me—and whoever made it, and put it on the trap—even knew of its existence—and Mr. Haliday was my master—and the man was dead—and he was a villain!

'I was living then at Quarry Place; and in the old quarry was a pond so deep that the boys used to say that far down the water was boiling hot, it was so near Hell.

'I softly opened the window, and, there in the dark, threw the bit of steel as far as I could into the quarry.

'No one ever knew, for I have never spoken a word of it till this very minute. I was not called at the inquest. Everyone was in a hurry; the coroner and the jury and the police. Our governor was in a hurry too, because we wanted to go on as usual at night; and too much talk of the tragedy would hurt business. So nothing was known; and all went on as usual. Except that after that Mrs. Haliday didn't stand in the wings during the harlequinade, and she was as loving to her old husband as a woman can be. It was him she used to watch now; and always with a sort of respectful adoration. She knew, though no one else did, except her husband —and me.'

When he finished there was a big spell of silence. The company had all been listening intently, so that there was no change except the cessation of Hempitch's voice. The eyes of all were now fixed on Mr. Wellesley Dovercourt. It was the *rôle* of the Tragedian to deal with such an occasion. He was quite alive to the privileges of his status, and spoke at once:

'H'm! Very excellent indeed! You will have to join the ranks of our profession, Mr. Master Machinist—the lower ranks, of course. A very thrilling narrative yours, and distinctly true. There may be some errors of detail, such as that Mrs. Haliday never flirted again. I . . . I knew John Haliday under, of course, his real name. But I shall preserve the secret you so judiciously suppressed. A very worthy person. He was stage carpenter at the Duke's Theatre, Bolton, where I first dared histrionic triumphs in the year—ah H'm! I saw quite a good deal of Mrs. Haliday at that time. And you are wrong about her. Quite wrong! She was a most attractive little woman—very!'

The Wardrobe Mistress here whispered to the Second Old Woman:

'Well, ma'am, they all seem agoin' of it tonight. I think they must have ketched the infection from Mr. Bloze. There isn't a bally word of truth in all Hempitch has said. I was there when the accident occurred—for it was an accident when Jim Bungnose, the clown, was killed. For he was a clown, not a 'arlequin; an' there wasn't no lovemakin' with Mrs. 'Aliday. God 'elp the woman as would try to make love to Jim; which she was the Strong Woman in a Circus, and could put up her dooks like a man. Moreover, there wasn't no Mrs. 'Aliday. The carpenter at Grimsby, where it is he means, was Tom Elrington, as he was my first 'usband. And as to Mr. Dovercourt rememberin'! He's a cure, he is; an' the Limit!'

* * *

The effect of the Master Machinist's story was so depressing that the M.C. tried to hurry things on; any change of sentiment would, he thought, be an advantage. So he bustled along:

'Now, Mr. Turner Smith, you are the next on the roster. It is a pity we have not an easel and a canvas and paint box here, or even some cartridge paper and charcoal, so that you might give us a touch of your art—what I may call a plastic diversion of the current of narrative genius which has been enlivening the snowy waste around us.' The artistic audience applauded this flight of metaphor—all except the young man from Oxford, who contented himself by saying loudly, 'Pip-pip!' He had heard something like it before at the Union.

THE SQUAW

NURNBERG AT THE time was not so much exploited as it has been since then. Irving had not been playing *Faust*, and the very name of the old town was hardly known to the great bulk of the travelling public. My wife and I being in the second week of our honeymoon, naturally wanted someone else to join our party, so that when the cheery stranger, Elias P. Hutcheson, hailing from Isthmian City, Bleeding Gulch, Maple Tree County, Neb. turned up at the station at Frankfort, and casually remarked that he was going on to see the most all-fired old Methuselah of a town in Yurrup, and that he guessed that so much travelling alone was enough to send an intelligent, active citizen into the melancholy ward of a daft house, we took the pretty broad hint and suggested that we should join forces. We found, on comparing notes afterwards, that we had each intended to speak with some diffidence or hesitation so as not to appear too eager, such not being a good compliment to the success of our married life; but the effect was entirely marred by our both beginning to speak at the same instant—stopping simultaneously and then going on together again. Anyhow, no matter how, it was done; and Elias P. Hutcheson became one of our party. Straightway Amelia and I found the pleasant benefit; instead of quarrelling, as we had been doing, we found that the restraining influence of a third party was such that we now took every opportunity of spooning in odd corners. Amelia declares that ever since she has, as the result of that experience, advised all her friends to take a friend on the honeymoon. Well, we 'did' Nurnberg together, and much enjoyed the racy remarks of our Transatlantic friend, who, from his quaint speech and his wonderful stock of adventures, might have stepped out of a novel. We kept for the last object of interest in the city to be visited the Burg, and on the day appointed for the visit strolled round the outer wall of the city by the eastern side.

The Burg is seated on a rock dominating the town and an immensely deep fosse guards it on the northern side. Nurnberg has been happy in that it was never sacked; had it been it would certainly not be so spick and span perfect as it is at present. The ditch has not been used for centuries, and now its base is spread with tea-gardens and orchards, of which some of the trees are of quite respectable growth. As we wandered round the wall, dawdling in the hot July sunshine, we often paused to admire the views spread before us, and in especial the great plain covered with towns and villages and bounded with a blue line of hills, like a landscape of Claude Lorraine. From this we always turned with new delight to the city itself, with its myriad of quaint old gables and acre-wide red roofs dotted with dormer windows, tier upon tier. A little to our right rose the towers of the Burg, and nearer still, standing grim, the Torture Tower, which was, and is, perhaps, the most interesting place in the city. For centuries the tradition of the Iron Virgin of Nurnberg has been handed down as an instance of the horrors of cruelty of which man is capable; we had long looked forward to seeing it; and here at last was its home.

In one of our pauses we leaned over the wall of the moat and looked down. The garden seemed quite fifty or sixty feet below us, and the sun pouring into it with an intense, moveless heat like that of an oven. Beyond rose the grey, grim wall seemingly of endless height, and losing itself right and left in the angles of bastion and counterscarp. Trees and bushes crowned the wall, and above again towered the lofty houses on whose massive beauty Time has only set the hand of approval. The sun was hot and we were lazy; time was our own, and we lingered, leaning on the wall. Just below us was a pretty sight—a great black cat lying stretched in the sun, whilst round her gambolled prettily a tiny black kitten. The mother would wave her tail for the kitten to play with, or would raise her feet and push away the little one as an encouragement to further play. They were just at the foot of the wall, and Elias P. Hutcheson, in order to help the play, stooped and took from the walk a moderate sized pebble.

'See!' he said, 'I will drop it near the kitten, and they will both wonder where it came from.'

'Oh, be careful,' said my wife; 'you might hit the dear little thing!'

'Not me, ma'am,' said Elias P. 'Why, I'm as tender as a Maine cherry-tree. Lor, bless ye, I wouldn't hurt the poor pooty little critter more'n I'd scalp a baby. An' you may bet your variegated socks on that! See, I'll drop it fur away on the outside so's not to go near her!' Thus saying, he leaned over and held his arm out at full length and dropped the stone. It may be that there is some attractive force which draws lesser matters to greater; or more probably that the wall was not plump but sloped to its base—we not noticing the inclination from above; but the stone fell with a sickening thud that came up to us through the hot air, right on the kitten's head, and shattered out its little brains then and there. The black cat cast a swift upward glance, and we saw her eyes like green fire fixed an instant on Elias P. Hutcheson; and then her attention was given to the kitten, which lay still with just a quiver of her tiny limbs, whilst a thin red stream trickled from a gaping wound. With a muffled cry, such as a human being might give, she bent over the kitten licking its wounds and moaning. Suddenly she seemed to realise that it was dead, and again threw her eyes up at us. I shall never forget the sight, for she looked the perfect incarnation of hate. Her green eyes blazed with lurid fire, and the white, sharp teeth seemed to almost shine through the blood which dabbled her mouth and whiskers. She gnashed her teeth, and her claws stood out stark and at full length on every paw. Then she made a wild rush up the wall as if to reach us, but when the momentum ended fell back, and further added to her horrible appearance for she fell on the kitten, and rose with her black fur smeared with its brains and blood. Amelia turned quite faint, and I had to lift her back from the wall. There was a seat close by in shade of a spreading plane-tree, and here I placed her whilst she composed herself. Then I went back to Hutcheson, who stood without moving, looking down on the angry cat below.

As I joined him, he said:

'Wall, I guess that air the savagest beast I ever see—'cept once when an Apache squaw had an edge on a half-breed what they nicknamed "Splinters" 'cos of the way he fixed up her papoose which he stole on a raid just to show that he appreciated the way they had given his mother the fire torture. She got that kinder look so set on her face that it jest seemed to grow there. She followed Splinters mor'n three year till at last the braves got him and handed him over to her. They did say that no man, white or Injun, had ever been so long a-dying under the tortures of the Apaches. The only time I ever see her smile was when I wiped her out. I kem on the camp just in time to see Splinters pass in his checks, and he wasn't sorry to go either. He was a hard citizen, and though I never could shake with him after that papoose business—for it was bitter bad, and he should have been a white man, for he looked like one—I see he had got paid out in full. Durn me, but I took a piece of his hide from one of his skinnin' posts an' had it made into a pocket-book. It's here now!' and he slapped the breast pocket of his coat.

Whilst he was speaking the cat was continuing her frantic efforts to get up the wall. She would take a run back and then charge up, sometimes reaching an incredible height. She did not seem to mind the heavy fall which she got each time but started with renewed vigour; and at every tumble her appearance became more horrible. Hutcheson was a kind hearted-man—my wife and I had both noticed little acts of kindness to animals as well as to persons—and he seemed concerned at the state of fury to which the cat had wrought herself.

'Wall, now!' he said, 'I du declare that that poor critter seems quite desperate. There! there! poor thing, it was all an accident—though that won't bring back your little one to you. Say! I wouldn't have had such a thing happen for a thousand! Just shows what a clumsy fool of a man can do when he tries to play! Seems I'm too darned slipperhanded to even play with a cat. Say Colonel!'

it was a pleasant way he had to bestow titles freely—'I hope your wife don't hold no grudge against me on account of this unpleasantness? Why, I wouldn't have had it occur on no account.'

He came over to Amelia and apologised profusely, and she with her usual kindness of heart hastened to assure him that she quite understood that it was an accident. Then we all went again to the wall and looked over.

The cat missing Hutcheson's face had drawn back across the moat, and was sitting on her haunches as though ready to spring. Indeed, the very instant she saw him she did spring, and with a blind unreasoning fury, which would have been grotesque, only that it was so frightfully real. She did not try to run up the wall, but simply launched herself at him as though hate and fury could lend her wings to pass straight through the great distance between them. Amelia, womanlike, got quite concerned, and said to Elias P. in a warning voice:

'Oh! you must be very careful. That animal would try to kill you if she were here; her eyes look like positive murder.'

He laughed out jovially. 'Excuse me, ma'am,' he said, 'but I can't help laughin'. Fancy a man that has fought grizzlies an' Injuns bein' careful of bein' murdered by a cat!'

When the cat heard him laugh, her whole demeanour seemed to change. She no longer tried to jump or run up the wall, but went quietly over, and sitting again beside the dead kitten began to lick and fondle it as though it were alive.

'See!' said I, 'the effect of a really strong man. Even that animal in the midst of her fury recognises the voice of a master, and bows to him!'

'Like a squaw!' was the only comment of Elias P. Hutcheson, as we moved on our way round the city fosse. Every now and then we looked over the wall and each time saw the cat following us. At first she had kept going back to the dead kitten, and then as the distance grew greater took it in her mouth and so followed. After a while, however, she abandoned this, for we saw her following all alone; she had evidently hidden the body somewhere. Amelia's alarm grew at the cat's persistence, and more than once she repeated her warning; but the American always laughed with amusement, till finally, seeing that she was beginning to be worried, he said:

'I say, ma'am, you needn't be skeered over that cat. I go heeled, I du!' Here he slapped his pistol pocket at the back of his lumbar region. 'Why sooner'n have you worried, I'll shoot the critter, right here, an' risk the police interferin' with a citizen of the United States for carryin' arms contrairy to reg'lations!' As he spoke he looked over the wall, but the cat on seeing him, retreated, with a growl, into a bed of tall flowers, and was hidden. He went on: 'Blest if that ar critter ain't got more sense of what's good for her than most Christians. I guess we've seen the last of her! You bet, she'll go back now to that busted kitten and have a private funeral of it, all to herself!'

Amelia did not like to say more, lest he might, in mistaken kindness to her, fulfil his threat of shooting the cat: and so we went on and crossed the little wooden bridge leading to the gateway whence ran the steep paved roadway between the Burg and the pentagonal Torture Tower. As we crossed the bridge we saw the cat again down below us. When she saw us her fury seemed to return, and she made frantic efforts to get up the steep wall. Hutcheson laughed as he looked down at her, and said:

'Goodbye, old girl. Sorry I injured your feelin's, but you'll get over it in time! So long!' And then we passed through the long, dim archway and came to the gate of the Burg.

When we came out again after our survey of this most beautiful old place which not even the well-intentioned efforts of the Gothic restorers of forty years ago have been able to spoil—though their restoration was then glaring white—we seemed to have quite forgotten the unpleasant episode of the morning. The old lime tree with its great trunk gnarled with the passing of nearly nine centuries, the deep well cut through the heart of the rock by those captives of old, and the lovely view from the city wall whence we heard, spread over almost a full quarter of an hour, the multitudinous chimes of the city, had all helped to wipe out from our minds the incident of the slain kitten.

We were the only visitors who had entered the Torture Tower that morning—so at least said the old custodian—and as we had the place all to ourselves were able to make a minute and more satisfactory survey than would have otherwise been possible. The custodian, looking to us as the sole source of his gains for the day, was willing to meet our wishes in any way. The Torture Tower is truly a grim place, even now when many thousands of visitors have sent a stream of life, and the joy that follows life, into the place; but at the time I mention it wore its grimmest and most gruesome aspect. The dust of ages seemed to have settled on it, and the darkness and the horror of its memories seem to have become sentient in a way that would have satisfied the Pantheistic souls of Philo or Spinoza. The lower chamber where we entered was seemingly, in its normal state, filled with incarnate darkness; even the hot sunlight streaming in through the door seemed to be lost in the vast thickness of the walls, and only showed the masonry rough as when the builder's scaffolding had come down, but coated with dust and marked here and there with patches of dark stain which, if walls could speak, could have given their own dread memories of fear and pain. We were glad to pass up the dusty wooden staircase, the custodian leaving the outer door open to light us somewhat on our way; for to our eyes the one long-wick'd, evil-smelling candle stuck in a sconce on the wall gave an inadequate light. When we came up through the open trap in the corner of the chamber overhead, Amelia held on to me so tightly that I could actually feel her heart beat. I must say for my own part that I was not surprised at her fear, for this room was even more gruesome than that below. Here there was certainly more light, but only just sufficient to realise the horrible surroundings of the place. The builders of the tower had evidently intended that only they who should gain the top should have any of the joys of light and prospect. There, as we had noticed from below, were ranges of windows, albeit of mediaeval smallness, but elsewhere in the tower were only a very few narrow slits such as were habitual in places of mediaeval defence. A few of these only lit the chamber, and these so high up in the wall that from no part could the sky be seen through the thickness of the walls. In racks, and leaning in disorder against the walls, were a number of headsmen's swords, great double-handed weapons with broad blade and keen edge. Hard by were several blocks whereon the necks of the victims had lain, with here and there deep notches where the steel had bitten through the guard of flesh and shored into the wood. Round the chamber, placed in all sorts of irregular ways, were many implements of torture which made one's heart ache to see—chairs full of spikes which gave instant and excruciating pain; chairs and couches with dull knobs whose torture was seemingly less, but which, though slower, were equally efficacious; racks, belts, boots, gloves, collars, all made for compressing at will; steel baskets in which the head could be slowly crushed into a pulp if necessary; watchmen's hooks with long handle and knife that cut at resistance—this a speciality of the old Nurnberg police system; and many, many other devices for man's injury to man. Amelia grew quite pale with the horror of the things, but fortunately did not faint, for being a little overcome she sat down on a torture chair, but jumped up again with a shriek, all tendency to faint gone. We both pretended that it was the injury done to her dress by the dust of the chair, and the rusty spikes which had upset her, and Mr. Hutcheson acquiesced in accepting the explanation with a kind-hearted laugh.

But the central object in the whole of this chamber of horrors was the engine known as the Iron Virgin, which stood near the centre of the room. It was a rudely-shaped figure of a woman, something of the bell order, or, to make a closer comparison, of the figure of Mrs. Noah in the children's Ark, but without that slimness of waist and perfect *rondeur* of hip which marks the aesthetic type of the Noah family. One would hardly have recognised it as intended for a human figure at all had not the founder shaped on the forehead a rude semblance of a woman's face. This machine was coated with rust without, and covered with dust; a rope was fastened to a ring in the front of the figure, about where the waist should have been, and was drawn through a pulley, fastened on the wooden pillar which sustained the flooring above. The custodian pulling this rope showed that a section of the front was hinged like a door at one side; we then saw that the engine was of considerable thickness, leaving just room enough inside for a man to be placed. The door was of equal thickness and of great weight, for it took the custodian all his strength, aided though he was by the contrivance of the pulley, to open it. This weight was partly due to the fact that the door was of manifest purpose hung so as to throw its weight downwards, so that it might shut of its own accord when the strain was released. The inside was honeycombed with rust—nay more, the rust alone that comes through time would hardly have eaten so deep into the iron walls; the rust of the cruel stains was deep indeed! It was only, however, when we came to look at the inside of the door that the diabolical intention was manifest to the full. Here were several long spikes, square and massive, broad at the base and sharp at the points, placed in such a position that when the door should close the upper ones would pierce the eyes of the victim, and the lower ones his heart and vitals. The sight was too much for poor Amelia, and this time she fainted dead off, and I had to carry her down the stairs, and place her on a bench outside till she recovered. That she felt it to the quick was afterwards shown by the fact that my eldest son bears to this day a rude birthmark on his breast, which has, by family consent, been accepted as representing the Nurnberg Virgin.

When we got back to the chamber we found Hutcheson still opposite the Iron Virgin; he had been evidently philosophising, and now gave us the benefit of his thought in the shape of a sort of exordium.

'Wall, I guess I've been learnin' somethin' here while madam has been gettin' over her faint. 'Pears to me that we're a long way behind the times on our side of the big drink. We uster think out on the plains that the Injun could give us points in tryin' to make a man uncomfortable; but I guess your old mediaeval law-and-order party could raise him every time. Splinters was pretty good in his bluff on the squaw, but this here young miss held a straight flush all high on him. The points of them spikes air sharp enough still, though even the edges air eaten out by what uster be on them.

It'd be a good thing for our Indian section to get some specimens of this here play-toy to send round to the Reservations jest to knock the stuffin' out of the bucks, and the squaws too, by showing them as how old civilisation lays over them at their best. Guess but I'll get in that box a minute jest to see how it feels.'

'Oh no! no!' said Amelia. 'It is too terrible!'

'Guess, ma'am, nothin's too terrible to the explorin' mind. I've been in some queer places in my time. Spent a night inside a dead horse while a prairie fire swept over me in Montana Territory—an' another time slept inside a dead buffler when the Comanches was on the war path an' I didn't keer to leave my kyard on them. I've been two days in a caved-in tunnel in the Billy Broncho gold mine in New Mexico, an' was one of the four shut up for three parts of a day in the caisson what slid over on her side when we were settin' the foundations of the Buffalo Bridge. I've not funked an odd experience yet, an' I don't propose to begin now!'

We saw that he was set on the experiment, so I said: 'Well, hurry up, old man, and get through it quick!'

'All right, General,' said he, 'but I calculate we ain't quite ready yet. The gentlemen, my predecessors, what stood in that thar canister, didn't volunteer for the office—not much! And I guess there was some ornamental tyin' up before the big stroke was made. I want to go into this thing fair and square, so I must get fixed up proper first. I dare say this old galoot can rise some string and tie me up accordin' to sample?'

This was said interrogatively to the old custodian, but the latter, who understood the drift of his speech, though perhaps not appreciating to the full the niceties of dialect and imagery, shook his head. His protest was, however, only formal and made to be overcome. The American thrust a gold piece into his hand, saying: 'Take it, pard! it's your pot; and don't be skeer'd. This ain't no necktie party that you're asked to assist in!' He produced some thin frayed rope and proceeded to bind our companion with sufficient strictness for the purpose. When the upper part of his body was bound, Hutcheson said:

'Hold on a moment, Judge. Guess I'm too heavy for you to tote into the canister. You just let me walk in, and then you can wash up regardin' my legs!'

Whilst speaking he had backed himself into the opening which was just enough to hold him. It was a close fit and no mistake. Amelia looked on with fear in her eyes, but she evidently did not like to say anything. Then the custodian completed his task by tying the American's feet together so that he was now absolutely helpless and fixed in his voluntary prison. He seemed to really enjoy it, and the incipient smile which was habitual to his face blossomed into actuality as he said:

'Guess this here Eve was made out of the rib of a dwarf! There ain't much room for a full-grown citizen of the United States to hustle. We uster make our coffins more roomier in Idaho territory. Now, Judge, you jest begin to let this door down, slow, on to me. I want to feel the same pleasure as the other jays had when those spikes began to move toward their eyes!'

'Oh no! no! no!' broke in Amelia hysterically. 'It is too terrible! I can't bear to see it!—I can't! I can't!' But the American was obdurate. 'Say, Colonel,' said he, 'why not take Madame for a little promenade? I wouldn't hurt her feelin's for the world; but now that I am here, havin' kem eight thousand miles, wouldn't it be too hard to give up the very experience I've been pinin' an' pantin' fur? A man can't get to feel like canned goods every time! Me and the Judge here'll fix up this thing in no time, an' then you'll come back, an' we'll all laugh together!'

Once more the resolution that is born of curiosity triumphed, and Amelia stayed holding tight to my arm and shivering whilst the custodian began to slacken slowly inch by inch the rope that held back the iron door. Hutcheson's face was positively radiant as his eyes followed the first movement of the spikes.

'Wall!' he said, 'I guess I've not had enjoyment like this since I left Noo York. Bar a scrap with a French sailor at Wapping—an' that warn't much of a picnic neither—I've not had a show fur real pleasure in this dod-rotted Continent, where there ain't no b'ars nor no Injuns, an' wheer nary man goes heeled. Slow there,

Judge! Don't you rush this business! I want a show for my money this game—I du!'

The custodian must have had in him some of the blood of his predecessors in that ghastly tower, for he worked the engine with a deliberate and excruciating slowness which after five minutes, in which the outer edge of the door had not moved half as many inches, began to overcome Amelia. I saw her lips whiten, and felt her hold upon my arm relax. I looked around an instant for a place whereon to lay her, and when I looked at her again found that her eye had become fixed on the side of the Virgin. Following its direction I saw the black cat crouching out of sight. Her green eyes shone like danger lamps in the gloom of the place, and their colour was heightened by the blood which still smeared her coat and reddened her mouth. I cried out:

'The cat! look out for the cat!' for even then she sprang out before the engine. At this moment she looked like a triumphant demon. Her eyes blazed with ferocity, her hair bristled out till she seemed twice her normal size, and her tail lashed about as does a tiger's when the quarry is before it. Elias P. Hutcheson when he saw her was amused, and his eyes positively sparkled with fun as he said:

'Darned if the squaw hain't got on all her war paint! Jest give her a shove off if she comes any of her tricks on me, for I'm so fixed everlastingly by the boss, that durn my skin if I can keep my eyes from her if she wants them! Easy there, Judge! Don't you slack that ar rope or I'm euchered!'

At this moment Amelia completed her faint, and I had to clutch hold of her round the waist or she would have fallen to the floor. Whilst attending to her I saw the black cat crouching for a spring, and jumped up to turn the creature out.

But at that instant, with a sort of hellish scream, she hurled herself, not as we expected at Hutcheson, but straight at the face of the custodian. Her claws seemed to be tearing wildly as one sees in the Chinese drawings of the dragon rampant, and as I looked I saw one of them light on the poor man's eye, and actually tear through it and down his cheek, leaving a wide band of red where the blood seemed to spurt from every vein.

With a yell of sheer terror which came quicker than even his sense of pain, the man leaped back, dropping as he did so the rope which held back the iron door. I jumped for it, but was too late, for the cord ran like lightning through the pulley-block, and the heavy mass fell forward from its own weight.

As the door closed I caught a glimpse of our poor companion's face. He seemed frozen with terror. His eyes stared with a horrible anguish as if dazed, and no sound came from his lips.

And then the spikes did their work. Happily the end was quick, for when I wrenched open the door they had pierced so deep that they had locked in the bones of the skull through which they had crushed, and actually tore him—it—out of his iron prison till, bound as he was, he fell at full length with a sickly thud upon the floor, the face turning upward as he fell.

I rushed to my wife, lifted her up and carried her out, for I feared for her very reason if she should wake from her faint to such a scene. I laid her on the bench outside and ran back. Leaning against the wooden column was the custodian moaning in pain whilst he held his reddening handerchief to his eyes. And sitting on the head of the poor American was the cat, purring loudly as she licked the blood which trickled through the gashed socket of his eyes.

I think no one will call me cruel because I seized one of the old executioner's swords and shore her in two as she sat.

CROOKEN SANDS

MR. ARTHUR FERNLEE MARKAM, who took what was known as the Red House above the Mains of Crooken, was a London merchant, and being essentially a cockney, thought it necessary when he went for the summer holidays to Scotland to provide an entire rig-out as a Highland chieftain, as manifested in chomolithographs and on the music-hall stage. He had once seen in the Empire the Great Prince—'The Bounder King'—bring down the house by appearing as 'The MacSlogan of that Ilk', and singing the celebrated Scotch song, 'There's naething like haggis to mak a mon dry!' and he had ever since preserved in his mind a faithful image of the picturesque and warlike appearance which he presented. Indeed, if the true inwardness of Mr. Markam's mind on the subject of his selection of Aberdeenshire as a summer resort were known, it would be found that in the foreground of the holiday locality which his fancy painted stalked the many hued figure of the MacSlogan of that Ilk. However, be this as it may, a very kind fortune—certainly so far as external beauty was concerned—led him to the choice of Crooken Bay. It is a lovely spot, between Aberdeen and Peterhead, just under the rock-bound headland whence the long, dangerous reefs known as The Spurns run out into the North Sea. Between this and the 'Mains of Crooken'—a village sheltered by the northern cliffs—lies the deep bay, backed with a multitude of bent-grown dunes where the rabbits are to be found in thousands. Thus at either end of the bay is a rocky promontory, and when the dawn or the sunset falls on the rocks of red syenite the effect is very lovely. The bay itself is floored with level sand and the tide runs far out, leaving a smooth waste of hard sand on which are dotted here and there the stake nets and bag nets of the salmon fishers. At one end of the bay there is a little group or cluster of rocks whose heads are raised something above high water, except when in rough weather the waves come over them green. At low tide they are exposed down to sand level; and here is perhaps the only little bit of dangerous sand on this part of the eastern coast. Between the rocks, which are apart about some fifty feet, is a small quicksand, which, like the Goodwins, is dangerous only with the incoming tide. It extends outwards till it is lost in the sea, and inwards till it fades away in the hard sand of the upper beach. On the slope of the hill which rises beyond the dunes, midway between the Spurs and the Port of Crooken, is the Red House. It rises from the midst of a clump of fir-trees which protect it on three sides, leaving the whole sea front open. A trim old-fashioned garden stretches down to the roadway, on crossing which a grassy path, which can be used for light vehicles, threads a way to the shore, winding amongst the sand hills.

When the Markam family arrived at the Red House after their thirty-six hours of pitching on the Aberdeen steamer *Ban Righ* from Blackwall, with the subsequent train to Yellon and drive of a dozen miles, they all agreed that they had never seen a more delightful spot. The general satisfaction was more marked as at that very time none of the family were, for several reasons, inclined to find favourable anything or any place over the Scottish border. Though the family was a large one, the prosperity of the business allowed them all sorts of personal luxuries, amongst which was a wide latitude in the way of dress. The frequency of the Markam girls' new frocks was a source of envy to their bosom friends and of joy to themselves.

Arthur Fernlee Markam had not taken his family into his confidence regarding his new costume. He was not quite certain that he should be free from ridicule, or at least from sarcasm, and as he was sensitive on the subject, he thought it better to be actually in the suitable environment before he allowed the full splendour to burst upon them. He had taken some pains to insure the completeness of the Highland costume. For the purpose he had paid many visits to 'The Scotch All-Wool Tartan Clothing Mart' which had been lately established in Copthall-court by the Messrs. MacCallum More and Roderick MacDhu. He had anxious consultations with the head of the firm—MacCallum as he called himself, resenting any such additions as 'Mr.' or 'Esquire'. The known stock of buckles, buttons, straps, brooches and ornaments of all kinds were examined in critical detail; and at last an eagle's feather of sufficiently magnificent proportions was discovered, and the equipment was complete. It was only when he saw the finished costume, with the vivid hues of the tartan seemingly modified into comparative sobriety by the multitude of silver fittings, the cairngorm brooches, the philibeg, dirk and sporran that he was fully and absolutely satisfied with his choice. At first he had thought of the Royal Stuart dress tartan, but abandoned it on the MacCallum pointing out that if he should happen to be in the neighbourhood of Balmoral it might lead to complications. The MacCallum, who, by the way, spoke with a remarkable cockney accent, suggested other plaids in turn; but now that the other question of accuracy had been raised, Mr. Markam foresaw difficulties if he should by chance find himself in the locality of the clan whose colours he had usurped. The MacCallum at last undertook to have, at Markam's expense, a special pattern woven which would not be exactly the same as any existing tartan, though partaking of the characteristics of many. It was based on the Royal Stuart, but contained suggestions as to simplicity of pattern from the Macalister and Ogilvie clans, and as to neutrality of colour from the clans of Buchanan, Macbeth, Chief of Macintosh and Macleod. When the specimen had been shown to Markam he had feared somewhat lest it should strike the eye of his domestic circle as gaudy; but as Roderick MacDhu fell into perfect ecstasies over its beauty he did not make any objection to the completion of the piece. He thought, and wisely, that if a genuine Scotchman like MacDhu liked it, it must be right—especially as the junior partner was a man very much of his own build and appearance. When the MacCallum was receiving his cheque—which, by the way, was a pretty stiff one—he remarked:

'I've taken the liberty of having some more of the stuff woven in case you or any of your friends should want it.' Markam was gratified, and told him that he should be only too happy if the beautiful stuff which they had originated between them should become a favourite, as he had no doubt it would in time. He might make and sell as much as he would.

Markam tried the dress on in his office one evening after the clerks had all gone home. He was pleased, though a little frightened, at the result. The MacCallum had done his work thoroughly, and there was nothing omitted that could add to the martial dignity of the wearer.

'I shall not, of course, take the claymore and the pistols with me on ordinary occasions,' said Markam to himself as he began to undress. He determined that he would wear the dress for the first time on landing in Scotland, and accordingly on the morning when the *Ban Righ* was hanging off the Girdle Ness lighthouse, waiting for the tide to enter the port of Aberdeen, he emerged from his cabin in all the gaudy splendour of his new costume. The first comment he heard was from one of his own sons, who did not recognise him at first.

'Here's a guy! Great Scott! It's the governor!' And the boy fled forthwith and tried to bury his laughter under a cushion in the saloon. Markam was a good sailor and had not suffered from the pitching of the boat, so that his naturally rubicund face was even more rosy by the conscious blush which suffused his cheeks when he had found himself at once the cynosure of all eyes. He could have wished that he had not been so bold for he knew from the cold that there was a big bare spot under one side of his jauntily worn Glengarry cap. However, he faced the group of strangers boldly. He was not, outwardly, upset even when some of their comments reached his ears.

'He's off his bloomin' chump,' said a cockney in a suit of exaggerated plaid.

'There's flies on him,' said a tall thin Yankee, pale with sea-sickness, who was on his way to take up his residence for a time as close as he could get to the gates of Balmoral.

'Happy thought! Let us fill our mulls; now's the chance!' said a young Oxford man on his way home to Inverness. But presently Mr. Markam heard the voice of his eldest daughter.

'Where is he? Where is he?' and she came tearing along the deck with her hat blowing behind her. Her face showed signs of agitation, for her mother had just been telling her of her father's condition; but when she saw him she instantly burst into laughter so violent that it ended in a fit of hysterics. Something of the same kind happened to each of the other children. When they had all had their turn Mr. Markam went to his cabin and sent his wife's maid to tell each member of the family that he wanted to see them at once. They all made their appearance, suppressing their feelings as well as they could. He said to them very quietly:

'My dears, don't I provide you all with ample allowances?'

'Yes, father!' they all answered gravely, 'no one could be more generous!'

'Don't I let you dress as you please?'

'Yes, father!'—this a little sheepishly.

'Then, my dears, don't you think it would be nicer and kinder of you not to try and make me feel uncomfortable, even if I do assume a dress which is ridiculous in your eyes, though quite common enough in the country where we are about to sojourn?' There was no answer except that which appeared in their hanging heads. He was a good father and they all knew it. He was quite satisfied and went on:

'There, now, run away and enjoy yourselves! We shan't have another word about it.' Then he went on deck again and stood bravely the fire of ridicule which he recognised around him, though nothing more was said within his hearing.

The astonishment and the amusement which his get-up occasioned on the *Ban Righ* was, however, nothing to that which it created in Aberdeen. The boys and loafers, and women with babies, who waited at the landing shed, followed *en masse* as the Markam party took their way to the railway station; even the porters with their old-fashioned knots and their new-fashioned barrows, who await the traveller at the foot of the gang-plank, followed in wondering delight. Fortunately the Peterhead train was just about to start, so that the martyrdom was not unnecessarily prolonged. In the carriage the glorious Highland costume was unseen, and as there were but few persons at the station at Yellon, all went well there. When, however, the carriage drew near the Mains of Crooken and the fisher folk had run to their doors to see who it was that was passing, the excitement exceeded all bounds. The children with one impulse waved their bonnets and ran shouting behind the carriage; the men forsook their nets and their baiting and followed; the women clutched their babies and followed also. The horses were tired after their long journey to Yellon and back, and the hill was steep, so that there was ample time for the crowd to gather and even to pass on ahead.

Mrs. Markam and the elder girls would have liked to make some protest or to do something to relieve their feelings of chagrin at the ridicule which they saw on all faces, but there was a look of fixed determination on the face of the seeming Highlander which awed them a little, and they were silent. It might have been that the eagle's feather, even when arising above the bald head, the cairngorm brooch even on the fat shoulder, and the claymore, dirk and pistols, even when belted round the extensive paunch and protruding from the stocking on the sturdy calf, fulfilled their existence as symbols of martial and terrifying import! When the party arrived at the gate of the Red House there awaited them a crowd of Crooken inhabitants, hatless and respectfully silent; the remainder of the population was painfully toiling up the hill. The silence was broken by only one sound, that of a man with a deep voice.

'Man! but he's forgotten the pipes!'

The servants had arrived some days before, and all things were in readiness. In the glow consequent on a good lunch after a hard journey all the disagreeables of travel and all the chagrin consequent on the adoption of the obnoxious costume were forgotten.

That afternoon Markam, still clad in full array, walked through the Mains of Crooken. He was all alone, for strange to say, his wife and both daughters had sick headaches, and were, as he was told, lying down to rest after the fatigue of the journey. His eldest son, who claimed to be a young man, had gone out by himself to explore the surroundings of the place, and one of the boys could not be found. The other boy, on being told that his father had sent for him to come for a walk, had managed—by accident, of course —to fall into the water butt, and had to be dried and rigged out afresh. His clothes not having been as yet unpacked this was of course impossible without delay.

Mr. Markam was not quite satisfied with his walk. He could not meet any of his neighbours. It was not that there were not enough people about, for every house and cottage seemed to be full; but the people when in the open were either in their doorways some distance behind him, or on the roadway a long distance in front. As he passed he could see the tops of heads and the whites of eyes in the windows or round the corners of doors. The only interview which he had was anything but a pleasant one. This was with an odd sort of old man who was hardly ever heard to speak except to join in the 'Amens' in the meeting-house. His sole occupation seemed to be to wait at the window of the post-office from eight o'clock in the morning till the arrival of the mail at one, when he carried the letter-bag to a neighbouring baronial castle. The remainder of his day was spent on a seat in a draughty part of the port, where the offal of the fish, the refuse of the bait, and the house rubbish was thrown, and where the ducks were accustomed to hold high revel.

When Saft Tammie beheld him coming he raised his eyes, which were generally fixed on the nothing which lay on the roadway opposite his seat, and, seeming dazzled as if by a burst of sunshine, rubbed them and shaded them with his hand. Then he started up and raised his hand aloft in a denunciatory manner as he spoke:

' "Vanity of vanities, saith the preacher. All is vanity." Mon, be warned in time! "Behold the lilies of the field, they toil not, neither do they spin, yet Solomon in all his glory was not arrayed like one of these." Mon! Mon! Thy vanity is as the quicksand which swallows up all which comes within its spell. Beware vanity! Beware the quicksand, which yawneth for thee, and which will swallow thee up! See thyself! Learn thine own vanity! Meet thyself face to face, and then in that moment thou shalt learn the fatal force of thy vanity. Learn it, know it, and repent ere the quicksand swallow thee!' Then without another word he went back to his seat and sat there immovable and expressionless as before.

Markam could not but feel a little upset by this tirade. Only that it was spoken by a seeming madman, he would have put it down to some eccentric exhibition of Scottish humour or impudence; but the gravity of the message—for it seemed nothing else—made such a reading impossible. He was, however, determined not to give in to ridicule, and although he had not yet seen anything in Scotland to remind him even of a kilt, he determined to wear his Highland dress. When he returned home, in less than half-an-hour, he found that every member of the family was, despite the headaches, out taking a walk. He took the opportunity afforded by their absence of locking himself in his dressing-room, took off the Highland dress, and, putting on a suit of flannels, lit a cigar and had a snooze. He was awakened by the noise of the family coming in, and at once donning his dress made his appearance in the drawing-room for tea.

He did not go out again that afternoon; but after dinner he put on his dress again—he had, of course dressed for dinner as usual—and went by himself for a walk on the sea-shore. He had by this time come to the conclusion that he would get by degrees accustomed to the Highland dress before making it his ordinary wear. The moon was up and he easily followed the path through the sand-hills, and shortly struck the shore. The tide was out and the beach firm as a rock, so he strolled southwards to nearly the end of the bay. Here he was attracted by two isolated rocks some little way out from the edge of the dunes, so he strolled towards them. When he reached the nearest one he climbed it, and, sitting there elevated some fifteen or twenty feet over the waste of sand, enjoyed the lovely, peaceful prospect. The moon was rising behind the headland of Pennyfold, and its light was just touching the top of the furthermost rock of the Spurs some threequarters of a mile out; the rest of the rocks were in dark shadow. As the moon rose over the headland, the rocks of the Spurs and then the beach by degrees became flooded with light.

For a good while Mr. Markam sat and looked at the rising moon and the growing area of light which followed its rise. Then he turned and faced eastwards and sat with his chin in his hand looking seawards, and revelling in the peace and beauty and freedom of the scene. The roar of London—the darkness and the strife and weariness of London life—seemed to have passed quite away, and he lived at the moment a freer and higher life. He looked at the glistening water as it stole its way over the flat waste of sand, coming closer and closer insensibly—the tide had turned. Presently he heard a distant shouting along the beach very far off.

'The fishermen calling to each other,' he said to himself and looked round. As he did so he got a horrible shock, for though just then a cloud sailed across the moon he saw, in spite of the sudden darkness around him, his own image. For an instant, on the top of the opposite rock he could see the bald back of the head and the Glengarry cap with the immense eagle's feather. As he staggered back his foot slipped, and he began to slide down towards the sand between the two rocks. He took no concern as to falling, for the sand was really only a few feet below him, and his mind was occupied with the figure or simulacrum of himself, which had already disappeared. As the easiest way of reaching *terra firma* he prepared to jump the remainder of the distance. All this had taken but a second, but the brain works quickly, and even as he gathered himself for the spring he saw the sand below him lying so marbly level shake and sliver in an odd way. A sudden fear overcame him; his knees failed, and instead of jumping he slid miserably down the rock, scratching his bare legs as he went. His feet touched the sand—went through it like water—and he was down below his knees before he realised that he was in a quicksand. Wildly he grasped at the rock to keep himself from sinking further, and fortunately there was a jutting spur or edge which he was able to grasp instinctively. To this he clung in grim desperation. He tried to shout, but his breath would not come, till after a great effort his voice rang out. Again he shouted, and it seemed as if the sound of his own voice gavc him new courage, for he was able to hold on to the rock for a longer time than he thought possible—though he held on only in blind desperation. He was, however, beginning to find his grasp weakening, when, joy of joys! his shout was answered by a rough voice from just above him.

'God be thankit, I'm nae too late!' and a fisherman with great thigh-boots came hurriedly climbing over the rock. In an instant he recognised the gravity of the danger, and with a cheering 'Haud fast, mon! I'm comin'!' scrambled down till he found a firm foothold. Then with one strong hand holding the rock above, he leaned down, and catching Markam's wrist, called out to him, 'Haud to me, mon! Haud to me wi' ither hond!'

Then he lent his great strength, and with a steady, sturdy pull, dragged him out of the hungry quicksand and placed him safe upon the rock. Hardly giving him time to draw breath, he pulled and pushed him—never letting him go for an instant—over the rock into the firm sand beyond it, and finally deposited him, still shaking from the magnitude of his danger, high upon the beach. Then he began to speak:

'Mon! but I was just in time. If I had no laucht at yon foolish lads and began to rin at the first you'd a bin sinkin' doon to the bowels o' the airth be the noo! Wully Beagrie thocht you was a ghaist, and Tom MacPhail swore ye was only like a goblin on a puddicksteel! "Na!" said I. "Yon's bu the daft Englishman—the loony that had escapit frae the waxwarks." I was thinkin' that bein' strange and silly—if not a wholemade feel—ye'd no ken the ways o' the quicksan'! I shouted till warn ye, and then ran to drag ye aff, if need be. But God be thankit, be ye fule or only half-daft wi' yer vanity, that I was no that late!' and he reverently lifted his cap as he spoke.

Mr. Markham was deeply touched and thankful for his escape from a horrible death; but the sting of the charge of vanity thus made once more against him came through his humility. He was about to reply angrily, when suddenly a great awe fell upon him as he remembered the warning words of the half-crazy letter-carrier:

'Meet thyself face to face, and repent ere the quicksand shall swallow thee!'

Here, too, he remembered the image of himself that he had seen and the sudden danger from the deadly quicksand that had followed. He was silent a full minute, and then said:

'My good fellow, I owe you my life!'

The answer came with reverence from the hardy fisherman, 'Na! Na! Ye owe that to God; but, as for me, I'm only too glad till be the humble instrument o' His mercy.'

'But you will let me thank you,' said Mr. Markam, taking both the great hands of his deliverer in his and holding them tight. 'My heart is too full as yet, and my nerves are too much shaken to let me say much; but, believe me, I am very, very grateful!' It was quite evident that the poor old fellow was deeply touched, for the tears were running down his cheeks.

The fisherman said, with a rough but true courtesy:

'Ay, sir! thank me ye will—if it'll do yer poor heart good. An' I'm thinking that if it were me I'd be thankful too. But, sir, as for me I need no thanks. I am glad, so I am!'

That Arthur Fernlee Markam was really thankful and grateful was shown practically later on. Within a week's time there sailed into Port Crooken the finest fishing smack that had ever been seen in the harbour of Peterhead. She was fully found with sails and gear of all kinds, and with nets of the best. Her master and men went away by the coach, after having left with the salmon-fisher's wife the papers which made her over to him.

As Mr. Markam and the salmon-fisher walked together along the shore the former asked his companion not to mention the fact that he had been in such imminent danger, for that it would only distress his dear wife and children. He said that he would warn them all of the quicksand, and for that purpose he, then and there, asked questions about it till he felt that his information on the subject was complete. Before they parted he asked his companion if he had happened to see a second figure, dressed like himself on the other rock as he had approached to succour him.

'Na! Na!' came the answer, 'there is nae sic another fule in these parts. Nor has there been since the time o' Jamie Fleeman—him that was fule to the Laird o' Udny. Why, mon! sic a heathenish dress as ye have on till ye has nae been seen in these pairts within the memory o' mon. An' I'm thinkin' that sic a dress never was for sittin' on the cauld rock, as ye done beyont. Mon! but do ye no fear the rheumatism or the lumbagy wi' floppin' doon on to the cauld stanes wi' yer bare flesh? I was thinking that it was daft ye waur when I see ye the mornin' doon be the port, but it's fule or eediot ye maun be for the like o' thot!' Mr. Markam did not care to argue the point, and as they were now close to his own home he asked the salmon-fisher to have a glass of whisky—which he did—and they parted for the night. He took good care to warn all his family of the quicksand, telling them that he had himself been in some danger from it.

All that night he never slept. He heard the hours strike one after the other; but try how he would he could not get to sleep. Over and over again he went through the horrible episode of the quicksand, from the time that Saft Tammie had broken his habitual silence to preach to him of the sin of vanity and to warn him. The question kept ever arising in his mind: 'Am I then so vain as to be in the ranks of the foolish?' and the answer ever came in the words of the crazy prophet: '"Vanity of vanities! All is vanity." Meet thyself face to face, and repent ere the quicksand shall swallow thee!' Somehow a feeling of doom began to shape itself in his mind that he would yet perish in that same quicksand, for there he had already met himself face to face.

In the grey of the morning he dozed off, but it was evident that he continued the subject in his dreams, for he was fully awakened by his wife, who said:

'Do sleep quietly! That blessed Highland suit has got on your brain. Don't talk in your sleep, if you can help it!' He was somehow conscious of a glad feeling, as if some terrible weight had been lifted from him, but he did not know any cause of it. He asked his wife what he had said in his sleep, and she answered:

'You said it often enough, goodness knows, for one to remember it—"Not face to face! I saw the eagle plume over the bald head!

There is hope yet! Not face to face!" Go to sleep! Do!' And then he did go to sleep, for he seemed to realise that the prophecy of the crazy man had not yet been fulfilled. He had not met himself face to face—as yet at all events.

He was awakened early by a maid who came to tell him that there was a fisherman at the door who wanted to see him. He dressed himself as quickly as he could—for he was not yet expert with the Highland dress—and hurried down, not wishing to keep the salmon-fisher waiting. He was surprised and not altogether pleased to find that his visitor was none other than Saft Tammie, who at once opened fire on him:

'I maun gang awa' t' the post; but I thocht that I would waste an hour on ye, and ca' roond just to see if ye waur still that fou wi' vanity as on the nicht gane by. An I see that ye've no learned the lesson. Well! the time is comin', sure eneucht! However I have all the time i' the marnins to my ain sel', so I'll aye look roond jist till see how ye gang yer ain gait to the quicksan', and then to the de'il! I'm aff till ma wark the noo!' And he went straightaway, leaving Mr. Markam considerably vexed, for the maids within earshot were vainly trying to conceal their giggles. He had fairly made up his mind to wear on that day ordinary clothes, but the visit of Saft Tammie reversed his decision. He would show them all that he was not a coward, and he would go on as he had begun—come what might. When he came to breakfast in full martial panoply the children, one and all, held down their heads and the backs of their necks became very red indeed. As, however, none of them laughed—except Titus, the youngest boy, who was seized with a fit of hysterical choking and was promptly banished from the room—he could not reprove them, but began to break his egg with a sternly determined air. It was unfortunate that as his wife was handing him a cup of tea one of the buttons of his sleeve caught in the lace of her morning wrapper, with the result that the hot tea was spilt over his bare knees. Not unnaturally, he made use of a swear word, whereupon his wife, somewhat nettled, spoke out:

'Well, Arthur, if you will make such an idiot of yourself with that ridiculous costume what else can you expect? You are not accustomed to it—and you never will be!' In answer he began an indignant speech with: 'Madam!' but he got no further, for now that the subject was broached, Mrs. Markam intended to have her say out. It was not a pleasant say, and, truth to tell, it was not said in a pleasant manner. A wife's manner seldom is pleasant when she undertakes to tell what she considers 'truths' to her husband. The result was that Arthur Fernlee Markam undertook, then and there, that during his stay in Scotland he would wear no other costume than the one she abused. Woman-like his wife had the last word—given in this case with tears:

'Very well, Arthur! Of course you will do as you choose. Make me as ridiculous as you can, and spoil the poor girls' chances in life. Young men don't seem to care, as a general rule, for an idiot father-in-law! But I must warn you that your vanity will some day get a rude shock—if indeed you are not before then in an asylum or dead!'

It was manifest after a few days that Mr. Markam would have to take the major part of his outdoor exercise by himself. The girls now and again took a walk with him, chiefly in the early morning or late at night, or on a wet day when there would be no one about; they professed to be willing to go out at all times, but somehow something always seemed to occur to prevent it. The boys could never be found at all on such occasions, and as to Mrs. Markam she sternly refused to go out with him on any consideration so long as he should continue to make a fool of himself. On the Sunday he dressed himself in his habitual broadcloth, for he rightly felt that church was not a place for angry feelings; but on Monday morning he resumed his Highland garb. By this time he would have given a good deal if he had never thought of the dress, but his British obstinacy was strong, and he would not give in. Saft Tammie called at his house every morning, and, not being able to see him nor to have any message taken to him, used to call back in the afternoon when the letter-bag had been delivered and watched for his going out. On such occasions he never failed to warn him against his vanity in the same words which he had used at the first. Before many days were over Mr. Markam had come to look upon him as little short of a scourge.

By the time the week was out the enforced partial solitude, the constant chagrin, and the never-ending brooding which was thus engendered, began to make Mr. Markam quite ill. He was too proud to take any of his family into his confidence, since they had in his view treated him very badly. Then he did not sleep well at night, and when he did sleep he had constantly bad dreams. Merely to assure himself that his pluck was not failing him he made it a practice to visit the quicksand at least once every day, and hardly ever failed to go there the last thing at night. It was perhaps this habit that wrought the quicksand with its terrible experience so perpetually into his dreams. More and more vivid these became, till on waking at times he could hardly realise that he had not been actually in the flesh to visit the fatal spot. He sometimes thought that he might have been walking in his sleep.

One night his dream was so vivid that when he awoke he could not believe that it had only been a dream. He shut his eyes again and again, but each time the vision, if it was a vision, or the reality, if it was a reality, would rise before him. The moon was shining full and yellow over the quicksand as he approached it; he could see the expanse of light shaken and disturbed and full of black shadows as the liquid sand quivered and trembled and wrinkled and eddied as was its wont between its pauses of marble calm. As he drew close to it another figure came towards it from the opposite side with equal footsteps. He saw that it was his own figure, his very self, and in silent terror, compelled by what force he knew not, he advanced—charmed as the bird is by the snake, mesmerised or hypnotised—to meet this other self. As he felt the yielding sand closing over him he awoke in the agony of death, trembling with fear, and, strange to say, with the silly man's prophecy seeming to sound in his ears: '"Vanity of vanities! All is vanity!" See thyself and repent ere the quicksand swallow thee!'

So convinced was he that this was no dream that he arose, early as it was, and dressing himself without disturbing his wife took his way to the shore. His heart fell when he came across a series of footsteps on the sands, which he at once recognised as his own. There was the same wide heel, the same square toe; he had no doubt now that he had actually been there, and half horrified, and half in a state of dreamy stupor, he followed the footsteps, and found them lost in the edge of the yielding quicksand. This gave him a terrible shock, for there were no return steps marked on the sand, and he felt that there was some dread mystery which he could not penetrate, and the penetration of which would, he feared, undo him.

In this state of affairs he took two wrong courses. Firstly he kept his trouble to himself, and, as none of his family had any clue to it, every innocent word or expression which they used supplied fuel to the consuming fire of his imagination. Secondly he began to read books professing to bear upon the mysteries of dreaming and of mental phenomena generally, with the result that every wild imagination of every crank or half-crazy philosopher became a living germ of unrest in the fertilising soil of his disordered brain. Thus negatively and positively all things began to work to a common end. Not the least of his disturbing causes was Saft Tammie, who had now become at certain times of the day a fixture at his gate. After a while, being interested in the previous state of this individual, he made inquiries regarding his past with the following result.

Saft Tammie was popularly believed to be the son of a laird in one of the counties round the Firth of Forth. He had been partially educated for the ministry, but for some cause which no one ever knew threw up his prospects suddenly, and, going to Peterhead in its days of whaling prosperity, had there taken service on a whaler. Here off and on he had remained for some years, getting gradually more and more silent in his habits, till finally his shipmates protested against so taciturn a mate, and he had found service amongst the fishing smacks of the northern fleet. He had worked for many years at the fishing with always the reputation of being 'a wee bit daft', till at length he had gradually settled down at Crooken, where the laird, doubtless knowing something of his family history, had given him a job which practically made him a pensioner. The minister who gave the information finished thus:

'It is a very strange thing, but the man seems to have some odd kind of gift. Whether it be that "second sight" which we Scotch people are so prone to believe in, or some other occult form of knowledge, I know not, but nothing of a disastrous tendency ever occurs in this place but the men with whom he lives are able to quote after the event some saying of his which certainly appears to have foretold it. He gets uneasy or excited—wakes up, in fact—when death is in the air!'

This did not in any way tend to lessen Mr. Markam's concern, but on the contrary seemed to impress the prophecy more deeply on his mind. Of all the books which he had read on his new subject of study none interested him so much as a German one, *Die Doppelgänger*, by Dr. Heinrich von Aschenberg, formerly of Bonn. Here he learned for the first time of cases where men had led a double existence—each nature being quite apart from the other—the body being always a reality with one spirit, and a simulacrum with the other. Needless to say that Mr. Markham realised this theory as exactly suiting his own case. The glimpse which he had of his own back the night of his escape from the quicksand—his own footmarks disappearing into the quicksand with no return steps visible—the prophecy of Saft Tammie about his meeting himself and perishing in the quicksand—all lent aid to the conviction that he was in his own person an instance of the *Doppelgänger*. Being then conscious of a double life he took steps to prove its existence to his own satisfaction. To this end on one night before going to bed he wrote his name in chalk on the soles of his shoes. That night he dreamed of the quicksand, and of his visiting it—dreamed so vividly that on waking in the grey of the dawn he could not believe that he had not been there. Arising, without disturbing his wife, he sought his shoes.

The chalk signatures were undisturbed! He dressed himself and stole out softly. This time the tide was in, so he crossed the dunes and struck the shore on the further side of the quicksand. There, oh, horror of horrors! he saw his own footprints dying into the abyss!

He went home a desperately sad man. It seemed incredible that he, an elderly commercial man, who had passed a long and uneventful life in the pursuit of business in the midst of roaring, practical London, should thus find himself enmeshed in mystery and horror, and that he should discover that he had two existences. He could not speak of his trouble even to his own wife, for well he knew that she would at once require the fullest particulars of that other life—the one which she did not know; and that she would at the start not only imagine but charge him with all manner of infidelities on the head of it. And so his brooding grew deeper and deeper still. One evening—the tide then going out and the moon being at the full—he was sitting waiting for dinner when the maid announced that Saft Tammie was making a disturbance outside because he would not be let in to see him. He was very indignant, but did not like the maid to think that he had any fear on the subject, and so told her to bring him in. Tammie entered, walking more briskly than ever with his head up and a look of vigorous decision in the eyes that were so generally cast down. As soon as he entered he said:

'I have come to see ye once again—once again; and there ye sit, still just like a cockatoo on a pairch. Weel, mon, I forgie ye! Mind ye that, I forgie ye!' And without a word more he turned and walked out of the house, leaving the master in speechless indignation.

After dinner he determined to pay another visit to the quicksand—he would not allow even to himself that he was afraid to go. And so, about nine o'clock, in full array, he marched to the beach, and passing over the sands sat on the skirt of the nearer rock. The full moon was behind him and its light lit up the bay so that its fringe of foam, the dark outline of the headland, and the stakes of the salmon-nets were all emphasised. In the brilliant yellow glow the lights in the windows of Port Crooken and in those of the distant castle of the laird trembled like stars through the sky. For a long time he sat and drank in the beauty of the scene, and his soul seemed to feel a peace that it had not known for many days. All the pettiness and annoyance and silly fears of the past weeks seemed blotted out, and a new holy calm took the vacant place. In this sweet and solemn mood he reviewed his late action calmly, and felt ashamed of himself for his vanity and for the obstinacy which had followed it. And then and there he made up his mind that the present would be the last time he would wear the costume which had estranged him from those whom he loved, and which had caused him so many hours and days of chagrin, vexation, and pain.

But almost as soon as he arrived at this conclusion another voice seemed to speak within him and mockingly to ask him if he should ever get the chance to wear the suit again—that it was too late—he had chosen his course and must now abide the issue.

'It is not too late,' came the quick answer of his better self; and full of the thought, he rose up to go home and divest himself of the now hateful costume right away. He paused for one look at the beautiful scene. The light lay pale and mellow, softening every outline of rock and tree and house-top, and deepening the shadows into velvety-black, and lighting, as with a pale flame, the incoming tide, that now crept fringelike across the flat waste of sand. Then he left the rock and stepped out for the shore.

But as he did so a frightful spasm of horror shook him, and for an instant the blood rushing to his head shut out all the light of the full moon. Once more he saw that fatal image of himself moving beyond the quicksand from the opposite rock to the shore. The shock was all the greater for the contrast with the spell of peace which he had just enjoyed; and, almost paralysed in every sense, he stood and watched the fatal vision and the wrinkly, crawling quicksand that seemed to writhe and yearn for something that lay between. There could be no mistake this time, for though the moon behind threw the face into shadow he could see there the same shaven cheeks as his own, and the small stubby moustache of a few weeks' growth. The light shone on the brilliant tartan, and on the eagle's plume. Even the bald space at one side of the Glengarry cap glistened, as did the cairngorm brooch on the shoulder and the tops of the silver buttons. As he looked he felt his feet slightly sinking, for he was still near the edge of the belt of quicksand, and he stepped back. As he did so the other figure stepped forward, so that the space between them was preserved.

So the two stood facing each other, as though in some weird fascination; and in the rushing of the blood through his brain Markam seemed to hear the words of the prophecy: 'See thyself face to face, and repent ere the quicksand swallow thee.' He did stand face to face with himself, he had repented—and now he was sinking in the quicksand! The warning and prophecy were coming true.

Above him the seagulls screamed, circling round the fringe of the incoming tide, and the sound being entirely mortal recalled him to himself. On the instant he stepped back a few quick steps, for as yet only his feet were merged in the soft sand. As he did so the other figure stepped forward, and coming within the deadly grip of the quicksand began to sink. It seemed to Markam that he was looking at himself going down to his doom, and on the instant the anguish of his soul found vent in a terrible cry. There was at the same instant a terrible cry from the other figure, and as Markam threw up his hands the figure did the same. With horror-struck eyes he saw him sink deeper into the quicksand; and then, impelled by what power he knew not, he advanced again towards the sand to meet his fate. But as his more forward foot began to sink he heard again the cries of the seagulls which seemed to restore his benumbed faculties. With a mighty effort he drew his foot out of the sand which seemed to clutch it, leaving his shoe behind, and then in sheer terror he turned and ran from the place, never stopping till his breath and strength failed him, and he sank half swooning on the grassy path through the sandhills.

* * *

Arthur Markam made up his mind not to tell his family of his terrible adventure—until at least such time as he should be complete master of himself. Now that the fatal double—his other self—had been engulfed in the quicksand he felt something like his old peace of mind.

That night he slept soundly and did not dream at all; and in the morning was quite his old self. It really seemed as though his newer and worser self had disappeared for ever; and strangely enough Saft Tammie was absent from his post that morning and never appeared there again, but sat in his old place watching nothing, as of old, with lack-lustre eye. In accordance with his resolution he did not wear his Highland suit again, but one evening tied it up in a bundle, claymore, dirk and philibeg and all, and bringing it secretly with him threw it into the quicksand. With a feeling of intense pleasure he saw it sucked below the sand, whch closed above it into marble smoothness. Then he went home and announced cheerily to his family assembled for evening prayers:

'Well! my dears, you will be glad to hear that I have abandoned my idea of wearing the Highland dress. I see now what a vain old fool I was and how ridiculous I made myself! You shall never see it again!'

'Where is it, father?' asked one of the girls, wishing to say something so that such a self-sacrificing announcement as her father's should not be passed in absolute silence. His answer was so sweetly given that the girl rose from her seat and came and kissed him. It was:

'In the quicksand, my dear! and I hope that my worser self is buried there along with it—for ever.'

The remainder of the summer was passed at Crooken with delight by all the family, and on his return to town Mr. Markam had almost forgotten the whole of the incident of the quicksand, and all touching on it, when one day he got a letter from the MacCullum More which caused him much thought, though he said nothing of it to his family, and left it, for certain reasons, unanswered. It ran as follows:

'The MacCallum More and Roderick MacDhu.
'The Scotch All-Wool Tartan Clothing Mart.
Copthall Court, E.C.,
30th September, 1892.

'Dear Sir,—I trust you will pardon the liberty which I take in writing to you, but I am desirous of making an inquiry, and I am informed that you have been sojourning during the summer in Aberdeenshire (Scotland, N.B.). My partner, Mr. Roderick MacDhu—as he appears for business reasons on our bill-heads and in our advertisements, his real name being Emmanuel Moses Marks of London—went early last month to Scotland (N.B.) for a tour, but as I have only once heard from him, shortly after his departure, I am anxious lest any misfortune may have befallen him. As I have been unable to obtain any news of him on making all inquiries in my power, I venture to appeal to you. His letter was written in deep dejection of spirit, and mentioned that he feared a judgment had come upon him for wishing to appear as a Scotchman on Scottish soil, as he had one moonlight night shortly after his arrival seen his "wraith". He evidently alluded to the fact that before his departure he had procured for himself a Highland costume similar to that which we had the honour to supply to you, with which, as perhaps you will remember, he was much struck. He may, however, never have worn it, as he was, to my own knowledge, diffident about putting it on, and even went so far as to tell me that he would at first only venture to wear it late at night or very early in the morning, and then only in remote places, until such time as he should get accustomed to it. Unfortunately he did not advise me of his route so that I am in complete ignorance of his whereabouts; and I venture to ask if you may have seen or heard of a Highland costume similar to your own having been seen anywhere in the neighbourhood in which I am told you have recently purchased the estate which you temporarily occupied. I shall not expect an answer to this letter unless you can give me some information regarding my friend and partner, so pray do not trouble to reply unless there be cause. I am encouraged to think that he may have been in your neighbourhood as, though his letter is not dated, the envelope is marked with the postmark of "Yellon", which I find is in Aberdeenshire, and not far from the Mains of Crooken.

I have the honour to be, dear sir,

Yours very respectfully,

JOSHUA SHEENY COHEN BENJAMIN

(The MacCallum More.)

THE GOMBEEN MAN
(from *The Snake's Pass*)

'GOD SAVE ALL here,' said the man as he entered.

Room was made for him at the fire. He no sooner came near it and tasted the heat than a cloud of steam arose from him.

'Man! but ye're wet,' said Mrs. Kelligan. 'One'd think ye'd been in the lake beyant!'

'So I have,' he answered, 'worse luck! I rid all the way from Galway this blessed day to be here in time, but the mare slipped coming down Curragh Hill and threw me over the bank into the lake. I wor in the wather nigh three hours before I could get out, for I was foreninst the Curragh Rock an' only got a foothold in a chink, an' had to hold on wid me one arm for I fear the other is broke.'

'Dear! dear! dear!' interrupted the woman. 'Sthrip yer coat off, acushla, an' let us see if we can do anythin'.'

He shook his head, as he answered:

'Not now, there's not a minute to spare. I must get up the Hill at once. I should have been there be six o'clock. But I mayn't be too late yit. The mare has broke down entirely. Can any one here lend me a horse?'

There was no answer till Andy spoke:

'Me mare is in the shtable, but this gintleman has me an' her for the day, an' I have to lave him at Carnaclif tonight.'

Here I struck in:

'Never mind me, Andy! If you can help this gentleman, do so: I'm better off here than driving through the storm. He wouldn't want to go on, with a broken arm, if he hadn't good reason!'

The man looked at me with grateful eagerness:

'Thank yer honour, kindly. It's a rale gintleman ye are! An' I hope ye'll never be sorry for helpin' a poor fellow in sore throuble.'

'What's wrong, Phelim?' asked the priest. 'Is there anything troubling you that any one here can get rid of?'

'Nothin', Father Pether, thank ye kindly. The throuble is me own intirely, an' no wan here could help me. But I must see Murdock tonight.'

There was a general sigh of commiseration; all understood the situation.

'Musha!' said old Dan Moriarty, *sotto voce.* 'An' is that the way of it! An' is he too in the clutches iv that wolf? Him that we all thought was so warrum. Glory be to God! but it's a quare wurrld it is; an' it's few there is in it that is what they seems. Me poor frind! is there any way I can help ye? I have a bit iv money by me that yer welkim to the lend iv av ye want it.'

The other shook his head gratefully:

'Thank ye kindly, Dan, but I have the money all right; it's only the time I'm in trouble about!'

'Only the time! me poor chap! It's be time that the divil helps Black Murdock an' the likes iv him, the most iv all! God be good to ye if he has got his clutch on yer back, an' has time on his side, for ye'll want it!'

'Well! anyhow, I must be goin' now. Thank ye kindly, neighbours all. When a man's in throuble, sure the goodwill of his frinds is the greatest comfort he can have.'

'All but one, remember that! all but one!' said the priest.

'Thank ye kindly, Father, I shan't forget. Thank ye Andy: an' you, too, young sir, I'm much beholden to ye. I hope, some day, I may have it to do a good turn for ye in return. Thank ye kindly again, and good night.' He shook my hand warmly, and was going to the door, when old Dan said:

'An' as for that black-jawed ruffian, Murdock—' He paused, for the door suddenly opened, and a harsh voice said:

'Murtagh Murdock is here to answer for himself!'—It was my man at the window.

There was a sort of paralysed silence in the room, through which came the whisper of one of the old women:

'Musha! talk iv the divil!'

Joyce's face grew very white; one hand instinctively grasped his riding switch, the other hung uselessly by his side. Murdock spoke:

'I kem here expectin' to meet Phelim Joyce. I thought I'd save him the throuble of comin' wid the money.' Joyce said in a husky voice:

'What do ye mane? I have the money right enough here. I'm sorry I'm a bit late, but I had a bad accident—bruk me arrum, an' was nigh dhrownded in the Curragh Lake. But I was goin' up to ye at once, bad as I am, to pay ye yer money, Murdock.' The Gombeen Man interrupted him:

'But it isn't to me ye'd have to come, me good man. Sure, it's the sheriff, himself, that was waitin' for ye', an' whin ye didn't come'—here Joyce winced; the speaker smiled—'he done his work.'

'What wurrk, acushla?' asked one of the women. Murdock answered slowly:

'He sould the lease iv the farrum known as the Shleenanaher in open sale, in accordance wid the terrums of his notice, duly posted, and wid warnin' given to the houldher iv the lease.'

There was a long pause. Joyce was the first to speak:

'Ye're jokin', Murdock. For God's sake say ye're jokin'! Ye tould me yerself that I might have time to git the money. An' ye tould me that the puttin' me farrum up for sale was only a matther iv forrum to let me pay ye back in me own way. Nay! more, ye asked me not to tell any iv the neighbours, for fear some iv them might want to buy some iv me land. An' it's niver so, that whin ye got me aff to Galway to rise the money, ye went on wid the sale, behind me back—wid not a soul by to spake for me or mine—an' sould up all I have! No! Murtagh Murdock, ye're a hard man I know, but ye wouldn't do that! Ye wouldn't do that!'

Murdock made no direct reply to him, but said seemingly to the company generally:

'I ixpected to see Phelim Joyce at the sale today, but as I had some business in which he was consarned, I kem here where I knew there'd be neighbours—an' sure so there is.'

He took out his pocket-book and wrote names, 'Father Pether Ryan, Daniel Moriarty, Bartholomew Moynahan, Andhrew

McGlown, Mrs. Katty Kelligan—that's enough! I want ye all to see what I done. There's nothin' undherhand about me! Phelim Joyce, I give ye formil notice that yer land was sould an' bought be me, for ye broke yer word to repay me the money lint ye before the time fixed. Here's the Sheriff's assignmint, an' I tell ye before all these witnesses that I'll proceed with ejectment on title at wanst.'

All in the room were as still as statues. Joyce was fearfully still and pale, but when Murdock spoke the word 'ejectment' he seemed to wake in a moment to frenzied life. The blood flushed up in his face and he seemed about to do something rash; but with a great effort controlled himself and said:

'Mr. Murdock, ye won't be too hard. I got the money today—it's here—but I had an accident that delayed me. I was thrown into the Curragh Lake and nigh drownded an' me arrum is bruk. Don't be so close as an hour or two—ye'll never be sorry for it. I'll pay ye all, and more, and thank ye into the bargain all me life; ye'll take back the paper, won't ye, for me childhren's sake—for Norah's sake?'

He faltered; the other answered with an evil smile:

'Phelim Joyce, I've waited years for this moment—don't ye know me betther nor to think I would go back on meself whin I have shtarted on a road? I wouldn't take yer money, not if ivery pound note was spread into an acre and cut up in tin-pound notes. I want yer land—I have waited for it, an' I mane to have it!—Now don't beg me any more, for I won't go back—an' tho' its many a grudge I owe ye, I square them all before the neighbours be refusin' yer prayer. The land is mine, bought be open sale; an' all the judges an' coorts in Ireland can't take it from me! An' what do ye say to that now, Phelim Joyce?'

The tortured man had been clutching the ash sapling which he had used as a riding whip, and from the nervous twitching of his fingers I knew that something was coming. And it came; for, without a word, he struck the evil face before him—struck as quick as a flash of lightning—such a blow that the blood seemed to leap out round the stick, and a vivid welt rose in an instant. With a wild, savage cry the Gombeen Man jumped at him; but there were others in the room as quick, and before another blow could be struck on either side both men were grasped by strong hands and held back.

Murdock's rage was tragic. He yelled, like a wild beast, to be let get at his opponent. He cursed and blasphemed so outrageously that all were silent, and only the stern voice of the priest was heard:

'Be silent Murtagh Murdock! Aren't you afraid that the God overhead will strike you dead? With such a storm as is raging as a sign of His power, you are a foolish man to tempt Him.'

The man stopped suddenly, and a stern dogged sullenness took the place of his passion. The priest went on:

'As for you, Phelim Joyce, you ought to be ashamed of yourself; ye're not one of my people, but I speak as your own clergyman would if he were here. Only this day has the Lord seen fit to spare you from a terrible death; and yet you dare to go back of His mercy with your angry passion. You had cause for anger—or temptation to it, I know—but you must learn to kiss the chastening rod, not spurn it. The Lord knows what He is doing for you as for others, and it may be that you will look back on this day in gratitude for His doing, and in shame for your own anger. Men, hold off your hands—let those two men go; they'll quarrel no more—before me at any rate, I hope.'

The men drew back. Joyce held his head down, and a more despairing figure or a sadder one I never saw. He turned slowly away, and leaning against the wall put his face between his hands and sobbed. Murdock scowled, and the scowl gave place to an evil smile as looking all around he said:

'Well, now that me work is done, I must be gettin' home.'

'An' get some wan to iron that mark out iv yer face,' said Dan. Murdock turned again and glared around him savagely as he hissed out:

'There'll be iron for some one before I'm done. Mark me well! I've never gone back or wakened yit whin I promised to have me own turn. There's thim here what'll rue this day yit! If I am the shnake on the hill—thin beware the shnake. An' for him what shtruck me, he'll be in bitther sorra for it yit—him an' his!' He turned his back and went to the door.

'Stop!' said the priest. 'Murtagh Murdock, I have a word to say to you—a solemn word of warning. Ye have today acted the part of Ahab towards Naboth the Jezreelite; beware of his fate! You have coveted your neighbour's goods—you have used your power without mercy; you have made the law an engine of oppression. Mark me! It was said of old that what measure men meted should be meted out to them again. God is very just. "Be not deceived, God is not mocked. For what things a man shall sow, those also shall he reap." Ye have sowed the wind this day—beware lest you reap the whirlwind! Even as God visited his sin upon Ahab the Samarian, and as He has visited similar sins on others in His own way—so shall He visit yours on you. You are worse than the land-grabber—worse than the man who only covets. Saintough is a virtue compared with your act! Remember the story of Naboth's vineyard, and the dreadful end of it. Don't answer me! Go and repent if you can, and leave sorrow and misery to be comforted by others—unless you wish to undo your wrong yourself. If you don't—then remember the curse that may come upon you yet!'

Without a word Murdock opened the door and went out, and a little later we heard the clattering of his horse's feet on the rocky road to Shleenanaher.

When it was apparent to all that he was really gone a torrent of commiseration, sympathy and pity broke over Joyce. The Irish nature is essentially emotional, and a more genuine and stronger feeling I never saw. Not a few had tears in their eyes, and one and all were manifestly deeply touched. The least moved was, to all appearance, poor Joyce himself. He seemed to have pulled himself together, and his sterling manhood and courage and pride stood by him. He seemed, however, to yield to the kindly wishes of his friends; and when we suggested that his hurt should be looked to, he acquiesced:

'Yes, if you will. Betther not go home to poor Norah and distress her with it. Poor child! she'll have enough to bear without that.'

His coat was taken off, and between us we managed to bandage the wound. The priest, who had some surgical knowledge, came to the conclusion that there was only a simple fracture. He splinted and bandaged the arm, and we all agreed that it would be better for Joyce to wait until the storm was over before starting for home. Andy said he could take him on the car, as he knew the road well, and that, as it was partly on the road to Carnaclif, we should only have to make a short detour and would pass the house of the doctor, by whom the arm could be properly attended to.

So we sat around the fire again, whilst, without, the storm howled and the fierce gusts which swept the valley seemed at times as if they would break in the door, lift off the roof, or in some way annihilate the time-worn cabin which gave us shelter.

There could, of course, be only one subject of conversation now, and old Dan simply interpreted the public wish, when he said:

'Tell us, Phelim, sure we're all friends here! how Black Murdock got ye in his clutches? Sure any wan of us would get you out of thim if he could.'

There was a general acquiescence. Joyce yielded himself, and said:

'Let me thank ye, neighbours all, for yer kindness to me and mine this sorraful night. Well! I'll say no more about that; but I'll tell ye how it was that Murdock got me into his power. Ye know that boy of mine, Eugene?'

'Oh! and he's the fine lad, God bless him! an' the good lad too!' —this from the women.

'Well! ye know too that he got on so well whin I sint him to school that Dr. Walsh recommended me to make an ingineer of him. He said he had such promise that it was a pity not to see him get the right start in life, and he gave me, himself, a letther to Sir George Henshaw, the great ingineer. I wint and seen him, and he said he would take the boy. He tould me that there was a big fee to be paid, but I was not to throuble about that—at any rate, that he himself didn't want any fee, and he would ask his partner if he would give up his share too. But the latther was hard up for money. He said he couldn't give up all the fee, but that he would take half iv it, provided it was paid down in dhry money. Well! the regular fee to the firm was five hundhred pounds, and as Sir George had giv up half an' only half th' other half was to be paid, that was possible. I hadn't got more'n a few pounds by me—for what wid dhrainin' and plantin' and fencin' and the payin' the boy's schoolin', and the girl's at the Nuns' in Galway, it had put me to the pin iv me collar to find the money up to now. But I didn't like to let the boy lose his chance in life for want of an effort, an' I put me pride in me pocket an' kem an' asked Murdock for the money. He was very smooth an' nice wid me—I know why now—an' promised he would give it at wanst if I would give him security on me land. Sure he joked an' laughed wid me, an' was that cheerful that I didn't misthrust him. He tould me it was only forrums I was signin' that'd never be used'—Here Dan Moriarty interrupted him:

'What did ye sign, Phelim?'

'There wor two papers. Wan was a writin' iv some kind, that in considheration iv the money lent an' his own land—which I was to take over if the money wasn't paid at the time appointed—he was to get me lease from me: an' the other was a power of attorney to Enther Judgment for the amount if the money wasn't paid at the right time. I thought I was all safe as I could repay him in the time named, an' if the worst kem to the worst I might borry the money from some wan else—for the lease is worth the sum tin times over—an' repay him. Well! what's the use of lookin' back, anyhow! I signed the papers—that was a year ago, an' one week. An' a week ago the time was up!' He gulped down a sob, and went on:

'Well! ye all know the year gone has been a terrible bad wan, an' as for me it was all I could do to hould on—to make up the money was impossible. Thrue the lad cost me next to nothin', for he arned his keep be exthra work, an' the girl, Norah, kem home from school and laboured wid me, an' we saved every penny we could. But it was all no use!—we couldn't get the money together anyhow. Thin we had the misfortin wid the cattle that ye all know of; an' three horses, that I sould in Dublin, up an' died before the time I guaranteed them free from sickness.' Here Andy struck in:

'Thrue for ye! Sure there was some dhreadful disordher in Dublin among the horse cattle, intirely; an' even Misther Docther

Perfesshinal Ferguson himself couldn't git undher it!' Joyce went on:

'An' as the time grew nigh I began to fear, but Murdock came down to see me whin I was alone, an' tould me not to throuble about the money an' not to mind about the sheriff, for he had to give him notice. "An'," says he, "I wouldn't, if I was you, tell Norah anythin' about it, for it might frighten the girl—for weemin is apt to take to heart things like that that's only small things to min like us." An' so, God forgive me, I believed him; an' I niver tould me child anything about it—even whin I got the notice from the sheriff. An' whin the Notice tellin' of the sale was posted up on me land, I tuk it down meself so that the poor child wouldn't be frightened—God help me!' He broke down for a bit, but then went on:

'But somehow I wasn't asy in me mind, an' whin the time iv the sale dhrew nigh I couldn't keep it to meself any longer, an' I tould Norah. That was only yisterday, and look at me today! Norah agreed wid me that we shouldn't trust the Gombeen, an' she sent me off to the Galway Bank to borry the money. She said I was an honest man an' farmed me own land, and that the bank might lind the money on it. An' sure enough whin I wint there this mornin' be appointment, wid the Coadjuthor himself to introduce me, though he didn't know why I wanted the money—that was Norah's idea, and the Mother Superior settled it for her—the manager, who is a nice gintleman, tould me at wanst that I might have the money on me own note iv hand. I only gave him a formal writin', an' I took away the money. Here it is in me pocket in good notes; they're wet wid the lake, but I'm thankful to say all safe. But it's too late, God help me!' Here he broke down for a minute, but recovered himself with an effort:

'Anyhow the bank that thrusted me musn't be wronged. Back the money goes to Galway as soon as iver I can get it there. If I am a ruined man I needn't be a dishonest wan! But poor Norah! God help her! it will break her poor heart.'

There was a spell of silence only broken by sympathetic moans. The first to speak was the priest.

'Phelim Joyce, I told you a while ago, in the midst of your passion, that God knows what He is doin', and works in His own way. You're an honest man, Phelim, and God knows it, and, mark me, He won't let you nor yours suffer. "I have been young," said the Psalmist, "and now am old; and I have not seen the just forsaken, nor his seed seeking bread." Think of that, Phelim!—may it comfort you and poor Norah. God bless her! but she's the good girl. You have much to be thankful for, with a daughter like her to comfort you at home and take the place of her poor mother, who was the best of women; and with such a boy as Eugene, winnin' name and credit, and perhaps fame to come, even in England itself. Thank God for His many mercies, Phelim, and trust Him.'

There was a dead silence in the room. The stern man rose, and coming over took the priest's hand.

'God bless ye, Father!' he said, 'it's the true comforter ye are.'

The scene was a most touching one; I shall never forget it. The worst of the poor man's trouble seemed now past. He had faced the darkest hour; he had told his trouble, and was now prepared to make the best of everything—for the time at least—for I could not reconcile to my mind the idea that that proud, stern man, would not take the blow to heart for many a long day, that it might even embitter his life.

Old Dan tried comfort in a practical way by thinking of what was to be done. Said he:

'Iv course, Phelim, it's a mighty throuble to give up yer own foine land an' take Murdock's bleak shpot instead, but I daresay ye will be able to work it well enough. Tell me, have ye signed away all the land, or only the lower farm? I mane, is the Cliff Fields yours or his?'

Here was a gleam of comfort evidently to the poor man. His face lightened as he replied:

'Only the lower farm, thank God! Indeed, I couldn't part wid the Cliff Fields, for they don't belong to me—they are Norah's, that her poor mother left her—they wor settled on her, whin we married, be her father, and whin he died we got them. But, indeed, I fear they're but small use be themselves; shure there's no wather in them at all, savin' what runs off me ould land; an' if we have to carry wather all the way down the hill from—from me new land'—this was said with a smile, which was a sturdy effort at cheerfulness—'it will be but poor work to raise anythin' there—ayther shtock or craps. No doubt but Murdock will take away the sthrame iv wather that runs there now. He'll want to get the cliff lands, too, I suppose.'

I ventured to ask a question:

'How do your lands lie compared with Mr. Murdock's?'

There was bitterness in his tone as he answered, in true Irish fashion:

'Do you mane me ould land, or me new?'

'The lands that were—that ought still to be yours,' I answered.

He was pleased at the reply, and his face softened as he replied:

'Well, the way of it is this. We two owns the West side of the hill between us. Murdock's land—I'm spakin' iv them as they are, till he gets possession iv mine—lies at the top iv the hill; mine lies below. My land is the best bit on the mountain, while the Gombeen's is poor soil, with only a few good patches here and there. Moreover, there is another thing. There is a bog which is high up the hill, mostly on his houldin', but my land is free from bog, except one end of the big bog, an' a stretch of dry turf, the best in the counthry, an' wid' enough turf to last for a hundhred years, it's that deep.'

Old Dan joined in:

'Thrue enough! that bog of the Gombeen's isn't much use anyhow. It's rank and rotten wid wather. Whin it made up its mind to sthay, it might have done betther!'

'The bog? Made up its mind to stay! What on earth do you mean?' I asked. I was fairly puzzled.

'Didn't ye hear talk already,' said Dan, 'of the shiftin' bog on the mountain?'

'I did.'

'Well, that's it! It moved an' moved an' moved longer than anywan can remimber. Me grandfather wanst tould me that whin he was a gossoon it wasn't nigh so big as it was when he tould me.

It hasn't shifted in my time, and I make bould to say that it has made up its mind to settle down where it is. Ye must only make the best of it, Phelim. I daresay ye will turn it to some account.'

'I'll try what I can do, anyhow. I don't mane to fould me arms an' sit down op-pawsit me property an' ate it!' was the brave answer.

For myself, the whole idea was most interesting. I had never before even heard of a shifting bog, and I determined to visit it before I left this part of the country.

By this time the storm was beginning to abate. The rain had ceased, and Andy said we might proceed on our journey. So after a while we were on our way; the wounded man and I sitting on one side of the car, and Andy on the other. The whole company came out to wish us God-speed, and with such comfort as good counsel and good wishes could give we ventured into the inky darkness of the night.

Andy was certainly a born car-driver. Not even the darkness, the comparative strangeness of the road, or the amount of whisky-punch which he had on board could disturb his driving in the least; he went steadily on. The car rocked and swayed and bumped, for the road was a bye one, and in but poor condition—but Andy and the mare went on alike unmoved. Once or twice only, in a journey of some three miles of winding bye-lanes, crossed and crossed again by lanes or water-courses, did he ask the way. I could not tell which was road-way and which water-way, for they were all water-courses at present, and the darkness was profound. Still, both Andy and Joyce seemed to have a sense lacking in myself, for now and again they spoke of things which I could not see at all. As, for instance, when Andy asked:

'Do we go up or down where the road branches beyant?' Or again: 'I disremimber, but is that Micky Dolan's ould apple three, or didn't he cut it down? an' is it Tim's fornent us on the lift?'

Presently we turned to the right, and drove up a short avenue towards a house. I knew it to be a house by the light in the windows, for shape it had none. Andy jumped down and knocked, and after a short colloquy, Joyce got down and went into the Doctor's house. I was asked to go too, but thought it better not to, as it would only have disturbed the Doctor in his work; and so Andy and I possessed our souls in patience until Joyce came out again, with his arm in a proper splint. And then we resumed our journey through the inky darkness.

However, after a while either there came more light into the sky, or my eyes became accustomed to the darkness, for I thought that now and again I beheld 'men as trees walking'.

Presently something dark and massive seemed outlined in the sky before us—a blackness projected on a darkness—and, said Andy, turning to me:

'That's Knockcalltecrore; we're nigh the foot iv it now, and pretty shortly we'll be at the enthrance iv the boreen, where Misther Joyce'll git aff.'

We plodded on for a while, and the hill before us seemed to overshadow whatever glimmer of light there was, for the darkness grew more profound than ever; then Andy turned to my companion:

'Sure, isn't that Miss Norah I see sittin' on the sthyle beyant?' I looked eagerly in the direction in which he evidently pointed, but for the life of me I could see nothing.

'No! I hope not,' said the father, hastily. 'She'd never come out in the shtorm. Yes! It is her, she sees us.'

Just then there came a sweet sound down the lane:

'Is that you, father?'

'Yes! My child; but I hope you've not been out in the shtorm.'

'Only a bit, father; I was anxious about you. Is it all right, father; did you get what you wanted?' She had jumped off the stile and had drawn nearer to us, and she evidently saw me, and went on in a changed and shyer voice:

'Oh! I beg your pardon, I did not see you had a stranger with you.'

This was all bewildering to me; I could hear it all—and a sweeter voice I never heard—but yet I felt like a blind man, for not a thing could I see, whilst each of the three others was seemingly as much at ease as in the daylight.

'This gentleman has been very kind to me, Norah. He has given me a seat on his car, and indeed he's come out of his way to lave me here.'

'I am sure we're all grateful to you, sir; but, father, where is your horse? Why are you on a car at all? Father, I hope you haven't met with any accident—I have been so fearful for you all the day.' This was spoken in a fainter voice; had my eyes been of service, I was sure I would have seen her grow pale.

'Yes, my darlin', I got a fall on the Curragh Hill, but I'm all right. Norah dear! Quick, quick! catch her, she's faintin'!—my God! I can't stir!'

I jumped off the car in the direction of the voice, but my arms sought the empty air. However, I heard Andy's voice beside me:

'All right! I have her. Hould up, Miss Norah; yer dada's all right, don't ye see him there, sittin' on my car. All right, sir, she's a brave girrul! she hasn't fainted.'

'I am all right,' she murmured, faintly; 'but, father, I hope you are not hurt?'

'Only a little, my darlin', just enough for ye to nurse me a while; I daresay a few days will make me all right again. Thank ye, Andy; steady now, till I get down; I'm feelin' a wee bit stiff.' Andy evidently helped him to the ground.

'Good night, Andy, and good night to you too, sir, and thank you kindly for your goodness to me all this night. I hope I'll see you again.' He took my hand in his uninjured one, and shook it warmly.

'Good night,' I said, and 'good-bye: I am sure I hope we shall meet again.'

Another hand took mine as he relinquished it—a warm, strong one—and a sweet voice said, shyly:

'Good night, sir, and thank you for your kindness to father.'

I faltered 'Good night,' as I raised my hat; the aggravation of the darkness at such a moment was more than I could equably bear. We heard them pass up the boreen, and I climbed on the car again.

The night seemed darker than ever as we turned our steps towards Carnaclif, and the journey was the dreariest one I had ever taken. I had only one thought which gave me any pleasure, but that was a pretty constant one through the long miles of damp, sodden road —the warm hand and the sweet voice coming out of the darkness, and all in the shadow of that mysterious mountain, which seemed to have become a part of my life. The words of the old story-teller came back to me again and again:

'The Hill can hould tight enough! A man has raysons—sometimes wan thing and sometimes another—but the Hill houlds him all the same!'

And a vague wonder grew upon me as to whether it could ever hold me, and how!

THE WATTER'S MOU'

I

IT THREATENED TO be a wild night. All day banks of sea-fog had come and gone, sweeping on shore with the south-east wind, which is so fatal at Cruden Bay, and indeed all along the coast of Aberdeenshire, and losing themselves in the breezy expanses of the high uplands beyond. As yet the wind only came in puffs, followed by intervals of ominous calm; but the barometer had been falling for days, and the sky had on the previous night been streaked with great 'mare's-tails' running in the direction of the dangerous wind. Up to early morning the wind had been south-westerly, but had then 'backed' to south-east; and the sudden change, no less than the backing, was ominous indeed. From the waste of sea came a ceaseless muffled roar, which seemed loudest and most full of dangerous import when it came through the mystery of the driving fog. Whenever the fog-belts would lift or disperse, or disappear inland before the gusts of wind, the sea would look as though swept with growing anger; for though there were neither big waves as during a storm, nor a great swell as after one, all the surface of the water as far as the eye could reach was covered with little waves tipped with white. Closer together grew these waves as the day wore on, the angrier ever the curl of the white water where they broke. In the North Sea it does not take long for the waves to rise; and all along the eastern edge of Buchan it was taken for granted that there would be wild work on the coast before the night was over.

In the little look-out house on the top of the cliff over the tiny harbour of Port Erroll the coastguard on duty was pacing rapidly to and fro. Every now and again he would pause, and, lifting a field-glass from the desk, sweep the horizon from Girdleness at the south of Aberdeen, when the lifting of the mist would let him see beyond the Scaurs, away to the north, where the high cranes of the Blackman quarries at Murdoch Head seemed to cleave the sky like gigantic gallows-trees.

He was manifestly in high spirits, and from the manner in which, one after another, he looked again and again at the Martini-Henry rifle in the rack, the navy revolver stuck muzzle down on a spike, and the cutlass in its sheath hanging on the wall, it was easy to see that his interest arose from something connected with his work as a coastguard. On the desk lay an open telegram smoothed down by his hard hands, with the brown envelope lying beside it. It gave some sort of clue to his excitement, although it did not go into detail. 'Keep careful watch tonight; run expected; spare no efforts; most important.'

William Barrow, popularly known as Sailor Willy, was a very young man to be a chief boatman in the preventive service, albeit that his station was one of the smallest on the coast. He had been allowed, as a reward for saving the life of his lieutenant, to join the coast service, and had been promoted to chief boatman as a further reward for a clever capture of smugglers, wherein he had shown not only great bravery, but much ability and power of rapid organisation.

The Aberdeen coast is an important one in the way of guarding on account of the vast number of fishing-smacks which, during the season, work from Peterhead up and down the coast, and away on the North Sea right to the shores of Germany and Holland. This vast coming and going affords endless opportunities for smuggling; and, despite of all vigilance, a considerable amount of 'stuff' finds its way to the consumers without the formality of the Custom House. The fish traffic is a quick traffic, and its returns come all at once, so that a truly enormous staff would be requisite to examine adequately the thousand fishing-smacks which use the harbour of Peterhead, and on Sundays pack its basins with a solid mass of boats. The coast-line for some forty miles south is favourable for this illicit traffic. The gneiss and granite formations broken up by every convulsion of nature, and worn by the strain and toil of ages into every conceivable form of rocky beauty, offers an endless variety of narrow creeks and bays where the daring, to whom the rocks and the currents and the tides are known, may find secret entrance and speedy exit for their craft. This season the smuggling had been chiefly of an overt kind—that is, the goods had been brought into the harbour amongst the fish and nets, and had been taken through the streets under the eyes of the unsuspecting Customs officers. Some of these takes were so large, that the authorities had made up their minds that there must be a great amount of smuggling going on. The secret agents in the German, Dutch, Flemish, and French ports were asked to make extra exertions in discovering the amount of the illicit trade, and their later reports were of an almost alarming nature. They said that really vast amounts of tobacco, brandy, rum, silks, laces, and all sorts of excisable commodities were being secretly shipped in the British fishing-fleet; and as only a very small proportion of this was discovered, it was manifest that smuggling to a large extent was once more to the fore. Accordingly precautions were doubled all along the east coast frequented by the fishing-fleets. Not only were the coastguards warned of the danger and cautioned against devices which might keep them from their work at critical times, but they were apprised of every new shipment as reported from abroad. Furthermore, the detectives of the service were sent about to parts where the men were suspected of laxity—or worse.

Thus it was that Sailor Willy, with the experience of two promotions for cause, and with the sense of responsibility which belonged to his office, felt in every way elated at the possibility of some daring work before him. He knew, of course, that a similar telegram had been received at every station on the coast, and that the chance of an attempt being made in Cruden Bay or its surroundings was a small one; but he was young and brave and hopeful, and with an adamantine sense of integrity to support him in his work. It was unfortunate that his comrade was absent, ill in the hospital at Aberdeen, and that the strain at present on the service, together with the men away on annual training and in the naval manoeuvres, did not permit of a substitute being sent to him. However, he felt strong enough to undertake any amount of duty—he was strong enough and handsome enough to have a good opinion of himself, and too brave and too sensible to let his head be turned by vanity.

As he walked to and fro there was in the distance of his mind—in that dim background against which in a man's mind a woman's form finds suitable projection—some sort of vague hope that a wild dream of rising in the world might be some time realised. He knew that every precaution in his power had been already taken, and felt that he could indulge in fancies without detriment to his work. He had signalled the coastguard at Whinnyfold on the south side of the Bay, and they had exchanged ideas by means of the signal language. His appliances for further signalling by day or night were in perfect order, and he had been right over his whole boundary since he had received the telegram seeing that all things were in order. Willy Barrow was not one to leave things to chance where duty was concerned.

His day-dreams were not all selfish. They were at least so far unselfish that the results were to be shared with another; for Willy Barrow was engaged to be married. Maggie MacWhirter was the daughter of an old fisherman who had seen days more prosperous than the present. He had once on a time owned a fishing-smack, but by degrees he had been compelled to borrow on her, till now, when, although he was nominal owner, the boat was so heavily mortgaged that at any moment he might lose his entire possession. That such an event was not unlikely was manifest, for the mortgagee was no other than Solomon Mendoza of Hamburg and Aberdeen, who had changed in like manner the ownership of a hundred boats, and who had the reputation of being as remorseless as he was rich. MacWhirter had long been a widower, and Maggie since a little girl had kept house for her father and her two brothers, Andrew and Niel. Andrew was twenty-seven—six years older than Maggie—and Niel had just turned twenty. The elder brother was a quiet, self-contained, hard working man, who now and again manifested great determination, though generally at unexpected times; the younger was rash, impetuous, and passionate, and though in his moments of quiescence more tender to those he cared for than was usual with men of his class, he was a never-ending source of anxiety to his father and his sister. Andrew, or Sandy as he was always called, took him with consistent quietness.

The present year, although a good one in the main, had been but poor for MacWhirter's boat. Never once had he had a good take of fish—not one-half the number of crans of the best boat; and the season was so far advanced, and the supply had been so plentiful, that a few days before, the notice had been up at Peterhead that after the following week the buyers would not take any more herring.

This notice naturally caused much excitement, and the whole fishing industry determined to make every effort to improve the shining hours left to them. Exertions were on all sides redoubled, and on sea and shore there was little idleness. Naturally the smuggling interest bestirred itself too; its chance for the year was in the rush and bustle and hurry of the coming and going fleet, and anything held over for a chance had to be ventured now or left over for a year—which might mean indefinitely. Great ventures were therefore taken by some of the boats; and from their daring the authorities concluded that either heavy bribes were given, or else that the goods were provided by others than the fishermen who undertook to run them. A few important seizures, however, made the men wary; and it was understood from the less frequent but greater importance of the seizures, that the price for 'running' had greatly gone up. There was much passionate excitement amongst those who were found out and their friends, and a general wish to discover the informers. Some of the smuggling fishermen at first refused to pay the fines until they were told who had informed. This position being unsupportable, they had instead paid the fines and cherished hatred in their hearts. Some of the more reckless and turbulent spirits had declared their intention of avenging themselves on the informers when they should be known. It was only natural that this feeling of rage should extend to the Customs officers and men of the preventive service, who stood between the unscrupulous adventurers and their harvest; and altogether matters had become somewhat strained between the fishermen and the authorities.

The Port Erroll boats, like those from Collieston, were all up at Peterhead, and of course amongst them MacWhirter's boat the *Sea Gull* with her skipper and his two sons. It was now Friday night, and the boats had been out for several days, so that it was pretty certain that there would be a full harbour at Peterhead on the Saturday. A marriage had been arranged to take place this evening between Thomas Keith of Boddam and Alice MacDonald, whose father kept the public-house The Jamie Fleeman on the northern edge of the Erroll estate. Though the occasion was to be a grand one, the notice of it had been short indeed. It was said by the bride's friends that it had been fixed so hurriedly because the notice of the closing of the fishing season had been so suddenly given out at Peterhead. Truth to tell, some sort of explanation was necessary, for it was only on Wednesday morning that word had been sent to the guests, and as these came from all sorts of places between Peterhead and Collieston, and taking a sweep of some ten miles inland, there was need of some preparation. The affair was to top all that had ever been seen at Port Erroll, and as The Jamie Fleeman was but a tiny place—nothing, in fact, but a wayside public-house—it was arranged that it was to take place in the new barn and storehouses Matthew Beagrie had just built on the inner side of the sandhills, where they came close to the Water of Cruden.

Throughout all the east side of Buchan there had for some time existed a wonder amongst the quiet-going people as to the strange prosperity of MacDonald. His public-house had, of course, a practical monopoly; for as there was not a licensed house on the Erroll estate, and as his was the nearest house of call to the port, he naturally got what custom there was going. The fishermen all along the coast for some seven or eight miles went to him either to drink or to get their liquor for drinking elsewhere; and not a few of the Collieston men on their Saturday journey home from Peterhead and their Sunday journey out there again made a detour to have a glass and a chat and a pipe, if time permitted, with 'Tammas Mac'—for such was his sobriquet. To the authorities he and his house were also sources of interest; for there was some kind of suspicion that some of the excellent brandy and cigars which he dispensed had arrived by a simpler road than that through the Custom House. It was at this house, in the good old days of smuggling, that the coastguards used to be entertained when a run was on foot, and where they slept off their drunkenness whilst the cargoes were being hidden or taken inland in the ready carts. Of course all this state of things had been altered, and there was as improved a decorum amongst the smugglers as there was a sterner rule and discipline amongst the coastguards. It was many a long year since Philip Kennedy met his death at Kirkton at the hands of the exciseman Anderson. Comparatively innocent deception was now the smugglers' only wile.

Tonight the whole country-side was to be at the wedding, and the dance which was to follow it; and for this occasion the lion was to lie down with the lamb, for the coastguards were bidden to the feast with the rest. Sailor Willy had looked forward to the dance with delight, for Maggie was to be there, and on the *Billy Ruffian*, which had been his last ship, he had been looked on as the best dancer before the mast. If there be any man who shuns a dance in which he knows he can shine, and at which his own particular girl is to be present, that man is not to be found in the Royal Naval Marine, even amongst those of them who have joined in the preventive service. Maggie was no less delighted, although she had a source of grief which for the present she had kept all to herself. Her father had of late been much disturbed about affairs. He had not spoken of them to her, and she did not dare to mention the matter to him; for old MacWhirter was a close-mouthed man, and did not exchange many confidences even with his own children. But Maggie guessed at the cause of the sadness—of the down-bent head when none were looking; the sleepless nights and the deep smothered groans which now and again marked his heavy sleep told the tale loudly enough to reach the daughter's ears. For the last few weeks, whenever her father was at home, Maggie had herself lain awake listening, listening, in increasing agony of spirit, for one of these half moans or for the sound of the tossing of the restless man. He was as gentle and kind to his daughter as ever; but on his leaving the last time there had been an omission on his part which troubled her to the quick. For the first time in his life he had not kissed her as he went away.

On the previous day Sailor Willy had said he would come to the wedding and the dance if his duties should permit him; and, when asked if he could spare a few rockets for the occasion, promised that he would let off three Board of Trade rockets, which he could now deal with as it was three months since he had used any. He was delighted at the opportunity of meeting the fisherfolk and his neighbours; for his officers had impressed on him the need of being on good terms with all around him, both for the possibility which it would always afford him of knowing how things were going on, and for the benefit of the rocket-service whenever there might be need of willing hands and hearts to work with him, for in the Board of Trade rocket-service much depends on voluntary aid. That very afternoon he had fixed the rockets on the wall of the barn with staples, so that he could fire them from below with a slow match, which he fixed ready. When he had got the telegram he had called in to Maggie and told her if he did not come to fetch her she was to go on to the wedding by herself, and that he would try to join her later. She had appeared a little startled when he told her he might not be present; but after a pause smiled, and said she would go, and that he was not to lose any time coming when he was free. Now that every arrangement was complete, and as he had between puffs of the sea-fog got a clean sweep of the horizon and saw that there was no sail of any kind within sight, he thought he might have a look through the village and keep in evidence so as not to create any suspicion in the minds of the people. As he went through the street he noticed that nearly every house door was closed—all the women were at the new barn. It was now eight o'clock, and the darkness, which is slow of coming in the North, was closing in. Down by the barn there were quite a number of carts, and the horses had not been taken out, though the wedding was not to be till nine o'clock, or perhaps even later; for Mrs. MacDonald had taken care to tell her friends that Keith might not get over from Boddam till late. Willy looked at the carts carefully—some idea seemed to have struck him. Their lettering shewed them to be from all parts round, and the names mostly of those who had not the best reputation. When his brief survey was finished he looked round and then went swiftly behind the barn so that no one might see him. As he went he muttered reflectively:

'Too many light carts and fast horses—too much silence in the barn—too little liquor going, to be all safe. There's something up here tonight.' He was under the lee of the barn and looked up where he had fixed the rockets ready to fire. This gave him a new idea.

'I fixed them low so as to go over the sandhills and not be noticeable at Collieston or beyond. They are now placed up straight and will be seen for fifty miles if the weather be clear.'

It was too dark to see very clearly, and he would not climb up to examine them lest he should be noticed and his purpose of acquiring information frustrated; but then and there he made up his mind that Port Erroll or its neighbourhood had been the spot chosen for the running of the smuggled goods. He determined to find out more, and straightway went round to the front and entered the room.

II

As soon as Sailor Willy was seen to enter, a large part of the gathering looked relieved, and at once began to chat and gabble in marked contrast to their previous gloom and silence. Port Erroll was well represented by its womankind, and by such of its men as were not away at the fishing; for it was the intention to mask the smuggling scheme by an assemblage at which all the respectability would be present. There appeared to be little rivalry between the two shoemakers, MacPherson and Beagrie, who chatted together in a corner, the former telling his companion how he had just been down to the lifeboat-house to see, as one of the Committee, that it was all ready in case it should be wanted before the night was over. Lang John and Lang Jim, the policemen of the place, looked sprucer even than usual, and their buttons shone in the light of the many paraffin lamps as if they had been newly burnished. Mitchell and his companions of the salmon fishery were grouped in another corner, and Andrew Mason was telling Mackay, the new flesher, whose shed was erected on the edge of the burn opposite John Reid's shop, of a great crab which he had taken that morning in a pot opposite the Twa Een.

But these and nearly all the other Port Erroll folk present were quiet, and their talk was of local interest; the main clack of tongues came from the many strange men who stood in groups near the centre of the room and talked loudly. In the midst of them was the bridegroom, more joyous than any, though in the midst of his laughter he kept constantly turning to look at the door. The minister from Peterhead sat in a corner with the bride and her mother and father—the latter of whom, despite his constant laughter, had an anxious look on his face. Sailor Willy was greeted joyously, and the giver of the feast and the bridegroom each rose, and, taking a bottle and glass, offered him a drink.

'To the bride', said he; but seeing that no one else was drinking, he tapped the bridegroom on the shoulder, 'Come, drink this with me, my lad!' he added. The latter paused an instant and then helped himself from MacDonald's bottle. Willy did not fail to notice the act, and holding out his glass said:

'Come, my lad, you drink with me! Change glasses in old style!' An odd pallor passed quickly across the bridegroom's face, but MacDonald spoke quickly:

'Tak it, mon, tak it!' So he took the glass, crying 'No heeltaps', threw back his head, and raised the glass. Willy threw back his head too, and tossed off his liquor, but, as he did so, took care to keep a sharp eye on the other, and saw him, instead of swallowing his liquor, pour it into his thick beard. His mind was quite made up now. They meant to keep him out of the way by fair means or foul.

Just then two persons entered the room, one of them, James Cruickshank of the Kilmarnock Arms, who was showing the way to the other, an elderly man with a bald head, keen eyes, a ragged grey beard, a hooked nose, and an evil smile. As he entered MacDonald jumped up and came over to greet him.

'Oh! Mr. Mendoza, this is braw! We hopit tae see ye the nicht, but we were that feared that ye wadna come.'

'Mein Gott, but why shall I not come—on this occasion of all—the occasion of the marriage of the daughter of mein goot frient, Tam Smack? And moreovers when I bring these as I haf promise. For you, mein frient Keith, this cheque, which one week you cash, and for you, my tear Miss Alice, these so bright necklace, which you will wear, ant which will sell if so you choose.'

As he spoke he handed his gifts to the groom and bride. He then walked to the corner where Mrs. Mac sat, exchanging a keen look with his host as he did so. The latter seemed to have taken his cue and spoke out at once.

'And now, reverend sir, we may proceed—all is ready.' As he spoke the bridal pair stood up, and the friends crowded round. Sailor Willy moved towards the door, and just as the parson opened his book, began to pass out. Tammas Mac immediately spoke to him:

'Ye're no gangin', Sailor Willy? Sure ye'll wait and see Tam Keith marrit on my lass?'

He instantly replied: 'I must go for a while. I have some things to do, and then I want to try to bring Maggie down for the dance!' and before anything could be said, he was gone.

The instant he left the door he slipped round to the back of the barn, and running across the sandhills to the left, crossed the wooden bridge, and hurrying up the roadway by the cottage on the cliff gained the watch-house. He knew that none of the company in the barn could leave till the service was over, with the minister's eye on them, without giving cause for after suspicion; and he knew, too, that as there were no windows on the south side of the barn, nothing could be seen from that side. Without a moment's delay he arranged his signals for the call for aid; and as the rockets whizzed aloft, sending a white glare far into the sky, he felt that the struggle had entered on its second stage.

The night had now set in with a darkness unusual in August. The swaithes of sea-mist whirled in by the wind came fewer and fainter, and at times a sudden rift through the driving clouds showed that there was starlight somewhere between the driving masses of mist and gloom. Willy Barrow once more tried all his weapons and saw that all his signals were in order. Then he strapped the revolver and the cutlass in his belt, and lit a dark lantern so that it might be ready in case of need. This done, he left the watch-house, locking the door behind him, and, after looking steadily across the Bay to the Scaurs beyond, turned and walked northward towards the Watter's Mou'. Between the cliff on the edge of this and the watch-house there was a crane used for raising the granite boulders quarried below, and when he drew near this he stopped instinctively and called out, 'Who is there?' for he felt, rather than saw, some presence. 'It is only me, Willy,' came a soft voice, and a woman drew a step nearer through the darkness from behind the shaft of the crane.

'Maggie! Why, darling, what brings you here? I thought you were going to the wedding!'

'I knew ye wadna be there, and I wanted to speak wi' ye'—this was said in a very low voice.

'How did you know I wouldn't be there?—I was to join you if I could.'

'I saw Bella Cruickshank hand ye the telegram as ye went by the Post Office, and—and I knew there would be something to keep ye. O Willy, Willy! why do ye draw awa frae me?' for Sailor Willy had instinctively loosened his arms which were round her and had drawn back—in the instant his love and his business seemed as though antagonistic. He answered with blunt truthfulness:

'I was thinking, Maggie, that I had no cause to be making love here and now. I've got work, mayhap, tonight!'

'I feared so, Willy—I feared so!' Willy was touched, for it seemed to him that she was anxious for him, and answered tenderly:

'All right, dear! All right! There's no danger—why, if need be, I am armed,' and he slipped his hand on the butt of the revolver in his belt. To his surprise Maggie uttered a deep low groan, and turning away sat on the turf bank beside her, as though her strength was failing her. Willy did not know what to say, so there was a space of silence. Then Maggie went on hurriedly:

'O my God! it is a dreadfu' thing to lift yer han' in sic a deadly manner against yer neighbours, and ye not knowing what woe ye may cause.' Willy could answer this time:

'Ay, lass! it's hard indeed, and that's the truth. But that's the very reason that men like me are put here that can and will do their duty no matter how hard it may be.'

Another pause, and then Maggie spoke again. Willy could not see her face, but she seemed to speak between gasps for breath.

'Ye're lookin' for hard wark the nicht?'

'I am!—I fear so.'

'I can guess that that telegram tellt ye that some boats would try to rin in somewhere the nicht.'

'Mayhap, lass. But the telegrams are secret, and I must not speak of what's in them.'

After a long pause Maggie spoke again, but in a voice so low that he could hardly hear her amid the roar of the breaking waves which came in on the wind:

'Willy, ye're not a cruel man!—ye wadna, if ye could help it, dae harm to them that loved ye, or work woe to their belongin's?'

'My lass! that I wouldn't.' As he answered he felt a horrible sinking of the heart. What did all this mean? Was it possible that

Maggie, too, had any interest in the smuggling? No, no! a thousand times no! Ashamed of his suspicion he drew closer and again put his arm around her in a protecting way. The unexpected tenderness overcame her, and, bursting into tears, she threw herself on Willy's neck and whispered to him between her sobs:

'O Willy, Willy! I'm in sic sair trouble, and there's nane that I can speak to. Nae! not ane in the wide warld.'

'Tell me, darling; you know you'll soon be my wife, and then I'll have a right to know all!'

'Oh, I canna! I canna! I canna!' she said, and taking her arms from round his neck she beat her hands wildly together. Willy was something frightened, for a woman's distress touches a strong man in direct ration to his manliness. He tried to soothe her as though she were a frightened child, and held her tight to him.

'There! there! my darling. Don't cry. I'm here with you, and you can tell me all your trouble.' She shook her head; he felt the movement on his breast, and he went on:

'Don't be frightened, Maggie; tell me all. Tell me quietly, and mayhap I can help ye out over the difficult places.' Then he remained silent, and her sobs grew less violent; at last she raised her head and dashed away her tears fiercely with her hand. She dragged herself away from him: he tried to stop her, but she said:

'Nae, nae, Willy dear; let me speak it in my ain way. If I canna trust ye, wha can I trust? My trouble is not for mysel.' She paused, and he asked:

'Who, then, is it for?'

'My father and my brothers.' Then she went on hurriedly, fearing to stop lest her courage should fail her, and he listened in dead silence, with a growing pain in his heart.

'Ye ken that for several seasons back our boat has had bad luck —we took less fish and lost mair nets than any of the boats; even on the land everything went wrong. Our coo died, and the shed was blawn doon, and then the blight touched the potatoes in our field. Father could dae naething, and had to borrow money on the boat to go on with his wark; and the debt grew and grew, till now he only owns her in name, and we never ken when we may be sold up. And the man that has the mortgage isn't like to let us off or gie time!'

'Who is he? His name?' said Willie hoarsely.

'Mendoza—the man frae Hamburg wha lends to the boats at Peterhead.'

Willy groaned. Before his eyes rose the vision of that hard, cruel, white face that he had seen only a few minutes ago, and again he saw him hand out the presents with which he had bought the man and woman to help in his wicked scheme. When Maggie heard the groan her courage and her hope arose. If her lover could take the matter so much to heart all might yet be well, and in the moment all the womanhood in her awoke to the call. Her fear had broken down the barriers that had kept back her passion, and now the passion came with all the force of a virgin nature. She drew Willy close to her—closer still—and whispered to him in a low sweet voice, that thrilled with emotion:

'Willy, Willy, darlin'; ye wouldna see harm come to my father —my father, my father!' and in a wave of tumultuous, voluptuous passion she kissed him full in the mouth. Willy felt for the moment half dazed. Love has its opiates that soothe and stun even in the midst of their activity. He clasped Maggie close in his arms, and for a moment their hearts beat together and their mouths breathed the same air. Then Willy drew back, but Maggie hung limp in his arms. The silence which hung in the midst of nature's tumult broke its own spell. Willy realised what and where he was: with the waves dashing below his feet and the night wind laden with drifting mist wreathing around him in the darkness, and whistling amongst the rocks and screaming sadly through the ropes and stays of the flagstaff on the cliff. There was a wild fear in his heart and a burning desire to know all that was in his sweetheart's mind.

'Go on, Maggie! go on!' he said. Maggie roused herself and again took up the thread of her story—this time in feverish haste. The moment of passion had disquieted and disturbed her. She seemed to herself to be two people, one of whom was new to her, and whom she feared, but woman-like, she felt that as she had begun so must she go on; and thus her woman's courage sustained her.

'Some weeks ago, father began to get letters frae Mr. Mendoza, and they aye upset him. He wrote answers and sent them away at once. Then Mr. Mendoza sent him a telegram frae Hamburg, and he sent a reply—and a month ago father got a telegram telling him to meet him at Peterhead. He was very angry at first and very low-spirited after; but he went to Peterhead, and when he cam back he was very still and quite pale. He would eat naething, and went to bed although it was only seven o'clock. Then there were more letters and telegrams, but father answered nane o' them—sae far as I ken—and then Mr. Mendoza cam to our hoose. Father got as pale as a sheet when he saw him, and then he got red and angry, and I thocht he was going to strike him; but Mr. Mendoza said not to frichten his daughter, and father got quiet and sent me oot on a message to the Nether Mill. And when I cam back Mr. Mendoza had gone, and father was sitting with his face in his hands, and he didna hear me come in. When I spoke, he started up and he was as white as a sheet, and then he mumbled something and went into his room. And ever since then he hardly spoke to any one, and seemed to avoid me a'thegither. When he went away the last time he never even kissed me. And so, Willy—so, I fear that that awfu' Mr Mendoza has made him dae something that he didna want to dae, and it's all breaking my heart!' and again she laid her head on her lover's breast and sobbed. Willy breathed more freely; but he could not be content to remain in doubt, and his courage was never harder tried than when he asked his next question.

'Then, Maggie, you don't know anything for certain?'

'Naething, Willy—but I fear.'

'But there may be nothing, after all!' Maggie's hopes rose again, for there was something in her lover's voice which told her that he was willing to cling to any straw, and once again her woman's nature took advantage of her sense of right and wrong. 'Please

God, Willy, there may be naething! but I fear much that it may be so; but we must act as if we didna fear. It wadna dae to suspect poor father without some cause. You know, Willy, the Earl has promised to mak him the new harbourmaster. Old Forgie is bedridden now, and when winter comes he'll no even be able to pretend to work, so the Earl is to pension him, and father will get the post and hae the hoose by the harbour, and you know that every one's sae glad, for they a' respect father.'

'Ay, lass,' interrupted Willy, 'that's true; and why, then, should we—you and me, Maggie—think he would do ill to please that damned scoundrel, Mendoza?'

'Indeed, I'm thinkin' that it's just because that he is respeckit that Mendoza wants him to help him. He kens weel that nane would suspeck father, and—' here she clipped her lover close in her arms once again, and her breath came hot in his face till it made him half drunk with a voluptuous intoxication—'he kens that father, my father, would never be harmt by my lover!'

Even then, at the moment when the tragedy of his life seemed to be accomplished, when the woman he loved and honoured seemed to be urging him to some breach of duty, Willy Barrow could not but feel that some responsibility for her action rested on him. That first passionate kiss, which had seemed to unlock the very gates of her soul—in which she had yielded herself to him—had some mysterious bond or virtue like that which abides in the wedding ring. The Maggie who thus acted was his Maggie, and in all that came of it he had a part. But his mind was made up; nothing—not Maggie's kisses or Maggie's fears—would turn him from his path of duty, and strong in this resolution he could afford to be silent to the woman in his arms. Maggie instinctively knew that silence could now be her best weapon, and said no word as they walked towards the guard-house, Willy casting keen looks seawards, and up and down the coast as they went. When they were so close that in its shelter the roar of the surge seemed muffled, Maggie again nestled close to her lover, and whispered in his ear as he looked out over Cruden Bay:

'The *Sea Gull* comes hame the nicht!' Willy quivered, but said nothing for a time that seemed to be endless. Then he answered—'They'll find it hard to make the Port tonight. Look! the waves are rolling high, and the wind is getting up. It would be madness to try it.' Again she whispered to him:

'Couldna she rin in somewhere else—there are other openings besides Port Erroll in Buchan!' Willy laughed the laugh of a strong man who knew well what he said:

'Other openings! Ay, lass, there are other openings; but the coble isn't built that can run them this night. With a south-east gale, who would dare to try? The Bullers, or Robies Haven, or Dunbuy, or Twa Havens, or Lang Haven, or The Watter's Mou'—why, lass, they'd be in matches on the rocks before they could turn their tiller or slack a sail.'

She interrupted him, speaking with a despairing voice:

'Then ye'll no hae to watch nane o' them the nicht?'

'Nay, Maggie. Port Erroll is my watch tonight; and from it I won't budge.'

'And the Watter's Mou'?' she asked, 'is that no safe wi'oot watch? it's no far frae the Port.' Again Willy laughed his arrogant, masculine laugh, which made Maggie, despite her trouble, admire him more than ever, and he answered:

'The Watter's Mou'? To try to get in there in this wind would be to court sudden death. Why, lass, it would take a man all he knew to get out from there, let alone get in, in this weather! And then the chances would be ten to one that he'd be dashed to pieces on the rocks beyond,' and he pointed to where a line of sharp rocks rose between the billows on the south side of the inlet. Truly it was a fearful-looking place to be dashed on, for the great waves broke on the rocks with a loud roaring, and even in the semi-darkness they could see the white lines as the waters poured down to leeward in the wake of the heaving wave. The white cluster of rocks looked like a ghostly mouth opened to swallow whatever might come in touch. Maggie shuddered; but some sudden idea seemed to strike her, and she drew away from her lover for a moment, and looked towards the black cleft in the rocks of which they could just see the top from where they stood—the entrance to the Watter's Mou'.

And then with one long, wild, appealing glance skyward, as though looking a prayer which she dared not utter even in her heart, Maggie turned towards her lover once more. Again she drew close to him, and hung around his neck, and said with many gasps and pauses between her words:

'If the *Sea Gull* should come in to the Port the nicht, and if ony attempt that ye feared should tak you away to Whinnyfold or to Dunbuy so that you might be a bit—only a wee bit—late to search when the boat cam in—'

She stopped affrighted, for Willy put her from him to arm's length, not too gently either, and said to her so sternly that each word seemed to smite her like the lash of a whip, till she shrunk and quivered and cowered away from him:

'Maggie, lass! What's this you're saying to me? It isn't fit for you to speak or me to hear! It's bad enough to be a smuggler, but what is it that you would make of me? Not only a smuggler, but a perjurer and a traitor too. God! am I mistaken? Is it you, Maggie, that would make this of me? Of me! Maggie MacWhirter, if this be your counsel, then God help us both! you are no fit wife for me!' In an instant the whole truth dawned on Maggie of what a thing she would make of the man she loved, whom she had loved at the first because he was strong and brave and true. In the sudden revulsion of her feelings she flung herself on her knees beside him, and took his hand and held it hard, and despite his efforts to withdraw it, kissed it wildly in the humility of her self-abasement, and poured out to him a passionate outburst of pleading for his forgiveness, of justification of herself, and of appeals to his mercy for her father.

'O Willy, Willy! dinna turn frae me this nicht! My heart is sae fu' o' trouble that I am nigh mad! I dinna ken what to dae nor where to look for help! I think, and think, and think, and everywhere there is nought but dark before me, just as there is blackness oot ower the sea, when I look for my father. And noo when I want ye to help me—ye that are all I hae, and the only ane on earth that I can look tae in my wae and trouble—I can dae nae mair than turn ye frae me! Ye that I love! oh, love more than my life or my soul! I must dishonour and mak ye hate me! Oh, what shall I dae? What shall I dae? What shall I dae?' and again she beat the palms of her hands together in a paroxysm of wild despair, whilst Willy looked on with his heart full of pain and pity, though his resolution never flinched. And then through the completeness of her self-abasement came the pleading of her soul from a depth of her nature even deeper than despair. Despair has its own bravery, but hope can sap the strongest resolution. And the pleadings of love came from the depths of that Pandora's box which we call human nature.

'O Willy, Willy! forgie me—forgie me! I was daft to say what I did! I was daft to think that ye would be so base!—daft to think that I would like you to so betray yoursel! Forgie me, Willy, forgie me, and tak my wild words as spoken not to ye but to the storm that maks me fear sae for my father! Let me tak it a' back, Willy darlin'—Willy, my Willy; and dinna leave me desolate here with this new shadow ower me!' Here, as she kissed his hand again, her lover stooped and raised her in his strong arms and held her to him. And then, when she felt herself in a position of security, the same hysterical emotion came sweeping up in her brain and her blood—the same self-abandonment to her lover overcame her—and the current of her thought once again turned to win from him something by the force of her woman's wile and her woman's contact with the man.

'Willy,' she whispered, as she kissed him on the mouth and then kissed his head on the side of his neck, 'Willy, ye have forgien me, I ken—and I ken that ye'll harm father nae mair than ye can help —but if—'

What more she was going to say she hardly knew herself. As for Willy, he felt that something better left unsaid was coming, and unconsciously his muscles stiffened till he held her from him rather than to him. She, too, felt the change, and held him closer—

closer still, with the tenacity induced by a sense of coming danger. Their difficulty was solved for them, for just on the instant when the suggestion of treachery to his duty was hanging on her lips, there came from the village below, in a pause between the gusts of wind, the fierce roar of a flying rocket. Up and up and up, as though it would never stop—up it rose with its prolonged screech, increasing in sound at the first till it began to die away in the aërial heights above, so that when the explosion came it seemed to startle a quietude around it. Up in the air a thousand feet over their heads the fierce glitter of the falling fires of red and blue made a blaze of light which lit up the coast-line from the Scaurs to Dunbuy, and with an instinctive intelligence Willy Barrow took in all he saw, including the many men at the little port below, sheltering under the sea-wall from the sweeping of the waves as they looked out seawards. Instinctively also he counted the seconds till the next rocket should be fired—one, two, three; and then another roar and another blaze of coloured lights. And then another pause, of six seconds this time! and then the third rocket sped aloft with its fiery message. And then the darkness seemed blacker than ever, and the mysterious booming of the sea to grow louder and louder as though it came through silence. By this time the man and the woman were apart no less in spirit than physically. Willy, intent on his work, was standing outside the window of the guard-house, whence he could see all around the Bay and up and down the coast, and at the same time command the whole of the harbour. His feet were planted wide apart, for on the exposed rock the sweep of the wind was strong, and as he raised his arm with his field-glass to search the horizon the wind drove back his jacket and showed the butt of his revolver and the hilt of his cutlass. Maggie stood a little behind him, gazing seawards, with no less eager eyes, for she too expected what would follow. Her heart seemed to stand still though her breath came in quick gasps, and she did not dare to make a sound or to encroach on the business-like earnestness of the man. For full a minute they waited thus, and then far off at sea, away to the south, they saw a faint blue light, and then another and another, till at the last three lights were burning in a row. Instantly from the town a single rocket went up—not this time a great Board of Trade rocket, laden with coloured fire, but one which left a plain white track of light behind it. Willy gazed seawards, but there was no more sign from the far-off ship at sea; the signal, whatever it was, was complete. The coastguard was uncertain as to the meaning, but to Maggie no explanation was necessary. There, away at sea, tossed on the stormy waters, was her father. There was danger round him, but a greater danger on the shore—every way of entrance was barred by the storm—save the one where, through his fatal cargo, dishonour lay in wait for him. She seemed to see her duty clear before her, and come what might she meant to do it: her father must be warned. It was with a faint voice indeed that she now spoke to her lover:

'Willy!'

His heart was melted at the faltering voice, but he feared she was trying some new temptation, so, coldly and hardly enough, he answered:

'What is it, lass?'

'Willy, ye wadna see poor father injured?'

'No, Maggie, not if I could help it. But I'd have to do my duty all the same.'

'And we should a' dae oor duty—whatever it might be—at a' costs?'

'Ay, lass—at all costs!' His voice was firm enough now, and there was no mistaking the truth of its ring. Maggie's hope died away. From the stern task which seemed to rise before her over the waste of the black sea she must not shrink. There was but one more yielding to the weakness of her fear, and she said, so timidly that Willy was startled, the voice and manner were so different from those he had ever known:

'And if—mind I say "if", Willy—I had a duty to dae and it was fu' o' fear and danger, and ye could save me frae it, wad ye?' As she waited for his reply, her heart beat so fast and so heavily that Willy could hear it; her very life, she felt, lay in his answer. He did not quite understand the full import of her words and all that they implied, but he knew that she was in deadly earnest, and he felt that some vague terror lay in his answer; but the manhood in him rose to the occasion—Willy Barrow was of the stuff of which heroes are made—and he replied:

'Maggie, as God is above us, I have no other answer to give! I don't know what you mean, but I have a shadow of a fear! I must do my duty whatever comes of it!' There was a long pause, and then Maggie spoke again, but this time in so different a voice that her lover's heart went out to her in tenfold love and passion, with never a shadow of doubt or fear.

'Willy, tak me in your arms—I am not unworthy, dear, though for a moment I did falter!' He clasped her close to him, and whispered when their lips had met:

'Maggie, my darling, I never loved you like now. I would die for you if I could do you good.'

'Hush, dear, I ken it weel. But your duty is not only for yoursel, and it must be done! I too hae a duty to dae—a grave and stern ane!'

'What is it? Tell me, Maggie dear!'

'Ye maunna ask me! Ye maun never ken! Kiss me once again, Willy, before I go—for oh, my love, my love! it may be the last!'

Her words were lost in the passionate embrace which followed. Then, when he least expected it, she suddenly tore herself away and fled through the darkness across the field which lay between them and her home, whilst he stood doggedly at his watch looking out for another signal between sea and shore.

III

When she got to the far side of the field, Maggie, instead of turning to the left, which would have brought her home, went down the sloping track to the right, which led to the rustic bridge crossing the Back Burn near the Pigeon Tower. Thence turning to the right she scrambled down the bank beside the ruined barley-mill, so as to reach the little plots of sea-grass—islands, except at low tide—between which the tide rises to meet the waters of the stream.

The whole situation of Cruden is peculiar. The main stream, the Water of Cruden, runs in a south-easterly direction, skirts the sandhills, and, swirling under the stone bridge, partly built with the ruins of the old church which Malcolm erected to celebrate his victory over Sueno, turns suddenly to the right and runs to sea over a stony bottom. The estuary has in its wash some dangerous outcropping granite rocks, nearly covered at high tide, and the mouth opens between the most northerly end of the sandhills and the village street, whose houses mark the slope of the detritus from the rocks. Formerly the Water of Cruden, instead of taking this last turn, used to flow straight on till it joined the lesser stream known as the Back Burn, and together the streams ran seawards. Even in comparatively recent years, in times of flood or freshet, the spate broke down or swept over the intervening tongue of land, and the Water of Cruden took its old course seaward. This course is what is known as the Watter's Mou'. It is a natural cleft—formed by primaeval fire or earthquake or some sort of natural convulsion, —which runs through the vast mass of red granite which forms a promontory running due south. Water has done its work as well as fire in the formation of the gully as it now is, for the drip and flow and rush of water that mark the seasons for countless ages have completed the work of the pristine fire. As one sees this natural mouth of the stream in the rocky face of the cliff, it is hard to realise that Nature alone has done the work.

At first the cleft runs from west to east, and broadens out into a wide bay of which on one side a steep grassy slope leads towards the new castle of Slains, and on the other rises a sheer bank, with tufts of the thick grass growing on the ledges, where the earth has been blown. From this the cleft opens again between towering rocks like what in America is called a cañon and tends seaward to the south between precipices two hundred feet high, and over a bottom of great boulders exposed at low water towards the northern end. The precipice to the left or eastward side is twice rent with great openings, through which, in time of storm, the spray and spume of the easterly gale piling the great waves into the Castle Bay are swept. These openings are, however, so guarded with masses of rock that the force of the wildest wave is broken before it can leap up the piles of boulders which rise from their sandy floors. At the very mouth the cleft opens away to the west, where the cliff falls back, and seaward of which rise great masses of black frowning rock, most of which only show their presence at high water by the angry patches of foam which even in calm weather mark them—for the current here runs fast. The eastern portal is composed of a giant mass of red granite, which, from its overhanging shape, is known as 'the Ship's Starn.' It lies somewhat lower than the cliff of which it is a part, being attached to it by a great sloping shelf of granite, over which, when the storm is easterly, the torrent of spray sent up by the dashing waves rolls down to join the foamy waves in the Watter's Mou.'

Maggie knew that close to the Barley Mill, safe from the onset of the waves—for the wildest waves that ever rise lose their force fretting and churning on the stony sides and bottom of the Watter's Mou'—was kept a light boat belonging to her brother, which he sometimes used when the weather was fine and he wanted to utilise his spare time in line fishing. Her mind was made up that it was her duty to give her father warning of what awaited him on landing—if she could. She was afraid to think of the danger, of the myriad chances against her success; but, woman-like, when once the idea was fixed in her mind she went straight on to its realisation. Truly, thought of any kind would have been an absolute barrier to action in such a case, for any one of the difficulties ahead would have seemed sufficient. To leave the shore at all on such a night, and in such a frail craft, with none but a girl to manage it; then to find a way, despite storm and current, out to the boat so far off at sea; and finally, to find the boat she wanted at all in the fret of such a stormy sea—a wilderness of driving mist—in such a night, when never a star even was to be seen: the prospect might well appal the bravest.

But to think was to hesitate, and to hesitate was to fail. Keeping her thoughts on the danger to her father, and seeing through the blackness of the stormy night his white, woe-laden face before her, and hearing through the tumult of the tempest his sobs as on that night when her fear for him began to be acute, she set about her work with desperate energy. The boat was moored on the northern side of the largest of the little islands of sea-grass, and so far in shelter that she could get all in readiness. She set the oars in their places, stepped the mast, and rigged the sail ready to haul up. Then she took a small spar of broken wood and knotted to it a piece of rope, fastening the other end of the rope, some five yards long, just under the thwarts near the centre of the boat, and just a little forward on the port side. The spar she put carefully ready to throw out of the boat when the sweep of the wind should take her sail—for without some such strain as it would afford, the boat would probably heel over. Then she guided the boat in the shallow water round the little island till it was stern on to the sea side. It was rough work, for the rush and recoil of the waves beat the boat back on the sandy bank or left her now and again dry till a new wave lifted her.

All this time she took something of inspiration from the darkness and the roar of the storm around her. She was not yet face to face with danger, and did not realise, or try to realise, its magnitude. In such a mystery of darkness as lay before, above, and around her, her own personality seemed as nought. Truly there is an instinct of one's own littleness which becomes consciously manifest in the times when Nature puts forth her might. The wind swept up the channel of the Watter's Mou' in great gusts, till the open bay where she stood became the centre of an intermittent whirlwind. The storm came not only from the Mouth itself, but through the great gaps in the eastern wall. It drove across the gully till high amongst the rocks overhead on both sides it seemed now and again to scream as a living thing in pain or anger. Great sheets of mist appeared out of the inky darkness beyond, coming suddenly as though like the great sails of ships driving up before the wind. With gladness Maggie saw that the sheets of fog were becoming fewer and thinner, and realised that so far her dreadful task was becoming possible. She was getting more inspired by the sound and elemental fury around her. There was in her blood, as in the blood of all the hardy children of the northern seas, some strain of those sturdy Berserkers who knew no fear, and rode the very tempest on its wings with supreme bravery. Such natures rise with the occasion, and now, when the call had come, Maggie's brave nature answered it. It was with a strong, almost an eager, heart that she jumped into the boat, and seizing the oars, set out on her perilous course. The start was difficult, for the boat was bumping savagely on the sand; but, taking advantage of a big wave, two or three powerful strokes took her out into deeper water. Here, too, there was shelter, for the cliffs rose steeply; and when she had entered the elbow of the gully and saw before her the whole length of the Watter's Mou', the drift of the wind took it over her head, and she was able to row in comparative calmness under the shadow of the cliffs. A few minutes took her to the first of the openings in the eastern cliff, and here she began to feel the full fury of the storm. The opening itself was sheer on each side, but in the gap between was piled a mass of giant boulders, the work of the sea at its wildest during the centuries of stress. On the farther side of these the waves broke, and sent up a white cloud of spume that drove instantly into the darkness beyond. Maggie knew that here her first great effort had to be made, and lending her strength pulled the boat through the turmoil of wind and wave. As she passed the cleft, driven somewhat more out into the middle of the channel, she caught, in a pause between the rush of the waves, a glimpse of the lighted windows of the castle on the cliff. The sight for an instant unnerved her, for it brought into opposition her own dreadful situation, mental and physical, with the happy faces of those clustered round the comforting light. But the reaction was helpful, for the little jealousy which was at the base of the idea was blotted out by the thought of that stern and paramount duty which she had undertaken. Not seldom in days gone by had women like her, in times of test and torment, taken their way over the red-hot ploughshares under somewhat similar stress of mind.

She was now under the shelter of the cliff, and gaining the second and last opening in the rocky wall: as the boat advanced the force of the waves became greater, for every yard up the Watter's Mou' the fretting of the rocky bottom and sides had broken their force. This was brought home to her roughly when the breaking of a coming wave threw a sheet of water over her as she bent to her oars. Chop! chop! went the boat into the trough of each succeeding wave, till it became necessary to bale out the boat or she might never even get started on her way. This done she rowed on, and now came to the second opening in the cliff. This was much wilder than the first, for outside of it, to the east, the waves of the North Sea broke in all their violence, and with the breaking of each a great sheet of water came drifting over the wall of piled-up boulders. Again Maggie kept out in the channel, and, pulling with all her might, passed again into the shelter of the cliff. Here the water was stiller, for the waves were breaking directly behind the sheltering cliff, and the sound of them was heard high overhead in the rushing wind.

Maggie drew close to the rock, and, hugging it, crept on her outward way. There was now only one danger to come, before her final effort. The great shelf of rock inside the Ship's Starn was only saved from exposure by its rise on the outer side; but here, happily, the waves did not break, they swept under the overhanging slope on the outer side, and then passed on their way; the vast depth of the water outside was their protection within. Now and then a wave broke on the edge of the Ship's Starn, and then a great wall of green water rose and rushed down the steep slope, but in the pause between Maggie passed along; and now the boat nestled on the black water, under the shelter of the very outermost wall of rock. The Ship's Starn was now her last refuge. As she hurriedly began to get the sail ready she could hear the whistling of the wind round the outer side of the rock and overhead. The black water underneath her rose and fell, but in some mysterious eddy or backwater of Nature's forces she rested in comparative calm on the very edge of the maelström. By contrast with the darkness of the Watter's Mou' between the towering walls of rock, the sea had some mysterious light of its own, and just outside the opening on the western side she could see the white water pouring over the sunken rocks as the passing waves exposed them, till once more they looked like teeth in the jaws of the hungry sea.

And now came the final struggle in her effort to get out to open water. The moment she should pass beyond the shelter of the Ship's Starn the easterly gale would in all probability drive her straight upon the outer reef of rocks amongst those angry jaws, where the white teeth would in an instant grind her and her boat to nothingness. But if she should pass this last danger she should be out in the open sea and might make her way to save her father. She held in her mind the spot whence she had seen the answering signal to the rockets, and felt a blind trust that God would help her in her difficulty. Was not God pleased with self-sacrifice? What could be better for a maid than to save her father from accomplished sin and the discovery which made sin so bitter to bear? 'Greater love hath no man than this, that a man lay down his life for his friend.' Besides there was Sailor Willy! Had not he —even he—doubted her; and might she not by this wild night's work win back her old place in his heart and his faith? Strong in this new hope, she made careful preparation for her great effort. She threw overboard the spar and got ready the tiller. Then having put the sheet round the thwart on the starboard side, and laid the loose end where she could grasp it whilst holding the tiller, she hoisted the sail and belayed the rope that held it. In the eddy of the storm behind the sheltered rock the sail hung idly for a few seconds, and in this time she jumped to the stern and held the tiller with one hand and with the other drew the sheet of the sail taut and belayed it. An instant after, the sail caught a gust of wind and the boat sprang, as though a living thing, out toward the channel. The instant the shelter was past the sail caught the full sweep of the easterly gale, and the boat would have turned over only for the strain from the floating span line, which now did its part well. The bow was thrown round towards the wind, and the boat began rushing through the water at a terrific pace. Maggie felt the coldness of death in her heart; but in that wild moment the bravery of her nature came out. She shut her teeth and jammed the tiller down hard, keeping it in place against her thigh, with the other leg pressed like a pillar against the side of the boat. The little craft seemed sweeping right down on the outer rocks; already she could see the white wall of water, articulated into white lines like giant hairs, rushing after the retreating waves, and a great despair swept over her. But at that moment the rocks on the western side of the Watter's Mou' opened so far that she caught a glimpse of Sailor Willy's lamp reflected through the window of the coastguard hut. This gave her new hope, and with a mighty effort she pressed the tiller harder. The boat sank in the trough of the waves, rose again, the spar caught the rush of the receding wave and pulled the boat's head a point round, and then the outer rock was passed, and the boat, actually touching the rock so that the limpets scraped her side, ran free in the stormy waves beyond.

Maggie breathed a prayer as with trembling hand she unloosed the rope of the floating spar; then, having loosened the sheet, she turned the boat's head south, and, tacking, ran out in the direction where she had seen the signal light of her father's boat.

By contrast with the terrible turmoil amid the rocks, the great waves of the open sea were safety itself. No one to whom the sea is an occupation ever fears it in the open; and this fisher's daughter, with the Viking blood in her veins, actually rejoiced as the cockle-shell of a boat, dipping and jerking like an angry horse, drove up and down the swell of the waves. She was a good way out now, and the whole coast-line east and west was opening up to her. The mist had gone by, or, if it lasted, hung amid the rocks inshore; and through the great blackness round she saw the lights in the windows of the castle, the glimmering lights of the village of Cruden, and far off the powerful light at Girdleness blazing out at intervals. But there was one light on which her eyes lingered fixedly—the dim window of the coastguard's shelter, where she knew that her lover kept his grim watch. Her heart was filled with gladness as she thought that by what she was doing she would keep pain and trouble from him. She knew now, what she had all along in her heart believed, that Sailor Willy would not flinch from any duty however stern and pain-laden to him it might be; and she knew, too, that neither her rugged father nor her passionate young brother would ever forgive him for that duty. But now she would not, could not, think of failing, but gripped the tiller hard, and with set teeth and fixed eyes held on her perilous way.

Time went by hour by hour, but so great was her anxiety that she never noted how it went, but held on her course, tacking again and again as she tried to beat her way to her father through the storm. The eyes of sea folk are not ordinary eyes—they can pierce the darkness wherein the vision of land folk becomes lost or arrested; and the sea and the sky over it, and the coast-line, however black and dim—however low-lying or distant—have lessons of their own. Maggie began by some mysterious instinct to find her way where she wanted to go, till little by little the coast-line, save for the distant lights of Girdleness and Boddam, faded out of sight. Lying as she was on the very surface of the water, she had the horizon rising as it were around her, and there is nearly always some slight sign of light somewhere on the horizon's rim. There came now and again rents in the thick clouding of the stormy sky, and at such moments here and there came patches of lesser darkness like oases of light in the desert of the ebon sea. At one such moment she saw far off to the port side the outline of a vessel well known on the coast, the revenue cutter which was the seaward arm of the preventive service. And then a great fear came over poor Maggie's heart; the sea was no longer the open sea, for her father was held in the toils of his enemies, and escape seaward became difficult or would be almost impossible, when the coming morn would reveal all the mysteries that the darkness hid. Despair, however, has its own courage, and Maggie was too far in her venture now to dread for more than a passing moment anything which might follow. She knew that the *Sea Gull* lay still to the front, and with a beating heart and a brain that throbbed with the eagerness of hope and fear she held on her course. The break in the sky which had shown her the revenue cutter was only momentary, and all was again swallowed up in the darkness; but she feared that some other such rent in the cloudy night might expose her father to his enemies. Every moment, therefore, became precious, and steeling her heart and drawing the sheet of her sail as tight as she dared, she sped on into the darkness—on for a time that seemed interminable agony. Suddenly something black loomed up ahead of her, thrown out against the light of the horizon's rim, and her heart gave a great jump, for something told her that the Powers which aid the good wishes of daughters had sent her father out of that wilderness of stormy sea. With her sea-trained eyes she knew in a few moments that the boat pitching so heavily was indeed the *Sea Gull.* At the same moment some one on the boat's deck saw her sail, and a hoarse muffled murmur of voices came to her over the waves in the gale. The coble's head was thrown round to the wind, and in that stress of storm and chopping sea she beat and buffeted, and like magic her way stopped, and she lay tossing. Maggie realised the intention of the manoeuvre, and deftly swung her boat round till she came under the starboard quarter of the fishing-boat, and in the shadow of her greater bulk and vaster sail, reefed though it was, found a comparative calm. Then she called out:

'Father! It's me—Maggie! Dinna show a licht, but try to throw me a rope.'

With a shout in which were mingled many strong feelings, her father leaned over the bulwark, and, with seaman's instinct of instant action, threw her a rope. She deftly caught it, and, making it fast to the bows of her boat, dropped her sail. Then someone threw her another rope, which she fastened round her waist. She threw herself into the sea, and, holding tight to the rope, was shortly pulled breathless on board the *Sea Gull*.

She was instantly the centre of a ring of men. Not only were her father and two brothers on board, but there were no less than six men, seemingly foreigners, in the group.

'Maggie!' said her father, 'in God's name, lass, hoo cam ye oot here? Were ye overta'en by the storm? God be thankit that ye met us, for this is a wild nicht to be oot on the North Sea by yer lanes.'

'Father!' said she, in a hurried whisper in his ear. 'I must speak wi' ye alane. There isna a moment to lose!'

'Speak on, lass.'

'No' before these strangers, father. I must speak alane!' Without a word, MacWhirter took his daughter aside, and, amid a muttered dissatisfaction of the strange men, signed to her to proceed. Then, as briefly as she could, Maggie told her father that it was known that a cargo was to be run that night, that the coastguard all along Buchan had been warned, and that she had come out to tell him of his danger.

As she spoke the old man groaned, and after a pause said: 'I maun tell the rest. I'm no' the maister here the noo. Mendoza has me in his grip, an' his men rule here!'

'But, father, the boat is yours, and the risk is yours. It is you'll be punished if there is a discovery!'

'That may be, lass, but I'm no' free.'

'I feared it was true, father, but I thocht it my duty to come!' Doubtless the old man knew that Maggie would understand fully what he meant, but the only recognition he made of her act of heroism was to lay his hand heavily on her shoulder. Then stepping forward he called the men round him, and in his own rough way told them of the danger. The strangers muttered and scowled; but Andrew and Neil drew close to their sister, and the younger man put his arm around her and pressed her to him. Maggie felt the comfort of the kindness, and laying her head on her brother's shoulder, cried quietly in the darkness. It was a relief to her pent-up feelings to be able to give way if only so far. When MacWhirter brought his tale to a close, and asked: 'And now, lads, what's to be done?' one of the strangers, a brawny, heavily-built man, spoke out harshly:

'But for why this? Was it not that this woman's lover was of the guard? In this affair the women must do their best too. This lover of the guard—' He was hotly interrupted by Neil:

'Tisna the part of Maggie to tak a hand in this at a'.'

'But I say it is the part of all. When Mendoza bought this man he bought all—unless there be traitors in his house!' This roused Maggie, who spoke out quickly, for she feared that her brother's passion might brew trouble:

'I hae nae part in this dreadfu' affair. It's no' by ma wish or ma aid that father has embarked in this—this enterprise. I hae naught to dae wi 't o' ony kind.'

'Then for why are you here?' asked the burly man, with a coarse laugh.

'Because ma father and ma brithers are in danger, danger into which they hae been led, or been forced, by ye and the like o' ye. Do ye think it was for pleasure, or, O my God! for profit either, that I cam oot this nicht—an' in that?' and as she spoke she pointed to where the little boat strained madly at the rope which held her. Then MacWhirter spoke out fiercely, so fiercely that the lesser spirits who opposed him were cowed:

'Leave the lass alane, I say! Yon's nane o' her doin'; and if ye be men ye'd honour her that cam oot in sic a tempest for the sake o' the likes o' me—o' us!'

But when the strangers were silent, Neil, whose passion had been aroused, could not be quieted, and spoke out with a growing fury which seemed to choke him:

'So Sailor Willy told ye the danger and then let ye come oot in this nicht! He'll hae to reckon wi' me for that when we get in.'

'He telt me naething. I saw Bella Cruickshank gie him the telegram, and I guessed. He doesna ken I'm here—and he maun never ken. Nane must ever ken that a warning cam the nicht to father!'

'But they'll watch for us comin' in.'

'We maun rin back to Cuxhaven,' said the quiet voice of Andrew, who had not yet spoken.

'But ye canna,' said Maggie; 'the revenue cutter is on the watch, and when the mornin' comes will follow ye; and besides, hoo can ye get to Cuxhaven in this wind?'

'Then what are we to dae, lass?' said her father.

'Dae, father? Dae what ye should dae—throw a' this poisonous stuff that has brought this ruin owerboard. Lichten yer boat as ye will lichten yer conscience, and come hame as ye went oot!'

The burly man swore a great oath.

'Nothing overboard shall be thrown. These belongs not to you but to Mendoza. If they be touched he closes on your boat and ruin it is for you!' Maggie saw her father hesitate, and feared that other counsels might prevail, so she spoke out as by an inspiration. There, amid the surges of the perilous seas, the daughter's heroic devotion and her passionate earnestness made a new calm in her father's life:

'Father, dinna be deceived. Wi' this wind onshore, an' the revenue cutter ootside an' the dawn no' far off ye canna escape. Noo in the darkness ye can get rid o' the danger. Dinna lose a moment. The storm is somewhat lesser just enoo. Throw a' owerboard and come back to yer old self! What if we be ruined? We can work; and shall a' be happy yet!'

Something seemed to rise in the old man's heart and give him strength. Without pause he said with a grand simplicity:

'Ye're reet, lass, ye're reet! Haud up the casks, men, and stave them in!'

Andrew and Neil rushed to his bidding. Mendoza's men protested, but were afraid to interfere, and one after another bales and casks were lifted on deck. The bales were tossed overboard and the heads of the casks stove in till the scuppers were alternately drenched with brandy and washed with the seas.

In the midst of this, Maggie, knowing that if all were to be of any use she must be found at home in the morning, quietly pulled her boat as close as she dared, and slipping down the rope managed to clamber into it. Then she loosed the painter; and the wind and waves took her each instant farther and farther away. The sky over the horizon was brightening every instant, and there was a wild fear in her heart which not even the dull thud of the hammers as the casks were staved in could allay. She felt that it was a race against time, and her over-excited imagination multiplied her natural fear; her boat's head was to home, steering for where she guessed was the dim light on the cliff, towards which her heart yearned. She hauled the sheets close—as close as she dared, for now speed was everything if she was to get back unseen. Well she knew that Sailor Willy on his lonely vigil would be true to his trust, and that his eagle eye could not fail to note her entry when once the day had broken. In a fever of anxiety she kept her eye on the Girdleness light by which she had to steer, and with the rise and fall of every wave as she swept by them, threw the boat's head a point to the wind and let it fall away again.

The storm had nearly spent itself, but there were still angry moments when the mist was swept in masses before fresh gusts. These, however, were fewer and fewer, and in a little while she ceased to heed them or even to look for them, and at last her eager eye began to discern through the storm the flickering lights of the little port. There came a moment when the tempest poured out the lees of its wrath in one final burst of energy, which wrapped the flying boat in a wraith of mist.

And then the tempest swept onward, shoreward, with the broken mist showing white in the springing dawn like the wings of some messenger of coming peace.

IV

Matters looked serious enough on the *Sea Gull* when the time came in which rather the darkness began to disappear than the light to appear. Night and day have their own mysteries, and their nascence is as distant and as mysterious as the origin of life. The sky and the waters still seemed black, and the circle in which the little craft lived was as narrow as ever; but here and there in sky and on sea were faint streaks perceptible rather than distinguishable, as though swept thither by the trumpet blast of the messenger of the dawn.

Mendoza's men did not stint their curses nor their threats, and Neil with passionate violence so assailed them in return that both MacWhirter and Andrew had to exercise their powers of restraint. But blood is hot, and the lives of lawless men are prone to make violence a habit; the two elder men were anxious that there should be no extension of the present bitter bickering. As for MacWhirter, his mind was in a whirl and tumult of mixed emotions. First came his anxiety for Maggie when she had set forth alone on the stormy sea with such inadequate equipment. Well the old fisherman knew the perils that lay before her in her effort to win the shore, and his heart was positively sick with anxiety when every effort of thought or imagination concerning her ended in something like despair. In one way he was happier than he had been for many months; the impending blow had fallen, and though he was ruined it had come in such a time that his criminal intent had not been accomplished. Here again his anxiety regarding Maggie became intensified, for was it not to save him that she had set forth on her desperate enterprise. He groaned aloud as he thought of the price that he might yet have to pay—that he might have paid already, though he knew it not as yet—for the service which had saved him from the after-consequences of his sin. He dared not think more on the subject, for it would, he feared, madden him, and he must have other work to engross his thoughts. Thus it was that the danger of collision between Neil and Mendoza's men became an anodyne to his pain. He knew that a quarrel among seamen and under such conditions would be no idle thing, for they had all their knives, and with such hot blood on all sides none would hesitate to use them. The whole of the smuggled goods had by now been thrown overboard, the tobacco having gone the last, the bales having been broken up. So heavy had been the cargo that there was a new danger in that the boat was too much lightened. As Mendoza had intended that force as well as fraud was to aid this venture he had not stuck at trifles. There was no pretence of concealment and even the ballast had made way for cask and box and bale. The *Sea Gull* had been only partially loaded at Hamburg, but when out of sight of port her cargo had been completed from other boats which had followed, till, when she started for Buchan, she was almost a solid mass of contraband goods. Mendoza's men felt desperate at this hopeless failure of the venture; and as Neil, too, was desperate, in a different way, there was a grim possibility of trouble on board at any minute.

The coming of the dawn was therefore a welcome relief, for it united—if only for a time—all on board to try to avert a common danger.

Lighter and lighter grew the expanse of sea and sky, until over the universe seemed to spread a cool, pearly grey, against which every object seemed to stand starkly out. The smugglers were keenly on the watch, and they saw, growing more clearly each instant out of the darkness, the black, low-lying hull, short funnel, and tapering spars of the revenue cutter about three or four miles off the starboard quarter. The preventive men seemed to see them at the same time, for there was a manifest stir on board, and the cutter's head was changed. Then MacWhirter knew it was necessary to take some bold course of action, for the *Sea Gull* lay between two fires, and he made up his mind to run then and there for Port Erroll.

As the *Sea Gull* drew nearer in to shore the waves became more turbulent, for there is ever a more ordered succession in deep waters than where the onward rush is broken by the undulations of the shore. Minute by minute the dawn was growing brighter and the shore was opening up. The *Sea Gull*, lightened of her load, could not with safety be thrown across the wind, and so the difficulty of her tacks was increased. The dawn was just shooting its first rays over the eastern sea when the final effort to win the little port came to be made.

The harbour of Port Erroll is a tiny haven of refuge won from the jagged rocks that bound the eastern side of Cruden Bay. It is sheltered on the northern side by the cliff which runs as far as the Watter's Mou', and separated from the mouth of the Water of Cruden, with its waste of shifting sands, by a high wall of concrete. The harbour faces east, and its first basin is the smaller of the two, the larger opening sharply to the left a little way in. At the best of times it is not an easy matter to gain the harbour, for only when the tide has fairly risen is it available at all, and the rapid tide which runs up from the Scaurs makes in itself a difficulty at such times. The tide was now at three-quarters flood, so that in as far as water was concerned there was no difficulty; but the fierceness of the waves which sent up a wall of white water all along the cliffs looked ominous indeed.

As the *Sea Gull* drew nearer to the shore, considerable commotion was caused on both sea and land. The revenue cutter dared not approach so close to the shore, studded as it was with sunken rocks, as did the lighter draughted coble; but her commander evidently did not mean to let this be to the advantage of the smuggler. A gun was fired to attract the authorities on shore, and signals were got ready to hoist.

The crowd of strangers who thronged the little port had instinctively hidden themselves behind rock and wall and boat, as the revelation of the dawn came upon them, so that the whole place presented the appearance of a warren when the rabbits are beginning to emerge after a temporary scare. There were not wanting, however, many who stood out in the open, affecting, with what nonchalance they could, a simple business interest at the little port. Sailor Willy was on the cliff between the guard-house and the Watter's Mou', where he had kept his vigil all the night long. As soon as possible after he had sent out his appeal for help the lieutenant had come over from Collieston with a boatman and three men, and these were now down on the quay waiting for the coming of the *Sea Gull*. When he had arrived, and had learned the state of things, the lieutenant, who knew of Willy Barrow's relations with the daughter of the suspected man, had kindly ordered him to watch the cliff, whilst he himself with the men would look after the port. When he had first given the order in the presence of the other coastguards, Willy had instinctively drawn himself up as though he felt that he, too, had come under suspicion, so the lieutenant took the earliest opportunity when they were alone of saying to Willy:

'Barrow, I have arranged your duties as I have done, not by any means because I suspect that you would be drawn by your sympathies into any neglect of duty—I know you too well for that—but simply because I want to spare you pain in case things may be as we suspect!'

Willy saluted and thanked him with his eyes as he turned away, for he feared that the fullness of his heart might betray him. The poor fellow was much overwrought. All night long he had paced the cliffs in the dull routine of his duty, with his heart feeling like a lump of lead, and his brain on fire with fear. He knew from the wildness of Maggie's rush away from him that she was bent on some desperate enterprise, and as he had no clue to her definite intentions he could only imagine. He thought and thought until his brain almost began to reel with the intensity of his mental effort; and as he was so placed, tied to the stake of his duty, that he could speak with no one on the subject, he had to endure alone, and in doubt, the darkness of his soul, tortured alike by hopes and fears, through all the long night. At last, however, the pain exhausted itself, and doubt became its own anodyne. Despair has its calms—the backwaters of fears—where the tired imagination may rest awhile before the strife begins anew.

With joy he saw that the storm was slackening with the coming of the dawn; and when the last fierce gust had swept by him, screaming through the rigging of the flagstaff overhead, and sweeping inland the broken fragments of the mist, he turned to the sea, now of a cool grey with the light of the coming dawn, and swept it far and wide with his glass. With gladness—and yet with an ache in his heart which he could not understand—he realised that there was in sight only one coble—the *Sea Gull*—he knew her well—running for the port, and farther out the hull and smoke, the light spars and swift lines of the revenue cutter, which was evidently following her. He strolled with the appearance of leisureliness, though his heart was throbbing, towards the cliff right over the little harbour, so that he could look down and see from close quarters all that went on. He could not but note the many strangers dispersed about, all within easy distance of a rush to the quay when the boat should land, or the way in which the lieutenant and his men seemed to keep guard over the whole place. At first the figures, the walls of the port, the cranes, the boats, and the distant headlands were silhouetted in black against the background of grey sea and grey sky; but as the dawn came closer each object began to stand out in its natural proportions. All kept growing clearer and yet clearer and more and more thoroughly outlined, till the moment came when the sun, shooting over the horizon, set every living thing whose eyes had been regulated to the strain of the darkness and the twilight blinking and winking in the glory of the full light of day.

Eagerly he searched the faces of the crowd with his glass for Maggie, but he could not see her anywhere, and his heart seemed to sink within him, for well he knew that it must be no ordinary cause which kept Maggie from being one of the earliest on the look-out for her father. Closer and closer came the *Sea Gull,* running for the port with a speed and recklessness that set both the smugglers and the preventive men all agog. Such haste and such indifference to danger sprang, they felt, from no common cause, and they all came to the conclusion that the boat, delayed by the storm, discovered by the daylight, and cut off by the revenue cutter, was making a desperate push for success in her hazard. And so all, watchers and watched, braced themselves for what might come about. Amongst the groups moved the tall figure of Mendoza, whispering and pointing, but keeping carefully hidden from the sight of the coastguards. He was evidently inciting them to some course from which they held back.

Closer and closer came the *Sea Gull,* lying down to the scuppers as she tacked; lightened as she was she made more leeway than was usual to so crank a boat. At last she got her head in the right direction for a run in, and, to the amazement of all who saw her, came full tilt into the outer basin, and, turning sharply round, ran into the inner basin under bare poles. There was not one present, smuggler or coastguard, who did not set down the daring attempt as simply suicidal. In a few seconds the boat stuck on the sandbank accumulated at the western end of the basin and stopped, her bows almost touching the side of the pier. The coastguards had not expected any such manœuvre, and had taken their place on either side of the entrance to the inner basin, so that it took them a few seconds to run the length of the pier and come opposite the boat. The crowd of the smugglers and the smugglers' friends was so great that just as Neil and his brother began to shove out a plank from the bows to step ashore there was so thick a cluster round the spot that the lieutenant as he came could not see what was going on. Some little opposition was made to his passing through the mass of people, which was getting closer every instant, but his men closed up behind, and together they forced a way to the front before any one from the *Sea Gull* could spring on shore. A sort of angry murmur—that deep undertone which marks the passion of a mass—arose, and the lieutenant, recognising its import, faced round like lightning, his revolver pointed straight in the faces of the crowd, whilst the men with him drew their cutlasses.

To Sailor Willy this appearance of action gave a relief from almost intolerable pain. He was in feverish anxiety about Maggie, but he could do nothing—nothing; and to an active and resolute man this feeling is in itself the worst of pain. His heart was simply breaking with suspense, and so it was that the sight of drawn weapons, in whatever cause, came like an anodyne to his tortured imagination. The flash of the cutlasses woke in him the instinct of action, and with a leaping heart he sprang down the narrow winding path that led to the quay.

Before the lieutenant's pistol the crowd fell back. It was not that they were afraid—for cowardice is pretty well unknown in Buchan—but authority, and especially in arms, has a special force with law-breakers. But the smugglers did not mean going back altogether now that their booty was so close to them, and the two bodies stood facing each other when Sailor Willy came upon the scene and stood beside the officers. Things were looking pretty serious when the resonant voice of MacWhirter was heard:

'What d'ye mean, men, crowdin' on the officers. Stand back, there, and let the coastguards come aboard an they will. There's naught here that they mayn't see.'

The lieutenant turned and stepped on the plank—which Neil had by this time shoved on shore—and went on board, followed by two of his men, the other remaining with the boatman and Willy Barrow on the quay. Neil went straight to the officer, and said:

'I want to go ashore at once! Search me an ye will!' He spoke so rudely that the officer was angered, and said to one of the men beside him:

'Put your hands over him and let him go,' adding, sotto voce, 'He wants a lesson in manners!' The man lightly passed his hands over him to see that he had nothing contraband about him, and, being satisfied on the point, stood back and nodded to his officer, and Neil sprang ashore, and hurried off towards the village.

Willy had, by this time, a certain feeling of relief, for he had been thinking, and he knew that MacWhirter would not have been so ready to bring the coastguards on board if he had any contraband with him. Hope did for him what despair could not, for as he instinctively turned his eyes over the waste of angry sea, for an instant he did not know if it were the blood in his eyes or, in reality, the red of the dawn which had shot up over the eastern horizon.

Mendoza's men, having been carefully searched by one of the coastguards, came sullenly on shore and went to the back of the crowd, where their master, scowling and white-faced, began eagerly to talk with them in whispers. MacWhirter and his elder son busied themselves with apparent nonchalance in the needful matters of the landing, and the crowd seemed holding back for a spring. The suspense of all was broken by the incoming of a boat sent off from the revenue cutter, which, driven by four sturdy oarsmen, and steered by the commander himself, swept into the outer basin of the harbour, tossing amongst the broken waves. In the comparative shelter of the wall it turned, and driving into the inner basin pulled up on the slip beyond where the *Sea Gull* lay. The instant the boat touched, six bluejackets sprang ashore, followed by the commander, and all seven men marched quietly but resolutely to the quay opposite the *Sea Gull's* bow. The oarsmen followed, when they had hauled their boat up on the slip. The crowd now abandoned whatever had been its intention, and fell back looking and muttering thunder.

By this time the lieutenant was satisfied that the coble contained nothing that was contraband, and, telling its master so, stepped on shore just as Neil, with his face white as a sheet, and his eyes blazing, rushed back at full speed. He immediately attacked Sailor Willy:

'What hae ye dune wi' ma sister Maggie?'

He answered as quietly as he could, although there shot through his heart a new pain, a new anxiety:

'I know naught of her. I haven't seen her since last night, when Alice MacDonald was being married. Is she not at home?'

'Dinna ye ken damned weel that she's no'. Why did ye send her oot?' And he looked at him with the menace of murder in his eyes. The lieutenant saw from the looks of the two men that something was wrong, and asked Neil shortly:

'Where did you see her last?' Neil was going to make some angry reply; but in an instant Mendoza stepped forward, and in a loud voice gave instruction to one of his men who had been on board the *Sea Gull* to take charge of her, as she was his under a bill of sale. This gave Neil time to think, and his answer came sullenly:

'Nane o' ye're business—mind yer ain affairs!' MacWhirter, when he had seen Neil come running back, had realised the worst, and leaned on the taffrail of the boat, groaning. Mendoza's man sprang on board, and, taking him roughly by the shoulder, said:

'Come, clear out here. This boat is to Mendoza; get away!' The old man was so overcome with his feelings regarding Maggie that he made no reply, but quietly, with bent form, stepped on the plank and gained the quay. Willy Barrow rushed forward and took him by the hand and whispered to him:

'What does he mean?'

'He means,' said the old man in a low, strained voice, 'that for me an' him, an' to warn us she cam oot last nicht in the storm in a wee bit boat, an' that she is no' to her hame!' and he groaned. Willy was smitten with horror. This, then, was Maggie's high and desperate purpose when she left him. He knew now the meaning of those despairing words, and the darkness of the grave seemed to close over his soul. He moaned out to the old man: 'She did not tell me she was going. I never knew it. O my God!' The old man, with the protective instinct of the old to the young, laid his hand on his shoulder, as he said to him in a broken voice:

'A ken it, lad! A ken it weel! She tell't me sae hersel! The sin is a' wi' me, though you, puir lad, must e'en bear yer share o' the pain!' The commander said quietly to the lieutenant:

'Looks queer, don't it—the coastguard and the smuggler whispering?'

'All right,' came the answer, 'I know Barrow; he is as true as steel, but he's engaged to the old man's daughter. But I gather there's something queer going on this morning about her. I'll find out. Barrow,' he added, calling Willy to him, 'what is it about MacWhirter's daughter?'

'I don't know for certain, sir; but I fear she was out at sea last night.'

'At sea,' broke in the commander; 'at sea last night—how?'

'She was in a bit fishin'-boat,' broke in MacWhirter. 'Neighbours, hae ony o' ye seen her this mornin'? 'Twas ma son Andra's boat, that he keeps i' the Downans!'—another name for the Watter's Mou'. A sad silence that left the angry roar of the waves as they broke on the rocks and on the long strand in full possession was the only reply.

'Is the boat back in the Watter's Mou'?' asked the lieutenant sharply.

'No,' said a fisherman. 'A cam up jist noo past the Barley Mill, an' there's nae boat there.'

'Then God help her, an' God forgie me,' said MacWhirter, tearing off his cap and holding up his hands, 'for A've killed her—her that sae loved her auld father, that she went oot alane in a bit boat i' the storm i' the nicht to save him frae the consequence o' his sin.' Willy Barrow groaned, and the lieutenant turned to him: 'Heart, man, heart! God won't let a brave girl like that be lost. That's the lass for a sailor's wife. 'Twill be all right—you'll be proud of her yet!'

But Sailor Willy only groaned despite the approval of his conscience; his words of last night came back to him. 'Ye're no fit wife for me!' Now the commander spoke out to MacWhirter:

'When did you see her last?'

'Aboot twa o'clock i' the mornin'.'

'Where?'

'Aboot twenty miles off the Scaurs.'

'How did she come to leave you?'

'She pulled the boat that she cam in alongside the coble, an' got in by hersel—the last I saw o' her she had hoisted her sail an' was running nor'west. . . . But A'll see her nae mair—a's ower wi' the puir, brave lass—an' wi' me, tae, that killed her—a's ower the noo—a's ower!' and he covered his face with his hands and sobbed. The commander said kindly enough, but with a stern gravity that there was no mistaking:

'Do I take it rightly that the girl went out in the storm to warn you?'

'Ay! Puir lass—'twas an ill day that made me put sic a task on her—God forgie me!' and there and then he told them all of her gallant deed.

The commander turned to the lieutenant, and spoke in the quick, resolute, masterful accents of habitual command:

'I shall leave you the bluejackets to help—send your men all out, and scour every nook and inlet from Kirkton to Boddam. Out with all the lifeboats on the coast! And you, men!' he turned to the crowd, 'turn out, all of you, to help! Show that there's some man's blood in you, to atone if you can for the wrong that sent this young girl out in a storm to save her father from you and your like!' Here he turned again to the lieutenant, 'Keep a sharp eye on that man—Mendoza, and all his belongings. We'll attend to him later on: I'll be back before night.'

'Where are you off to, Commander?'

'I'm going to scour the sea in the track of the storm where that gallant lass went last night. A brave girl that dared what she did for her father's sake is not to be lost without an effort; and, by God, she shan't lack it whilst I hold Her Majesty's command! Boatswain, signal the cutter full steam up—no, you! We mustn't lose time, and the boatswain comes with me. To your oars, men!'

The seamen gave a quick, sharp 'Hurrah!' as they sprang to their places, whilst the man of the shore party to whom the order had been given climbed the sea-wall and telegraphed the needful orders; the crowd seemed to catch the enthusiasm of the moment, and scattered right and left to make search along the shore. In a few seconds the revenue boat was tossing on the waves outside the harbour, the men laying to their work as they drove her along, their bending oars keeping time to the swaying body of the commander, who had himself taken the tiller. The lieutenant said to Willy with thoughtful kindness:

'Where would you like to work on the search? Choose which part you will!' Willy instinctively touched his cap as he answered sadly:

'I should like to watch here, sir, if I may. She would make straight for the Watter's Mou'!'

V

The search for the missing girl was begun vigorously, and carried on thoroughly and with untiring energy. The Port Erroll lifeboat was got out and proceeded up coast, and a telegram was sent to Kirkton to get out the lifeboat there, and follow up the shore to Port Erroll. From either place a body of men with ropes followed on shore keeping pace with the boat's progress. In the meantime the men of each village and hamlet all along the shore of Buchan from Kirkton to Boddam began a systematic exploration of all the openings on the coast. Of course there were some places where no search could at present be made. The Bullers, for instance, was well justifying its name with the wild turmoil of waters that fretted and churned between its rocky walls, and the neighbourhood of the Twa Een was like a seething caldron. At Dunbuy, a great sheet of foam, perpetually renewed by the rush and recoil of the waves among the rocks, lay like a great white blanket over the inlet, and effectually hid any flotsam or jetsam that might have been driven thither. But on the high cliffs around these places, on every coign of vantage, sat women and children, who kept keen watch for aught that might develop. Every now and again a shrill cry would bring a rush to the place and eager eyes would follow the pointing hand of the watcher who had seen some floating matter; but in every case a few seconds and a little dispersing of the shrouding foam put an end to expectation. Throughout that day the ardour of the searchers never abated. Morning had come rosy and smiling over the waste of heaving waters, and the sun rose and rose till its noonday rays beat down oppressively. But Willy Barrow never ceased from his lonely vigil on the cliff. At dinner-time a good-hearted woman brought him some food, and in kindly sympathy sat by him in silence, whilst he ate it. At first it seemed to him that to eat at all was some sort of wrong to Maggie, and he felt that to attempt it would choke him. But after a few mouthfuls the human need in him responded to the occasion, and he realised how much he wanted food. The kindly neighbour then tried to cheer him with a few words of hope, and a many words of Maggie's worth, and left him, if not cheered, at least sustained for what he had to endure.

All day long his glass ranged the sea in endless, ever-baffled hope. He saw the revenue boat strike away at first towards Girdleness, and then turn and go out to where Maggie had left the *Sea Gull*; and then under full steam churn her way north-west through the fretted seas. Now and again he saw boats, far and near, pass on their way; and as they went through that wide belt of sea where Maggie's body might be drifting with the wreckage of her boat, his heart leaped and fell again under stress of hope and despair. The tide fell lower and ever lower, till the waves piling into the estuary roared among the rocks that paved the Watter's Mou'. Again and again he peered down from every rocky point in fear of seeing amid the turmoil—what, he feared to think. There was ever before his eyes the figure of the woman he loved, spread out rising and falling with the heaving waves, her long hair tossing wide and making an aureole round the upturned white face. Turn where he would, in sea or land, or in the white clouds of the summer sky, that image was ever before him, as though it had in some way burned into his iris.

Late in the afternoon, as he stood beside the crane, where he had met Maggie the night before, he saw Neil coming towards him, and instinctively moved from the place, for he felt that he would not like to meet on that spot, for ever to be hallowed in his mind, Maggie's brother with hatred in his heart. So he moved slowly to meet him, and when he had got close to the flagstaff waited till he should come up, and swept once again the wide horizon with his glass—in vain. Neil, too, had begun to slow his steps as he drew nearer. Slower and slower he came, and at last stood close to the man whom in the morning he had spoken to with hatred and murder in his heart.

All the morning Neil had worked with a restless, feverish activity, which was the wonder of all. He had not stayed with the searching party with whom he had set out; their exhaustive method was too slow for him, and he soon distanced them, and alone scoured the whole coast as far as Murdoch Head. Then in almost complete despair, for his mind was satisfied that Maggie's body had never reached that part of the shore, he had retraced his steps almost at a run, and, skirting the sands of Cruden Bay, on whose wide expanse the breakers still rolled heavily and roared loudly, he glanced among the jagged rocks that lay around Whinnyfold and stretched under the water away to the Scaurs. Then he came back again, and the sense of desolation complete upon him moved his passionate heart to sympathy and pity. It is when the soul within us feels the narrow environments of our selfishness that she really begins to spread her wings.

Neil walked over the sandhills along Cruden Bay like a man in a dream. With a sailor's habit he watched the sea, and now and again had his attention attracted by the drifting masses of seaweed torn from its rocky bed by the storm. In such tossing black masses he sometimes thought that Maggie's body might lie, but his instinct of the sea was too true to be long deceived. And then he began to take himself to task. Hitherto he had been too blindly passionate to be able to think of anything but his own trouble; but now, despite what he could do, the woe-stricken face of Sailor Willy would rise before his inner eye like the embodiment or the wraith of a troubled conscience. When once this train of argument had been started, the remorseless logic which is the mechanism of the spirit of conscience went on its way unerringly. Well he knew it was the ill-doing of which he had a share, and not the duty that Willy owed, that took his sister out alone on the stormy sea. He knew from her own lips that Willy had neither sent her nor even knew of her going, and the habit of fair play which belonged to his life began to exert an influence. The first sign of his change of mind was the tear which welled up in his eye and rolled down his cheek. 'Poor Maggie! Poor Willy!' he murmured to himself, half unconsciously, 'A'll gang to him an' tak it a' back!' With this impulse on him he quickened his steps, and never paused till he saw Willy Barrow before him, spy-glass to eye, searching the sea for any sign of his lost love. Then his fears, and the awkwardness which a man feels at such a moment, no matter how poignant may be the grief which underlies it, began to trip him up. When he stood beside Willy Barrow, he said, with what bravery he could:

'I tak it a' back, Sailor Willy! Ye werena to blame! It was oor daein'! Will ye forgie me?' Willy turned and impulsively grasped the hand extended to him. In the midst of his overwhelming pain this was some little gleam of sunshine. He had himself just sufficient remorse to make the assurance of his innocence by another grateful. He knew well that if he had chosen to sacrifice his duty Maggie would never have gone out to sea, and though it did not even occur to him to repent of doing his duty, the mere temptation—the mere struggle against it, made a sort of foothold where flying remorse might for a moment rest. When the eyes of the two men met, Willy felt a new duty rise within his. He had always loved Neil, who was younger than himself, and was Maggie's brother, and he could not but see the look of anguish in the eyes that were so like Maggie's. He saw there something which in one way transcended his own pain, and made him glad that he had not on his soul the guilt of treachery to his duty. Not for the wide world would he have gazed into Maggie's eyes with such a look as that in his own. And yet—and yet—there came back to him with an overpowering flood of anguish the thought that, though the darkness had mercifully hidden it, Maggie's face, after she had tempted him, had had in it something of the same expression. It is a part of the penalty of being human that we cannot forbid the coming of thoughts, but it is a glory of humanity that we can wrestle with them and overcome them. Quick on the harrowing memory of Maggie's shame came the thought of Maggie's heroic self-devotion: her true spirit had found a way out of shame and difficulty, and the tribute of the lieutenant, 'That's the lass for a sailor's wife!' seemed to ring in Willy's ears. As far as death was concerned, Willy Barrow did not fear it for himself, and how could he feel the fear for another. Such semblance of fear as had been in his distress was based on the selfishness which is a part of man's love, and in this wild hour of pain and distress became a thing of naught. All this reasoning, all this sequence of emotions, passed in a few seconds, and, as it seemed to him all at once, Willy Barrow broke out crying with the abandon which marks strong men when spiritual pain breaks down the barriers of their pride. Men of Willy's class seldom give way to their emotions. The prose of life is too continuous to allow of any habit of prolonged emotional indulgence; the pendulum swings back from fact to fact and things go on as before. So it was with Sailor Willy. His spasmodic grief was quick as well as fierce, like an April shower; and in a few seconds he had regained his calm. But the break, though but momentary, had relieved his pent-up feelings, and his heart beat more calmly for it. Then some of the love which he had for Maggie went out to her brother, and as he saw that the pain in his face did not lessen, a great pity overcame him and he tried to comfort Neil.

'Don't grieve, man. Don't grieve. I know well you'd give your heart's blood for Maggie'—he faltered as he spoke her name, but with a great gulp went on bravely: 'There's your father—her father, we must try and comfort him. Maggie,' here he lifted his cap reverently, 'is with God! We, you and I, and all, must so bear ourselves that she shall not have died in vain.' To Sailor Willy's tear-blurred eyes, as he looked upward, it seemed as if the great white gull which perched as he spoke on the yard of the flagstaff over his head was in some way an embodiment of the spirit of the lost girl, and, like the lightning phantasmagoria of a dream, there flitted across his mind many an old legend and eerie belief gained among the wolds and barrows of his Yorkshire home.

There was not much more to be said between the men, for they understood each other, and men of their class are not prone to speak more than is required. They walked northwards, and for a long time they stood together on the edge of the cliff, now and again gazing seawards, and ever and anon to where below their feet the falling tide was fretting and churning amongst the boulders at the entrance of the Watter's Mou'.

Neil was unconsciously watching his companion's face and following his thoughts, and presently said, as though in answer to something that had gone before: 'Then ye think she'll drift in here, if onywhere?' Willy started as though he had been struck, for there seemed a positive brutality in the way of putting his own secret belief. He faced Neil quickly, but there was nothing in his face of any brutal thought. On the contrary, the lines of his face were so softened that all his likeness to his sister stood out so markedly as to make the heart of her lover ache with a fresh pang—a new sense, not of loss, but of what he had lost. Neil was surprised at the manner of his look, and his mind working back gave him the clue. All at once he broke out:

'O Willy mon, we'll never see her again! Never! never! till the sea gies up its dead; what can we dae, mon? what can we dae? what can we dae?'

Again there was a new wrench to Sailor Willy's heart. Here were almost Maggie's very words of the night before, spoken in the same despairing tone, in the same spot, and by one who was not only her well-beloved brother, but who was, as he stood in this abandonment of his grief, almost her living image. However, he did not know what to say, and he could do nothing but only bear in stolid patient misery the woes that came upon him. He did all that could be done—nothing—but stood in silent sympathy and waited for the storm in the remorseful young man's soul to pass. After a few minutes Neil recovered somewhat, and, pulling himself together, said to Willy with what bravery he could:

'A'll gang look after father. A've left him ower lang as't is!' The purpose of Maggie's death was beginning to bear fruit already.

He went across the field straight towards where his father's cottage stood under the brow of the slope towards the Water of Cruden. Sailor Willy watched him go with sadness, for anything that had been close to Maggie was dear to him, and Neil's presence had been in some degree an alleviation of his pain.

During the hours that followed he had one gleam of pleasure—something that moved him strangely in the midst of his pain. Early in the morning the news of Maggie's loss had been taken to the Castle, and all its household had turned out to aid vigorously in the search. In his talk with the lieutenant and his men, and from the frequent conversation of the villagers, the Earl had gathered pretty well the whole truth of what had occurred. Maggie had been a favourite with the ladies of the Castle, and it was as much on her account as his own that the Mastership of the Harbour had been settled prospectively on MacWhirter. That this arrangement was to be upset since the man had turned smuggler was taken for granted by all, and already rumour and surmise were busy in selecting a successor to the promise. The Earl listened but said nothing. Later on in the day, however, he strolled up the cliff where Willy paced on guard, and spoke with him. He had a sincere regard and liking for the fine young fellow, and when he saw his silent misery his heart went out to him. He tried to comfort him with hopes, but, finding that there was no response in Willy's mind, confined himself to praise of Maggie. Willy listened eagerly as he spoke of her devotion, her bravery, her noble spirit, that took her out on such a mission; and the words fell like drops of balm on the seared heart of her lover. But the bitterness of his loss was too much that he should be altogether patient, and he said presently:

'And all in vain! All in vain! she lost, and her father ruined, his character gone as well as all his means of livelihood—and all in vain! God might be juster than to let such a death as hers be in vain!'

'No, not in vain!' he answered solemnly, 'such a deed as hers is never wrought in vain. God sees and hears, and His hand is strong and sure. Many a man in Buchan for many a year to come will lead an honester life for what she has done; and many a woman will try to learn her lesson in patience and self-devotion. God does not in vain put such thoughts into the minds of His people, or into their hearts the noble bravery to carry them out.'

Sailor Willy groaned. 'Don't think me ungrateful, my lord,' he said, 'for your kind words— but I'm half wild with trouble, and my heart is sore. Maybe it is as you say—and yet—and yet the poor lass went out to save her father and here he is, ruined in means, in character, in prospects—for who will employ him now just when he most wants it. Everything is gone—and she gone too that could have helped and comforted him!'

As he spoke there shot through the mind of his comforter a thought followed by a purpose not unworthy of that ancestor, whose heroism and self-devotion won an earldom with an ox-yoke as its crest, and the circuit of a hawk's flight as its dower. There was a new tone in the Earl's voice as he spoke:

'You mean about the harbour-mastership! Don't let that distress you, my poor lad. MacWhirter has lapsed a bit, but he has always borne an excellent character, and from all I hear he was sorely tempted. And, after all, he hasn't done—at least completed—any offence. Ah!' and here he spoke solemnly, 'poor Maggie's warning did come in time. Her work was not in vain, though God help us all! she and those that loved her paid a heavy price for it. But even if MacWhirter had committed the offence, and it lay in my power, I should try to prove that her noble devotion was not without its purpose—or its reward. It is true that I might not altogether trust MacWhirter until, at least, such time as by good service he had re-established his character. But I would and shall trust the father of Maggie MacWhirter, that gave her life for him; and well I know that there isn't an honest man or woman in Buchan that won't say the same. He shall be the harbour-master if he will. We shall find in time that he has reared again the love and respect of all men. That will be Maggie's monument; and a noble one too in the eyes of God and of men!'

He grasped Willy's hand in his own strong one, and the hearts of both men, the gentle and the simple, went out each to the other, and became bound together as men's hearts do when touched with flame of any kind.

When he was alone Willy felt somehow more easy in his mind. The bitterest spirit of all his woe—the futility of Maggie's sacrifice—was gone, exorcised by the hopeful words and kind act of the Earl, and the resilience of his manhood began to act.

And now there came another distraction to his thoughts—an ominous weather change. It had grown colder as the day went on, but now the heat began to be oppressive, and there was a deadly stillness in the air; it was manifest that another storm was at hand. The sacrifice of the night had not fully appeased the storm-gods. Somewhere up in that Northern Unknown, where the Fates weave their web of destiny, a tempest was brewing which would soon boil over. Darker and darker grew the sky, and more still and silent and oppressive grew the air, till the cry of a sea-bird or the beating of the waves upon the rocks came as distinct and separate things, as though having no counterpart in the active world. Towards sunset the very electricity of the air made all animate nature so nervous that men and women could not sit quiet, but moved restlessly. Susceptible women longed to scream out and vent their feelings, as did the cattle in the meadows with their clamorous lowing, or the birds wheeling restlessly aloft with articulate cries. Willy Barrow stuck steadfastly to his post. He had some feeling—some presentiment, that there would soon be a happening—what, he knew not; but, as all his thoughts were of Maggie, it must surely be of her. It might have been that the thunderous disturbance wrought on a system overtaxed almost beyond human endurance, for it was two whole nights since he had slept. Or it may have been that the recoil from despair was acting on his strong nature in the way that drives men at times to desperate deeds, when they rush into the thick of battle, and, fighting, die. Or it may simply have been that the seaman in him spoke through all the ways and offices of instinct and habit, and that with the foreknowledge of coming stress woke the power that was to combat with it. For great natures of the fighting kind move with their surroundings, and the spirit of the sailor grew with the storm pressure whose might he should have to brave.

Down came the storm in one wild, frenzied burst. All at once the waters seemed to rise, throwing great sheets of foam from the summit of the lifting waves. The wind whistled high and low, and screamed as it swept through the rigging of the flagstaff. Flashes of lightning and rolling thunderclaps seemed to come together, so swift their succession. The rain fell in torrents, so that within a few moments the whole earth seemed one filmy sheet, shining in the lightning flashes that rent the black clouds, and burn and rill and runlet roared with rushing water. All through the hamlet men and women, even the hardiest, fled to shelter—all save the one who paced the rocks above the Watter's Mou', peering as he had done for many an hour down into the depths below him in the pauses of his seaward glance. Something seemed to tell him that Maggie was coming closer to him. He could feel her presence in the air and the sea; and the memory of that long, passionate kiss, which had made her his, came back, not as a vivid recollection, but as something of the living present. To and fro he paced between the flagstaff and the edge of the rocks; but each turn he kept further and further from the flagstaff, as though some fatal fascination was holding him to the Watter's Mou'. He saw the great waves come into the cove tumbling and roaring, dipping deep under the lee of the Ship's Starn in wide patches of black, which in the dark silence of their onward sweep stood out in strong contrast to the white turmoil of the churning waters under his feet. Every now and again a wave greater than all its fellows—what fishermen call the 'sailor's wave' —would ride in with all the majesty of resistless power, shutting out for a moment the jagged whiteness of the submerged rocks, and sweeping up the cove as though the bringer of some royal message from the sea.

As one of these great waves rushed in, Willy's heart beat loudly, and for a second he looked around as though for some voice, from whence he knew not, which was calling to him. Then he looked down and saw, far below him, tossed high upon the summit of the wave, a mass that in the gloom of the evening and the storm looked like a tangle of wreckage—spar and sail and rope—twirling in the rushing water round a dead woman, whose white face was set in an aureole of floating hair. Without a word, but with the bound of a panther, Willy Barrow sprang out on the projecting point of rock, and plunged down into the rushing wave whence he could meet that precious wreckage and grasp it tight.

Down in the village the men were talking in groups as the chance of the storm had driven them to shelter. In the rocket-house opposite the Salmon Fisher's store had gathered a big cluster, and they were talking eagerly of all that had gone by. Presently one of them said:

'Men, oughtn't some o' us to gang abeen the rocks and bide a wee wi' Sailor Willy? The puir lad is nigh daft wi' his loss, an 'a wee bit companionship wouldna be bad for him.' To which a sturdy youth answered as he stepped out:

'A'll go bide wi' him. It must be main lonely for him in the guard-house the nicht. An' when he's relieved, as A hear he is to be, by Michael Watson ower frae Whinnyfold, A'll gang wi' him or tak him hame wi' me. Mither'll be recht glad to thole for him!' and drawing his oilskin closer round his neck he went out in the storm. As he walked up the path to the cliff the storm seemed to fade away—the clouds broke, and through the wet mist came gleams of fading twilight; and when he looked eastwards from the cliff the angry sea was all that was of storm, for in the sky was every promise of fine weather to come. He went straight to the guard-house and tried to open the door, but it was locked; then he went to the side and looked in. There was just sufficient light to see that the place was empty. So he went along the cliff looking for Willy. It was now light enough to see all round, for the blackness of the sky overhead had passed, the heavy clouds being swept away by the driving wind; but nowhere could he see any trace of the man he sought. He went all along the cliff up the Watter's Mou', till, following the downward trend of the rock, and plashing a way through the marsh—now like a quagmire, so saturated was it with the heavy rainfall—he came to the shallows opposite the Barley Mill. Here he met a man from The Bullers, who had come along by the Castle, and him he asked if he had seen Willy Barrow on his way. The decidedly negative answer 'A've seen nane. It's nae a night for ony to be oot that can bide wi'in!' made him think that all might not be well with Sailor Willy, and so he went back again on his search, peering into every hole and cranny as he went. At the flagstaff he met some of his companions, who, since the storm had passed, had come to look for weather signs and to see what the sudden tempest might have brought about. When they heard that there was no sign of the coastguard they separated, searching for him, and shouting lest he might have fallen anywhere and could hear their voices.

All that night they searched, for each minute made it more apparent that all was not well with him; but they found no sign. The waves still beat into the Watter's Mou' with violence, for though the storm had passed the sea was a wide-stretching mass of angry waters, and curling white crowned every wave. But with the outgoing tide the rocky bed of the cove broke up the waves, and they roared sullenly as they washed up the estuary.

In the grey of the morning a fisher-boy rushed up to a knot of men who were clustered round the guard-house and called to them:

'There's somethin' wollopin' aboot i' the shallows be the Barley Mill! Come an' get it oot! It looks like some ane!' So there was a rush made to the place. When they got to the islands of sea-grass the ebbing tide had done its work, and stranded the 'something' which had rolled amid the shallows.

There, on the very spot whence the boat had set sail on its warning errand, lay its wreckage, and tangled in it the body of the noble girl who had steered it—her brown hair floating wide and twined round the neck of Sailor Willy, who held her tight in his dead arms.

The requiem of the twain was the roar of the breaking waves and the screams of the white birds that circled round the Watter's Mou'.